Friends Like These

ALSO BY KIMBERLY McCREIGHT

Reconstructing Amelia

Where They Found Her

A Good Marriage

Friends Like These

A Novel

Kimberly McCreight

HARPER LARGE PRINT
An Imprint of HarperCollins*Publishers*

This is a work of fiction. Names, characters, places, and incidents are products of the author's imagination or are used fictitiously and are not to be construed as real. Any resemblance to actual events, locales, organizations, or persons, living or dead, is entirely coincidental.

HarperCollins books may be purchased for educational, business, or sales promotional use. For information, please e-mail the Special Markets Department at SPsales@harpercollins.com.

FIRST HARPER LARGE PRINT EDITION

ISBN: 978-0-06-320759-2

Library of Congress Cataloging-in-Publication Data is available upon request.

21 22 23 24 25 LSC 10 9 8 7 6 5 4 3 2 1

For the friends who saved me long ago.
For the ones who still do.

No friendship is an accident.

—O. Henry, *Heart of the West*

Prologue

You were the one who started it. So, in a way, you're responsible for how it ended. "That's ridiculous," you'd say. And maybe it is unfair to blame you, under the circumstances. But at this point, all I can do is tell the truth. Anyway, no one could have predicted the exact way things would unfold. Certainly not me. All the heartbreak, all those lives with so much potential, gone in a flash.

Too much loyalty—that's the real problem. Best friends are supposed to stand by you, no matter what. They disregard your occasionally disagreeable nature and off-putting eccentricities and accept the whole of you. That's the beauty of real friendship. But close friends can also let you get away with too much. And what feels like total acceptance, what masquerades as unconditional love, can turn toxic. Especially if what your friend really wants is a partner in crime, someone to excuse their own bad behavior. Because letting you be your worst self just so you can be terrible together is cruelty, not kindness. And it's got nothing to do with love.

Not that I ever thought you were cruel. I thought you were funny and smart and so gorgeous that it made my chest ache. God, how I loved you. Not in a sexual way, I just worshipped you. And, let's face it, you never did love me back in quite the same way. Maybe I decided I couldn't accept that. Maybe I realized that it wasn't actually love you were showing me, no matter how many times you called it that. Pity perhaps, but not love. And so I chose *me* over *us*. Because while the us felt good in the moment, I knew it would destroy me eventually.

But I am only one person. I won't take the fall for everything that's happened. And when you have a group of friends like these—beautiful and dynamic and smart and opinionated—things can get very complicated. Especially with the endless overlapping connections and all that history, there are so many ways that desire can go sideways.

It's like gripping a tinderbox. Sooner or later, it's bound to explode in your hands.

Alice

It was that girl in my art history class who told me. The one with the stringy brown hair and the ironic princess T-shirts who's really sweet. But also really annoying. Arielle. Or Erin. Or something. She started talking at me on our way out of class. She does that a lot. Always looking for an angle into my group of friends. We're that way at Vassar: sought after. Of course, people only see our impeccable exterior—our beautiful faces and just-so clothes, the way we flow like floodwater into a room, claiming every inch as our own.

Did you hear? *Her breath was hot and damp against my ear and smelled of spearmint gum and onions.* They found a body. *She sounded scared but a little excited, too. The corners of her mouth were twitching.*

What are you talking about? *I asked.* Where?

Right in front of Main Building.

Who is it? *I asked.*

Her face brightened. She liked being the one who knew something. The person with the inside scoop. She probably thought it would be a foot in the door with the cool kids.

He doesn't go to school here. They think maybe somebody killed him. *A beat later she admitted she'd made that part up.* Actually, they think he fell from the roof of Main Building. That he's the burglar.

Dead. Dead. Dead. Of course he was by the time they found him. I tried to suck in a mouthful of air, but it was no use. This would be a thing we could never take back. Something that could not be fixed. Somebody was dead, and it was all our fault.

I already knew: it would haunt us forever.

Ten Years Later
Detective Julia Scutt

Sunday, 4:27 a.m.

I pull my car to a stop behind the second cruiser parked at the top of the long, curved driveway. One still has its lights on, flickering against the trees. More cars are at the scene a couple miles down the road. All the cars we've got will be out on this one. That's not a whole lot in Kaaterskill, a small Catskills town that's a thirty-minute drive from its namesake waterfall.

Thus far the details of the accident, or whatever it is, are scarce. There's a passenger dead and the driver is missing, injured presumably, given the blood on the open driver's door. But the vehicle is deep in the woods, too far away from the point of impact. Suggests something other than an accident.

So while the patrolmen and the search teams comb the woods, looking for the missing driver, I've come here in the wee hours of Sunday morning. To this house where their friends are. Old friends from college, I've been told. Weekenders. That they're weekenders would be obvious from the house, a high-end remodel—spires and turrets and a wraparound porch, all gleaming. Even the driveway's smooth, round gravel looks pricey. They're up from the city—Brooklyn, Manhattan, doesn't matter. The weekend hipsters are all the same—millennials with an excess of money, liberal politics, and particular tastes. Locals hate them, but, man, do they love the money they spend.

Weekenders being involved complicates the investigation, especially if whatever happened turns out to be more than your average car wreck. We do have our share of crime these days, most of it starting or ending in opioids; they're everywhere in the Catskills. And if somebody up for the weekend from Manhattan is dead, the *New York Times* will be all over it. Boss sure as hell doesn't want that.

As I open the car door, it starts to rain. Drops, heavy and big as marbles, pelt the windshield. *Shit.* Rain's not good if we need to resort to dogs.

I square my shoulders as I make my way up the driveway. It's hard to establish authority on a scene when you're a woman, harder still when you look like "a cheerleader with a gun"—some DWI actually said that to me once. But I've got excellent instincts, and I'm not afraid to sink my teeth in until I knock against bone. That's what the lieutenant used to say. That was before he blew his head off in his driveway while his wife slept inside—opioids don't discriminate.

Next month, Chief Seldon decides who takes over the detective bureau. As far as I'm concerned, that person should be me. I've got the highest clearance rate. But Seldon's got his doubts. When you're a woman, anything questionable in your past—even things that weren't your fault—and *unstable* gets written onto you like a tattoo.

I take one last breath before I open the front door. I've got this, whatever it is. I know I do. Just so long as I keep myself in the here and now.

Maeve

Friday, 7:05 p.m.

Through the car window the trees were finally coming into focus, first the branches and then the individual leaves, already burnt orange at their edges. For nearly two hours, the woods had been nothing more than brown and green streaks as the three of us hurtled past, headed upstate on the twisty Taconic.

I'd been thinking of the first time I drove that way to Vassar. How nervous I'd felt—nervous and alive. College was a new beginning, a chance finally to be anybody I wanted to be. And I'd seized it, hadn't I? I'd learned so much about myself, not to mention getting a world-class education. But most important, I'd made this incredible group of friends. Where would any of us be now without one another? A complicated question always, hindsight and history being what they are. But complicated for us especially. What was never complicated, though, was our love. We were fiercely devoted to each other from the very start.

That was probably because none of us had great relationships with our real families. I was the only actual orphan, though. Orphan by choice—I was honest about that. I'd cut my parents out of my life because they were emotionally and physically abusive—I'd shared a few of the more shocking details. But my friends never judged. They accepted me completely, even though the estrangement had left me desperate for financial aid and constantly short on cash.

But right now we weren't headed back to Vassar's campus, despite the familiar switchbacks of the Taconic. We were going an unfortunate additional fifty miles north, deep into the Catskill Mountains. Jonathan had bought a weekend house in Kaaterskill, of all places. Not somewhere I would have ever chosen to go. But there was absolutely no opting out of this weekend. It was all hands on deck for Keith.

So here I was, ready to do what I was best at: looking on the bright side. And the bright side of this weekend was that we were going to get Keith help. That I might also have the chance to pump Jonathan for a little information about Bates would just be a side benefit.

Jonathan had introduced us. He'd met Bates back at Horace Mann, which meant that I had Jonathan to thank for both my boyfriend and my very, very good job in public relations at the Cheung Charitable Foundation, an offshoot of his father's hedge fund.

I think my friends were convinced that I was with Bates because of his money. That I was trying to claw back the life of luxury I'd lost when I severed ties with my parents. But Bates had given up Goldman Sachs to work at the Robin Hood foundation. He volunteered at the Boys & Girls Club. I'd even signed up myself, thanks to him. Being with Bates had already made me a better person, and he hadn't judged me for the stories I told him about the brutality of my childhood. Because he was a kind, nonjudgmental person. For the first time in my life, I thought maybe I could really be myself with someone. I wasn't all the way there yet, but I was working on it.

I pressed the button in the center console to slide the passenger window down and breathed in the Hudson Valley air, which smelled of distant fireplaces and dried leaves.

"I can't believe you're getting married," I said, looking over at Jonathan. His intense brown eyes were fixed on the road, lips pressed together. Oh, that had come out wrong. Negative almost. I reached over and put a hand on his. "I mean, I'm happy for you."

That was true—I *was* happy for Jonathan. He deserved to finally be with someone worthy of his generosity. Because Jonathan could be too generous, even with us. I'd warned him countless times: giving people too much all but guarantees they'll never really love you.

Jonathan smiled, but it seemed a little forced. "I'm happy for me, too."

"When is the actual wedding, anyway, and where?" I asked, digging for my phone in my oversize Hammitt bag—nice but not too flashy.

Flashy was tactless when you worked at a foundation. Bates was right about that. I typed out a quick text—Miss you already—and hit send. Bates had been working so hard this past week. It made complete sense that he hadn't invited me back to his place after dinner last night. Still, it was hard to shake the queasy feeling I'd woken up with. Especially now that I hadn't heard from him all day. It didn't help that I was already on edge. I still couldn't shake that anonymous email. I just needed to stop fixating—it was the only solution.

"We haven't set an exact date. In May or June, I think." Jonathan waved a hand. "And in the city probably. You know my parents: God forbid they leave Manhattan."

"You *think* May or June?" Stephanie asked from the back seat, finally off the conference call that had kept us largely silenced up front for nearly an hour. "You'd better get the details nailed down, Jonathan, or the New York City wedding machine will eat you alive."

I was a tiny bit jealous at the thought of Jonathan planning a wedding. Bates and I had only been together four months—way too early to be thinking about a proposal, obviously. But maybe I *was* hoping for a little forward momentum. That was the problem with getting so much of what you wanted—you just ended up wanting more.

"Peter and I like to be spontaneous," Jonathan said.

"That makes sense," I said, though I wasn't sure it exactly did.

"How much farther is your house anyway?" Stephanie asked. "Because no offense, but it's like a submarine back here. Did you know you were paying more to get your passengers extra carsick?"

Stephanie had been razzing Jonathan ever since he pulled up in the brand-new Tesla. The expensive car was somewhat out of character. Jonathan didn't usually advertise his wealth, which even by Vassar's privileged standards was eye-popping. Jonathan's father believed that earning money was far more important than letting people know you had it. Which I think was his real issue with Jonathan: he wasn't ambitious enough, especially compared to his completely lovely, but thoroughly hard-charging older sisters.

"We're less than fifteen minutes away." Jonathan adjusted his hands slightly on the wheel. He was definitely worried—about the weekend, about Keith. We all were.

"Okay, but I'm warning you, I haven't eaten all day." Stephanie's low blood sugar had a way of turning her prickly but always funny observations into barbs that actually drew blood.

I looked down at my hundred-dollar acrylics, resting on my perfect weekend slacks—Theory, on sale from Saks. In college, Stephanie had sometimes scolded me about being too focused on appearances—expensive things, beautiful people—and maybe I had been a little superficial. But back then I didn't quite look the way I did now, and all I could ever think was: What a privilege to be above caring about such things. Sometimes I still felt that way. I mean, look at Jonathan—he didn't care about making money because he didn't have to.

I focused again on the view out the window. In every direction, trees and more trees, their gnarled trunks and branches full of spectacular leaves crowding out the sun. Lovely, but a little ominous. I put my phone back in my bag.

"We should use the time we have left to, you know, strategize," Jonathan said. "Derrick and Keith can't be far behind us."

"Strategize?" Stephanie scoffed.

When I glanced back, she was sunk low in the back seat, the sleeves of her fashionable suit jacket pushed up, heels kicked off. Her arms were crossed tight in a pretty good impersonation of a sullen child. Stephanie had always been as tall and striking as a supermodel, though, and going natural these days only enhanced her large amber eyes, high cheekbones, and light brown skin. But Stephanie's beauty had always been of the absurdly unattainable variety: pointless to covet. Though sometimes, I still did.

Jonathan eyed Stephanie in the rearview. "If this is going to work, we really need to be a united front."

"We're united, we're united," she said. "Keith obviously has to go to rehab. There's no doubt about that."

"And we'll get him to go," I said, sounding way more confident than I felt. After all, I'd been the one who'd talked Keith into it the last time. I saw the look in his eye when he said it was a one-time-only deal. He'd meant it.

"Wait, what the hell is that?" Stephanie pointed a long finger between us at the left-hand side of the windshield.

Set up on a hill back from the road was an ancient-looking farmhouse that had completely collapsed in on itself. What remained was a hull of splintered boards, broken windows, peeling picket fencing—all of it left there to decompose. Almost as menacing was the run-down building in front, low and rectangular and tilting to the left, like a short stretch of makeshift motel rooms jerry-rigged from plywood and other scrap. People were living there, too, from the looks of it: some kind of light inside, a door slightly ajar. There were clothes strewn about outside and a big pile of garbage at one end—bottles, cans, food containers.

As we passed, I caught sight of a large bonfire around back. Two thin, hunched figures stood nearby in the glow.

"I can't believe people are living there," I said. "I mean—that's so sad."

Jonathan shrugged. "There are a lot of opioids up here, and not everyone has friends like us to swoop in. Or the means to pay for rehab. *Keith* doesn't have the means to pay for rehab."

"I've got to be honest, Jonathan, this is less charming than I pictured," Stephanie said. "Kind of like a horror movie, and you know the Black friend always dies first in those."

"No one's dying," I said. "Don't even joke about that."

"Um, not really joking," she went on. "Remind me again, Jonathan, why you bought a place here, when you could have used your piles of money to buy one, I don't know, literally *anywhere* else?"

"Funny, Maeve asked the same thing—more than once." He shot a look in my direction.

"Hey, I was only trying to help," I said, lifting my hands. "I wanted to make sure you'd thought it through, that's all. It is kind of off the beaten path up here." And that was absolutely true.

"Peter and I talked about Montauk, but that's always such a scene."

"So you opted for meth alley instead?" Stephanie muttered.

"Our friends, Justin and Bill, just bought a house a few towns over. You know, they own that restaurant on Perry Street?" When Jonathan glanced over, I nodded. But I'd never heard Jonathan mention a Justin or a Bill before. "Anyway, they've been married forever."

They were probably more Peter's friends. It wasn't that Jonathan was antisocial, but compared to life-of-the-party Peter, with his washboard abs and irresistible surfer charm, *everyone* was an introvert.

The trees were giving way to houses now that we were approaching town, set close together and on the small side, but at least not falling down. There was a Cumberland Farms gas station up on the right. As we slowed to a stop at a red light in front, a wiry old white guy standing at the pumps wearing a baseball hat and a long-sleeved Gatorade T-shirt glared menacingly at our car. When we met eyes, I looked away.

"You know, their coffee isn't actually half bad," Jonathan said brightly. "When Peter told me that, I laughed. And we got into a fight about me being a snob. I don't know, maybe I am. Anyway, Peter was right about the coffee. The people who work there are nice, too. Unfortunately, not everyone in Kaaterskill is so friendly to weekenders."

"What does that mean?" I asked, unable to resist reaching in to check my phone for a reply from Bates. Nothing yet.

"The locals aren't the most progressive bunch, that's all, and weekenders, myself included, can be demanding and tone-deaf. Like this car." A flicker of emotion passed over Jonathan's face. He shook his head. "Driving it up here is kind of like waving an asshole flag."

"At least you're up here spending money," Stephanie said diplomatically. "They've got to want that."

"They'd like the upside without the downside. Like everybody," Jonathan said. "Anyway, we're not far from the house now, and it *is* charming, Stephanie. Wait until you see the fireplaces."

"Okay, but you better have snacks," she said. "And if I spot one MAGA hat, I'm hightailing it out of Dodge."

We turned left down the main street, lined with charming shops—Perch Pilates, Patisserie Lenox, De Marchin Antiques, TEA: A Salon. The wood-frame storefronts were brightly painted and had cute, funky signage. But in between there were darkened doorways and boarded-up storefronts, cropping up more frequently as we drove on, like an infection beginning to spread.

"This downtown *is* adorable, Jonathan," I said. "We should come back later and walk around."

"Will the scenic tour be before or after we stuff Keith in the trunk and drive him to Bright Horizons?" Stephanie asked, her tone more sad now than sarcastic.

"Come on, we did it before without resorting to force," I offered. "And if we can't get Keith all the way convinced, there's always next weekend, right? At least we'll have opened up a dialogue."

"Oh, no, no. Keith has to go, *this weekend*," Jonathan said nervously. "By Monday. Otherwise, my dad's calling back the loan. If he does that, Keith will lose the gallery—you get that, right? He thought the loan was 'criminally indulgent' *before* he found out Keith was an addict. Now he's beside himself. As far as he's concerned, it's shameful for me to even have a friend like Keith. It's even more shameful for me to let my dad be taken advantage of in this way. The only way he might hold off is if Keith's in rehab."

I wasn't surprised that Jonathan's father was angry. I'd be angry, too. Keith was definitely using some of Jonathan's money to purchase drugs, either directly or indirectly.

"Maybe your dad is right," Stephanie said. "Keith is a bigger mess now than I've ever seen him. It's like he's trying to kill himself."

"Are you really surprised?" Jonathan asked.

"It's been ten years—how long is Alice going to be Keith's excuse for everything?" Stephanie asked.

"I don't know," Jonathan said. "Forever?"

"We all loved her," Stephanie went on. "And we all feel awful about what happened, but there has to be a line somewhere."

"Yeah, but Keith was *in* love with her," I offered. "Kind of makes sense that he's in the worst place."

"And is Alice our excuse for enabling him?" Stephanie asked. "We feel so guilty that we're killing Keith with kindness?"

We all stayed quiet for a long time.

"Rehab," I said decisively. "We just need to get him in, and then we can let the professionals take over. This time it'll take."

And I truly believed it might. The last time we talked Keith into it—or *I* talked Keith into it—was probably too soon. It was only about a year after graduation, eighteen months after the car Alice was driving had been spotted abandoned near the Kingston-Rhinecliff Bridge. Sixteen months after her death was officially declared a suicide, though her body had not been found. I pictured it now, a skeleton, bright white and worn smooth, wedged forever between boulders at the bottom of the Hudson River. I shuddered.

"Maeve is right," Jonathan said. "We just need to get Keith into Bright Horizons. That's all. And we can do that. I know we can."

The sunset was streaking the sky orange as Jonathan slowed the car at a tall, perfectly manicured hedge. Beyond it were the tops of dozens of towering trees. It wasn't until we turned down the gravel driveway that the house itself finally came into view: a stunning Queen Anne, complete with spindle-topped turrets, second-floor balconies, and a massive wraparound porch. Four perfect wooden rocking chairs sat on either side of the hunter-green front door. My breath caught.

As we drove closer, I could see that the windows looked especially grand for that kind of older home, as though the remodel had involved enlarging them. The house's sharp, clean edges—the perfectly squared-off roof, the precisely rectangular front steps—gave it an unexpectedly modern feel. Some lights were already on inside, warm and inviting in the quickly vanishing light. Peter had arranged to have the place ready for our arrival, Jonathan had told us on the drive. Peter might not have been perfect, but he was good at taking care of Jonathan.

"I'm so glad you and Peter found each other," I said. "What you have together—it's . . ."

Enviable. But Jonathan was my friend. I *was* happy for him.

"He's lucky to have you, Jonathan. We all are." Stephanie reached forward and hugged Jonathan fiercely from behind. That was how Stephanie always got you—without warning, she'd shed her armor. "True love—at least one of us has found it."

"Come on, Derrick has Beth," Jonathan deadpanned.

And for the first time since we left the city, we all started to laugh.

Detective Julia Scutt

Sunday, 4:32 a.m.

Officer Nick Fields is in the entryway, hand already on his gun as I step inside the house. For Christ's sake. Fields should never be on a door. Old for a patrol officer, with a salt-and-pepper mustache and heavy gut, he's too jumpy for the field.

I meet his eyes. "Where are they?"

"Through there." He hooks a chubby thumb over his shoulder toward the open doorway. "Seem pretty shaken up."

"Understandable." One of their friends is dead, another missing, and we don't even know yet who is who. I nod at Fields as I pass. "Don't shoot anyone."

As I walk through the parlor area, I take in the expensive rugs, the just-right coffee-table books. One wall is covered in bold blue-striped wallpaper; a brightly upholstered antique armchair sits along a narrow side table. Everything is perfectly mismatched in the way rich people seem to love—smart, but homey. And expensive as hell.

Most locals would resent these people for every square inch of it. I get that. But I also know that having money doesn't make people monsters, necessarily. That's because I left Hudson, where I grew up—across the river and slightly bigger than Kaaterskill—for college at UCLA, then a year of working at a tech start-up in San Francisco. I only did all that for my mom. I've always known I was going to be a police officer—here, in Kaaterskill. When I came home to enroll in the academy, my mom demanded to know why I'd take such a dangerous, low-paying job when I had endless options. Of course we both knew the answer to that question. We were just good at pretending otherwise.

And just like that my mind is headed there. To the whole thing. *Dammit.* Lately, my brain has a hair trigger. It's that stupid podcast. Last episode just aired a couple weeks ago, and there's been a lot of talk about it around town. It's hard to avoid. But I'll be damned if someone else's sick idea of entertainment is going to turn me inside out after all this time. I've been fine. I am fine. And I intend to stay that way.

I walk into a large living room. There are two red leather couches facing each other, two females—one white, one Black—and an East Asian male seated close together, late twenties, early thirties. They're attractive and well put together, glamorous, even—their clothes, their affect. But visibly upset, eyes glassy and red-rimmed. I glance up at Officers Tarzian and Cartright standing on the far side of the room, nod in their direction.

I turn back to the three on the couch. "Detective Julia Scutt."

They introduce themselves: Stephanie Allen, Jonathan Cheung, Maeve Travis.

"Have you figured out who you found yet?" Stephanie asks, her gold-flecked eyes narrowing sharply. It sounds just shy of an accusation. All we do know for sure at the moment is that Derrick Chism and Keith Lazard—two white males, both thirty years old, both approximately five foot ten—are missing, though one of them is presumably the deceased.

"It's Derrick's car. He'd have been in the driver's seat, right?" Jonathan says glancing at his friends. He's wearing one of those knit beanies that the hipsters love. It highlights his elegant cheekbones and full mouth. Still, it looks a little ridiculous on him.

"Except Derrick told me Keith drove up here," Stephanie says.

"If you brought us down there we could identify them," Jonathan offers.

"Can't do that unfortunately. The area isn't secure. We could have a suspect at large." This is true, but even if it wasn't there's no way I'd be bringing them to the scene. Their mere presence could corrupt the investigation and render them useless as witnesses. That's assuming they aren't suspects themselves, which I haven't remotely ruled out.

"So, you don't think this was an accident?" Stephanie asks.

"The positioning of the car is off," I say.

"What does that mean?" Jonathan again.

"Like perhaps not the product of an accident," I say. "I could try to have pictures taken, see if you can identify your friend that way, but you should know that there has been significant facial damage. It might make an identification impossible regardless."

I'm not looking to upset them, but I do need their focus off the ID. It matters, of course, but not as much at the moment as me getting a sense of what the hell happened here.

"That's awful," Maeve says, looking queasy as she stares down and twists the rings on her delicate, perfectly manicured hands. She's more put-together than the other two—her tailored outfit, the nails. Trying harder maybe because she's not quite as attractive. She's the kind of woman you're convinced you know, but just can't remember from where. "I don't think I want to see the pictures."

They are all quiet for a moment then, looking pained. I do feel bad for them. They are clearly upset.

"Listen, at least let's run fingerprints, and see if we can spare you. They don't need to have a criminal record to be in the system. Some licensing, background checks for certain employers . . ."

I let the silence stretch out, see if someone jumps in to offer an arrest record.

"Couldn't you just compare the fingerprints on some of their things here?" Jonathan asks.

"That's actually much harder than you'd think. DNA works much better, but according to the officers"—I nod in Cartright and Tarzian's direction—"their toothbrushes and such are all together in the one bathroom. There's no way to know whose is whose. Unless you can tell them apart?"

They all shake their heads.

"If all else fails we'll go to their home residences to collect reference DNA. But let's just take this one step at a time. Your other friend may turn up any second. I know this is difficult, but I'd ask for your patience. In the meantime, if you could give this officer your full names, addresses, dates of birth. And whatever you know for your two friends. That would be helpful."

I motion to Cartright, who hesitates—like I couldn't be asking him to do something so menial. Cartright is a Seldon stooge. When I glare at him, he finally steps forward with a pad and pen.

"Run a full two-seven on everyone," I say.

I mean a complete background check, and for each one of them, not just the two men in the car. I hope Cartright gets the distinction. Right now we need all the information we can get.

"So where do you think the one who—" Jonathan's voice cuts out. "Whoever didn't get killed, where are they?"

"Search teams are combing the woods," I offer. "We'll find them."

"But how many police officers do you even have around here?" Stephanie pushes to her feet and begins to pace. “Every one of them needs to be out there looking for—it’s either Keith or Derrick. They could be running out of time.” She stops pacing and crosses her arms, scowling at me. “If something happens to them because you moved too slow, you will be held accountable.”

I swallow back my irritation. “Don’t worry. We have plenty of men. There’s a specialized search-and-rescue team from State headed—”

“This was my idea,” Jonathan says. He looks shrunken suddenly. Like he’s dissolving into the couch. “Coming up here, I mean. This is my house. We were here for my bachelor party.”

A bachelor party? Well, now, that does put a different spin on things.

“What happened didn’t have anything to do with your bachelor party.” Stephanie’s tone is sharp, her jaw clenched. “It’s irrelevant.”

“I just want to be sure she has all the facts.” He levels his eyes at Stephanie. Maybe not quite the pushover he seems.

“Oh God,” Maeve says, turning ashen. “I just, I don’t understand. This is so—they were *just* here.”

“That’s exactly why we need your help.”

“These are our best friends.” Stephanie looks at the others, then back at me. “We’ll tell you anything you want to know.”

Stephanie

Friday, 7:22 p.m.

I watched Jonathan march up the front steps in his skinny jeans and bright orange cashmere sweater—Peter's influence. Left to his own devices, Jonathan dressed like a POW from a Brooks Brothers catalog—all outsized price-point and undersized fashion sense. I felt an absurd pang of jealousy. Now I wanted a boyfriend to pick out my clothes?

"Do we know what time Keith and Derrick are supposed to be here?" Maeve asked.

I looked back toward the road, dead quiet in the dark. The light had vanished all at once in the trees. "Do we even know for sure they left the city?" Keith often randomly disappeared, didn't call back—

ghosted us. Classic addict nonsense. We needed to be prepared.

"Keith texted earlier today about the bachelor party," Jonathan said as he fumbled around for the right key. "Said he was looking forward to it. So that's encouraging."

"Speaking of which, how long are we planning to keep up the whole bachelor-party charade?" I asked. "Isn't that just . . . delaying the inevitable?"

"Maybe we would have worked out those details if you hadn't been on the phone the *entire* car ride," Maeve singsonged. But her eyes widened immediately when I squinted at her. "I was just teasing, come on."

Maeve never could bear the thought of anyone being even a little mad at her. She was going to have to toughen up if she was going to survive as an Upper East Side trophy wife. Those women could be ruthless. Then again, her fellow debutantes from Charleston probably hadn't been especially cuddly either.

And Maeve was right about the call; I should have rescheduled. I buried myself in work when I didn't feel like dealing, a trick I'd learned from my workaholic professor parents. And the past few weeks, I'd definitely been avoiding things.

"Sorry about the conference call," I said. "That was obnoxious."

"Let me text Keith to see where they are," Maeve offered. Her face sank for a second as she looked at her phone—something about Bates, probably—but she managed to smile again as she punched out a quick text.

Jonathan swung open the front door. "Welcome to Locust Grove!" he intoned with a bow, waving us inside.

The house smelled of honeysuckle with a hint of lemon, or maybe just earth-friendly cleaning products. The furniture and fixtures were a balance of modern flair and rough-hewn farmhouse, an abstract rug in the entryway under a round antique-looking table piled with an eclectic mix of art books and a stone urn filled with fresh apples. It was all beautiful, of course, like everywhere Jonathan had ever lived. But the decor looked more personal. As if each item had been lovingly selected.

"It's gorgeous, Jonathan," I said, and it was.

But I felt hollow, looking around. I couldn't help but compare it to my own sleek Midtown apartment, the one I'd rented only because it was close to my office. My furniture all from one of those casual-chic furniture outlets that's in every suburban mall and, conveniently, online. It was a nice apartment with a nice gym that I never used and nice doormen whose names I didn't know, filled with things just nice enough that I could have somebody over without feeling embarrassed—not that I ever did.

Jonathan smiled as he surveyed the room. "Peter did all of it himself. You should have seen the place when we bought it. It was a disaster."

There was a sudden, odd rustling sound from the living room. A mouse? We all peered tentatively.

"Boo!"

I jerked back, banging my head into the wall behind me. When I looked up, there was a man in the doorway, laughing. For a moment, my brain refused to place his face.

But then—Finch. Yep, that was definitely him. Keith's star artist. Right there, in the flesh. Awesome.

"Sorry, sorry!" Keith appeared next to Finch—eyes wide, brown hair roguishly unkempt, suit jacket and jeans, green-checked button-down. His gallery uniform. "That was Finch's bad idea."

"Keith, what the hell?" Maeve shouted with admirable force.

"Come on, it was funny," Finch said, grinning slyly and flashing his perfect teeth, thankfully not in my direction.

Caught in a halo of light from the living room behind him, Finch's thick, shoulder-length brown hair looked streaked with gold, his green eyes twinkling. He was a striking man, there was no denying it. But he was too manicured, with his $300 white T-shirts, just-so scruffy beard, and perennially bronzed skin. He was also obnoxiously arrogant.

The last time I'd seen Finch was a month earlier, at a reception in his honor at Cipriani's. I'd gone because Keith had said they needed bodies. Of course, when I arrived at the end of a brutal workday, there were already hundreds of people in attendance. Typical Keith—he needed you desperately until he forgot all about you. Finch had greeted me with a too-tight hug before pronouncing my dress "adventurous" in a tone that made me want to ask what he meant and also made me want to tell him off. I couldn't remember now if I'd said anything back. I couldn't remember much from that night, except for the way it ended.

Now I kept blinking at Finch as though that might make him disappear. Keith had probably sniffed out that we were up to something and brought along Finch as a human shield. What a disaster.

Derrick appeared then, sheepish at the back of the living room, where he'd evidently been squirreled away this entire time. He ran an exasperated hand over his brown hair, longer now and shaggier, but in an appealing way. I was always surprised by how good Derrick looked these days, so much better than he had in college. He'd come into his own over the years.

"I told them not to do it," Derrick said, sounding very much like the disapproving literature professor he was. He pushed his tortoise-framed glasses up the bridge of his nose. "They wouldn't listen to me."

No one ever listened to Derrick.

"Where's your car, Derrick?" Jonathan's brow pinched angrily as he looked toward the driveway. "And how did you guys get in? You didn't break a window or something, did you?"

"We parked up the road and walked back. And break a window, seriously?" Keith looked wounded.

"No need to break and enter anyway when we had these." Finch dangled a set of keys in the air. His other hand was hooked around the molding above the living room entryway as he stretched his long body forward, tattooed bicep flexing. On purpose, no doubt. "You shouldn't leave 'em under the mat." As usual, he was leaning into his southern drawl. "Down in Arkansas that's an open invitation to come on inside. Right, Derrick?"

"I literally have no idea what you're talking about, Finch," Derrick said. "It was your dumb idea to come in, and Keith's idiotic decision to go along with it."

"Aw, Keith has to listen to me. You know that, Derrick," Finch said. "Because without me, there is no him. Right, Keith?"

"Absolutely," Keith said, as if he couldn't have cared less how much Finch demeaned him. He probably wasn't even listening. For all I knew, he was high out of his mind at that very moment. Actually, he definitely was. "Come on, Steph." Keith stepped closer to me. "Even you thought it was a little funny. You're smiling on the inside."

"I am not," I said, softening despite myself when Keith wrapped an arm around my waist and kissed me on the cheek.

Keith had that effect on people—all people. Men, women, gay, straight, or anything else. Being even briefly in the center of his attention was like staring into the setting sun. You couldn't pull your eyes away, even after they began to burn.

I could still remember the night freshman year Keith had come to find me in the library, dragging me out to his studio to see a painting.

"Please," he had begged. "I just finished the first in the series. And it's amazing." He got down on his paint-splattered knees in front of my desk, deep in the library stacks. The same desk I worked at every night, so everyone *always* knew exactly where to come find me. And come they did. Something I must have secretly enjoyed—because I could have moved around to avoid being found. "You *need* to see it."

"*Me*, or someone? Because if you just want someone to say it's great, we can skip the hike over there," I said. "It's great, Keith. I'm sure it is."

"No, *you.* You, specifically, need to see it," he said, his eyes dancing. "It'll be worth it. I promise."

Begrudgingly I'd gone with him, heading across the dark campus to his art studio at nearly midnight. And there, set up in his studio under a spotlight, was a huge canvas, a painting of me as a little girl, facing a vast and roiling sea. I'd told my friends the story about my parents not watching—consumed as they both were grading term papers on the beach—as three-year-old me ran right out into the waves and almost drowned. To me, the story explained everything anyone needed to know about my family—the subtle heartbreak of benign neglect. Most people didn't get it. But Keith had—it was all right there in that painting.

"It's beautiful," I said, my throat seizing. And it was, the bright blue and white electrifying around the small figure. The little me.

Keith was smiling as he looked at the painting. "I'm going to do one for everyone. A family of origin series.

Hopefully, the other ones live up." He wrapped an arm around me as we stared at the painting, my feet floating above the floor. "You know, just because your parents don't have feelings, that doesn't mean you can't."

"I feel things," I said quietly, still staring at the painting.

"I mean for another living, breathing person," Keith said. "You can let yourself do that. There's still time to be whoever you want to be."

My throat had felt too tight to object. Keith was the only person who'd ever seen my perfection for what it was: a locked and lonely box. He was the only one who ever called me out on anything.

It was dangerously easy to get swept up in Keith's huge, wild heart, even when you were just his friend. Poor Alice had never stood a chance. But that hadn't stopped me from judging her, had it? Love, of all trivial things, I'd thought. All those times I'd told Alice to grow up and get over Keith, to stop being such a drama queen. Yes, I'd been trying to help, but in retrospect it seemed so callous. What had I known about anything back then? What did I know now?

"Still working yourself to death for the man, huh?" When I turned, Finch was standing at my side, eyeing me pointedly. "Because you've seemed *awfully* busy."

He was bound to say something. Finch's entire artistic career was built on provocation. The key was to ignore him. Narcissists tire easily.

"Stephanie, can you come here for a second?" Jonathan called, trying and failing to sound nonchalant.

"If you'll excuse me. Jonathan needs me," I said to Finch as I slid past him into the living room.

"It's just a waste, that's all," Finch called after me. "You don't know what you're missing."

I did not turn back around.

"Hello, Stephanie? Over here, please. *Now.*" Jonathan waved me over.

"You were going to show me the fireplace, right?" I called out, hoping it might remind him to stay calm. Freaking out about Finch being there was obviously not going to help anything. "I won't complain the rest of the weekend if you get me in front of a fireplace."

"Right." Jonathan put a hand on my arm. "Somehow I doubt you will stop complaining, but there are actually *four* fireplaces. You and Maeve even have one in your room, which also has a view of the Hudson and the incredible sunset. You'll see tomorrow. Anyway, it's the very best room in the house, so naturally I gave it to the two of you."

"What's this about a fireplace?" Maeve asked as she joined us.

"Hey now," Finch said, slithering over with alarming speed. "Shouldn't we be drawing straws for the best room? Unless maybe you ladies *want* to share."

"We're good, thanks," Maeve said, cheerfully oblivious.

Maeve somehow gave everyone the benefit of the doubt, despite all she'd been through. It was one of the many reasons I worried about Bates. Jonathan had said he was a "solid guy," but Jonathan didn't always have the best taste in men. And I mean, *Bates*? But Maeve was utterly smitten. She claimed it was because Bates was kind and funny, and he'd been nice enough when I met him. But he was also *very* good-looking and *very* rich, and Maeve got mesmerized by sparkly surfaces. I blamed her awful family. Maeve had cut them out of her life, but they'd still left their mark.

"Finch is just playing. We'll take whatever room you've got," Keith said, slapping Jonathan on the back before heading to the far side of the living room. It only took him opening a couple cabinets to find the bar. "Ah, here it is. Nice setup, Jonathan."

"Solid call, Keith." Finch plopped himself down on one of the red leather couches. "After that drive, I could use a fucking cocktail."

Drinks. Exactly the way to kick off any intervention. Maeve and I exchanged a look as she dutifully headed over to where Keith was crouched. I watched her try to distract him from the alcohol, tilting her head to the side and smiling sweetly. But Keith was fixated. From far away he looked like such shit, too. None of us knew exactly what he was using. It had started with pot and then Xanax and Ativan. At some point he'd moved on to Oxy or Percocet or something. God only knew the extent of it these days. Forget Jonathan's dad and the loan and the gallery, Keith might be dead soon if we didn't get him into rehab.

I wondered sometimes what would have become of us if we'd just called the police that night on the roof. I'd wanted to, at least at first. Until I'd been reminded of the cost to everyone's future—mine most importantly. But if we had called someone, Alice might still be alive—she and Keith still together. Instead, that night was still reverberating through all of us—Jonathan with his pathological generosity, Derrick marrying miserable Beth, me working myself numb, and Maeve—well Maeve deserved to be happy, finally. She'd been through enough for one lifetime.

I did wonder if Maeve had gotten the most recent email from Alice's mom. She'd sent similar ones to all of us previously—usually once or twice a year—resurfacing to blame us for what had happened to Alice. Though this latest message had a newly threatening tone: *I know what you did.* Still, there was nothing to do but wait for Alice's mom to retreat back into her grief. So far, she always had. Usually we talked about the messages. At least Maeve and I did. But this time neither of us had said a word. I think we were tacitly agreeing that it would be too much to face on top of the intervention.

"You've got a problem with somebody having a drink at seven p.m. on a Friday night?" Finch smiled wryly when I looked at him. Evidently he'd been watching me watch Keith. "You only like to have one kind of fun?"

"Fuck you, Finch," I said before heading away again, across the room. So much for not taking the bait.

"What the hell is Finch doing here?" I whispered to Derrick, who was standing at a window looking out.

He shrugged. "Being a jerk? Isn't that all Finch ever does?"

"Did you know he was coming?" It sounded like an accusation. Maybe it was, a little bit.

Derrick and Finch had known each other since they were kids back in Arkansas, though they'd grown up on opposite sides of the tracks, literally. Derrick's family was wealthy by local standards, Finch the product of abject poverty. Something else for the art world to eat up. Derrick actually introduced Keith to Finch, back when Finch hadn't yet been paid a dime for his art and

Keith was still starting out. Despite that, Derrick didn't seem to like Finch very much. I never could figure out why he'd helped him in the first place. Though that was Derrick: nice to a fault.

"Of course I didn't *know* Finch was coming. Don't you think I would have warned you guys?" Derrick said. "I was already at the gallery to get Keith when Finch showed up. He asked what we were doing—Keith had a weekend bag. And then he was asking to come like he always does. You know the only reason he wants to hang out with us is because we won't let him. If we just said yes once in a while, he'd probably lose interest."

"Did Finch know *all* of us were going to be here?" I asked—I couldn't help it. "Or did he think it was just the three of you?"

"Don't know. I definitely said it was Jonathan's bachelor party and that Finch shouldn't come. But you know Keith, Finch gets what Finch wants." Derrick shook his head in disgust. "I would have pushed back harder, but I was worried Keith might get suspicious. If Finch finds out about the drugs, he'll fire Keith for sure. Finch's dad was a meth addict. We can't do an intervention with him here. It'll have to wait."

Not that it mattered what Finch found out, because he'd already fired Keith. But I was the only one who knew that. And given the way I'd found out, it wasn't like I could tell anyone.

"Except we can't wait," I said. "Keith has to get checked into Bright Horizons by Monday, or Jonathan's dad is going to call in his loan."

Derrick closed his eyes. "Great."

I looked out the window. In the side yard a bunch of boards had been stacked in a tall triangle, like someone had prepped the site for a bonfire.

"What's that?" I asked, tapping my finger against the pane.

Derrick kept his eyes on the boards. "I was just trying to figure that out myself."

"What's up with the pyre?" I called across the room to Jonathan.

Jonathan made his way over to look. "That's—" He recoiled, only for a split second, but it was unmistakable. "That's . . . I have absolutely no idea what that is. They're putting in a deck off the master bedroom at the back, must be related."

"But, like, arranged like that?" Derrick asked. "It's kind of . . . weird, don't you think?"

"No." Jonathan laughed awkwardly. "I'm sure Peter just forgot to tell me about it, whatever it is. He's been working so hard on the house and his book. You know what that's like, Derrick. He's consumed—I mean, in a good way. A great way."

"I thought Peter was a web designer," I said. Before that I could have sworn I'd heard actor.

As far as I was concerned, they all had one translation: gold digger. Though I tried to keep that opinion to myself. Jonathan did seem genuinely happy, and Peter did seem genuinely devoted to him. There was a possibility I was being overprotective.

"Web designing was just a day job. Peter has always been a writer. And he is so talented," Jonathan said, eyes still scrutinizing the wood. He turned to Derrick. "A big-name literary agent compared him to David Foster Wallace, and he's not even finished with the first draft. Derrick, you have to read it—you're going to love it."

"Sounds interesting," Derrick said tightly. Notably not saying he would read it.

Derrick would never actually say no, though. He'd admitted to me once that this was because both his parents had been alcoholics. His survival had always been predicated on accommodating people.

"Oh, good. I knew you'd be willing to help, Derrick. Maybe read it and pass it on to your agent?" Jonathan was as generous with his connections as he was with his money, even when those connections were us. "Peter was so nervous you'd say no. Anyway, thank you for helping him. You know how hard it is to break into the writing world."

"Right, yeah. Definitely," Derrick said with forced politeness. "I'd be happy to read it."

"I'll text Peter about those boards, too—I'm sure they're nothing. He runs a very tight ship with the renovation." Jonathan typed out a quick text, hit send, and tucked his phone back in his pocket. Then he leaned in close to whisper, "Now, come on. Help me get Keith stashed away upstairs so we can regroup. The clock is ticking."

Two Weeks Earlier

It's strange being back on campus after all these years. It looks much smaller than I recall, which is the way of all things, I suppose—swelling to outsize importance in your memory. It's more beautiful, too, the grounds so lush and leafy, the flower beds overflowing with red and pink blooms. That's the thing about youth: beauty being so readily available, it's easily overlooked.

I sit on a bench and watch the students walking this way and that, bright-eyed and fresh-faced. Hopeful. It's only just after Labor Day, the start of a new semester. They are so naive and open still, rushing headlong with the reckless confidence of youth. They don't know yet that danger will lie in the most ordinary places, tucked deep within the very best things. Like love and loyalty and friendship. Everyone thinks love will be the thing that saves them, and yet it leaves so much destruction in its wake.

But as much as I feel worried for all those young, eager, naive faces, I also feel sorry for myself. For what's already been lost. What I could lose still. I didn't ask for any of this, certainly not this sudden fork in the road. I know I can't ignore it, but I'm also not quite sure what to do. And so I'm doing this: watching, hoping an answer will come.

After a while, I push myself up off the bench in the center of the quad. Following the sidewalk as it curves past the library and the chapel, I finally stop at another bench across from the English building, Sanders Classroom. I sit down again and watch the door. I'm earlier than I planned. Derrick's class doesn't even finish until 5:00 p.m., but he'll be coming out right after that. He's a punctual, responsible guy, always has been. He lives an hour's train ride away these days, with his wife. Married young, which isn't much of a surprise. Derrick was a grown-up early on. The fact that he is also now old enough to be a full-fledged Vassar professor himself is still hard to wrap my head around. All those years gone, and yet in so many ways time is frozen still.

Finally the door to the building opens and out the students pour, laughing, in twos and threes. Eventually there's a pause in the stream, and a moment later there is Derrick, walking quickly, bag in hand. He looks good. Older, of course, but he's no longer the nerdy, ghostly pale writer he once was—he is legitimately an almost-hot literature professor, fair skin tanned, stride much more assured. He even looks taller. I feel relieved seeing him. Derrick is a kind person, always has been—even if, in a way, you could say it was his terrible decision at the very end that was the actual key to everything. Literally and figuratively. Like handing a match to someone soaked in gasoline. Were it not for him being so generous with his car, everything could have been different. That's what everyone thinks, even if they'd never say it to Derrick's face. I'm the one person in the world who knows it isn't true.

Anyway, with a situation like this, it's far too complicated to point a finger in a single direction. No matter how much better that would feel.

Derrick is only a few yards from the door when a young blond woman bounces out behind him. She has on jeans and a very tight midriff top that barely covers her breasts. She's so beautiful and bright, she glows.

"Derrick!" she calls out as she rushes after him.

He stops, dutiful but a little annoyed maybe. A professor trying to stay patient with an overeager student. Derrick must be beloved on campus—young, talented, kind. Handsome. And he is an actual acclaimed novelist. It's no surprise if the students, the girls especially, chase after him. Still, it is something to watch firsthand.

Derrick and the young woman begin to walk side by side, talking seriously. And for a moment I feel guilty for judging her by her long legs and large breasts. She's probably a gifted, dedicated student, merely trying to do a good job. I really have gotten old.

But then I see it—she reaches over and runs a finger along Derrick's hip. It's a quick gesture, one that I might have missed were it not for the way Derrick smiles in response. As they continue on, their sexual chemistry is all I can see.

Oh, Derrick. Come on.

I stay sitting, watching them from afar. And as Derrick and his student disappear into the distance, my disappointment in him is slowly replaced by something else—relief. It's proof: no one is truly innocent. And so it's only fair that no one is truly free.

Keith

Friday, 7:39 p.m.

I handed Finch his drink and sat down next to him on that neon couch. Who the hell buys a couch that fucking bright red? The glare was like a nail in my temple. Or maybe it wasn't the couch. My head had been pounding ever since I got into Derrick's car. Into the *driver's* seat. God only knows why I asked to drive, but I did. And of course Derrick said okay. He's my yes man, just like I'm Finch's.

The headache always started first for me, even before I was all the way down. Soon my head would feel pinched in a vise, tighter and tighter until my thoughts would barely be making it through. And then I'd get turned around. And turned around. Already the room was starting to spin.

Goddamn Jace. If he'd just called me back before we'd left, I wouldn't feel like such shit right now. Because these days that's what using was about for me: not feeling like shit. There was no getting high anymore, not really. Oxy gets into your bones and eats away the marrow. The artist I'd first used with had warned me I'd be aching to fill that emptiness forever. Of course, that hadn't stopped me from giving it a try. What I hadn't considered was just how much it would suck living this way. Not to mention how fucking expensive it would be. These days, I could only go a couple hours before I needed to do a few lines. Lately, it was costing me almost $4,000 a week. That's why people switched to heroin. Not me, not yet. But I'd glimpsed it on the horizon.

Right now, it had been four hours. If I went six or eight, things were going to get bad, fast.

I reached for the glass of Macallan winking up at me from the coffee table. Monogrammed glass. House with a name. *Locust Grove.* Only Jonathan. A second later, when I looked down at my hand, the glass was empty. I didn't remember taking a sip. Couldn't taste even a trace on my lips. Gone with everything else down the not-high rabbit hole.

"Dude, Keith, are you even listening?" Finch asked.

He'd been talking—Finch was always talking, and I was always supposed to be listening. Actually, I was supposed to be fucking entertained. Luckily, I was good at pretending. That was my job. And under the circumstances, I needed to be extra nice to Finch. But that was easier said than done when my joints felt like they were being pried apart with a screwdriver.

I looked over at poor, sweet Maeve, who'd somehow gotten roped into our conversation. Maeve was a genuinely good person, despite her shitty childhood. She'd been physically abused, I was pretty sure, maybe even sexually, though she'd never gotten into specifics with me. It had made her origin painting almost impossible. In the end I'd painted Maeve with us, or the suggestion of us—hands, feet, an arm. Not alone. But not with them. Never with them.

Maeve was brave, too. She'd been the one to chase after me as I'd stormed off from Alice's funeral in a rage. Alice's nutso mom had screamed some vicious, halfway accurate stuff about Alice's death being my fault. And so I'd taken it upon myself to tell her to fuck off, at her own daughter's funeral.

"Today is the worst day," Maeve said when she'd finally caught up with me. "But tomorrow will be better."

Maeve had been wrong about things getting better. I'd known it then. I knew it now. But I loved her for believing in a version of the future where I made it through in one piece—where I made it through at all. Because the truth was, I'd always been irrational, impulsive, selfish—even before what happened to Alice. And, sure, my parents had spent my childhood fixated on hating each other, but they'd never laid a hand on my sister or me. And my sister Samantha was happy, well-adjusted. Normal. She was a doctor for God's sake, happily married to Christina for four years now, a baby on the way. So what was my excuse for being such a mess?

"Hello, Keith." Finch snapped his fingers in my face.

"Yeah, I'm listening, Finch," I lied. "I'm always listening."

"Maeve, seriously, you had to be there," Finch went on, now that he had my full attention, that dickhead laugh stuck in the back of his throat. "She was the hottest girl in that club, and she was *all* over Keith. Probably would have gone down on him right there. And the motherfucker *falls asleep*. Just passes out. Boom, head on the table."

Maeve's eyes widened. She didn't want to hear about this. She didn't want me to be this way. Neither did I. Who fucking wanted this?

"Yeah, but she got her revenge," I managed to add. "She put six hundred dollars' worth of bottles on my card. Sent them to other tables on her way out."

Maeve eyed me. "Keith, God, that's so much money."

She was right. So much money I didn't have. So much money owed to all the wrong people—like the esteemed Serpentine Gallery in London, or my humorless friends from Staten Island.

"Good thing I keep you rich as shit, huh?" Finch reached over and clamped a hand around the back of my neck. He loved to joke about how much money I'd made from him. And by joke, I mean he loved to say vicious shit that he definitely believed. And he *had* made me a lot of money—it was just long gone now.

My phone rang then, super loud inside my jacket pocket. Jace—it had to be. Maybe he'd drive up from the city and deliver if I paid him enough. Of course, that would require actual cash. But that was a detail. I'd work it out.

"Probably London calling with your fucking specs," I said as I stood. "I'll be right back."

"London?" Finch shouted after me as I started across the room. "It's after midnight there, you fucker!"

It definitely wasn't London calling. Six weeks ago, the Serpentine Gallery had canceled Finch's show. Canceled it because *I* owed them money for setup on a previous show. Fucking artist of mine that needed a whole second level constructed for his installation—complete with an elevator. I'd agreed to pay 70 percent of the cost. The show was a huge success—buzz, reviews. But no one had bought a fucking thing. That was how I'd landed in my current predicament, borrowing from Peter to pay Paul—where Peter is an actual mobster whose wife likes to overpay for art she doesn't understand. And Paul turns out to be me, jamming all the money up my nose.

Outside on the porch, it was cold as shit and dark, the only light from the one small bulb overhead, a wall of darkness beyond. I was freezing in my short sleeves. I wiped a hand across my face as my nose began to run. When you came down, your insides also liquefied.

"Hey, what's up, man?" I answered. Jace and I were tight. Weren't we? Maybe he'd even front me the cash. "Jace, man, are you there?"

"We see you. You're standing on the porch of a white house in Kaaterskill." A man's voice—slow and steady and dead fucking calm. "And you have a hand on the back of your head."

My heart slammed against my ribs. I looked around—I did have a hand on my head, standing under that bright porch light. I knew who they were, of course. This wasn't the first time they'd called. They'd come by the gallery, too.

"I'm going to pay you," I said.

"Yeah, you are. By the end of business tomorrow. Or we're coming after your friends." The line went dead.

Pound, pound. pound, went the jackhammer in my chest. I put a hand on the side of the house to steady myself. *Holy fuck*. My friends? But of course a criminal in a $2,000 suit can figure a workaround for your own death wish. I looked over my shoulder toward the windows to see if anyone inside had been watching. The world looked stretched and far away, like I was staring through a tube. I could just make out Finch still talking to Maeve inside. Her arms were wrapped protectively around her body.

I tried to breathe. I owed $80,000, plus interest, and it was three months past due. How much time did I honestly think they were going to give me? The cable company got revenge faster than that.

I stared down at my feet for a long time before finally pulling my Marlboros from my pocket. I tapped one out and stuck it in my mouth, lit it, and inhaled. When I exhaled, the smoke expanded into an outsize cloud. Okay. I was going to be okay. Actually, I felt a little sharper. Nothing like a little death threat to clear out the haze. I'd figure something out. I always did.

Maybe if I was just straight with Finch about the Serpentine situation, he'd see the humor in it. Maybe he'd even lend me the 80K. After all, Finch understood irony. He'd built an entire career on fucking with people—the millennial Brooklyn Banksy known for high-impact, satirical conceptual art. These days it was usually video combined with large sculptural elements and paintings, not nearly as edgy as it once was now that it was mostly paid for by generous corporate sponsors. But Finch had become famous for the things he'd once done without permission. Like repainting overnight a series of huge Nike billboards on West Broadway in SoHo, replacing the punchy JUST DO IT with directives like FEEL FAT AND INADEQUATE. BE STRESSED AND INHUMAN. ACCEPT YOU WILL NEVER BE ENOUGH. The black-and-white billboards had been the talk of the city for at least a week, during which time one comedy of errors after another—orchestrated by Finch—had kept them from being painted over. It was clever as hell. You had to give that to Finch; he was always clever. Maybe he'd appreciate me being clever.

Except what was clever about fucking over your most important artist? No, I wasn't thinking clearly. Finch was going to go ballistic when he heard about the Serpentine. He'd been excited—it was a prestige thing. I couldn't tell Finch. And I could not ask Jonathan for more money either. He'd already done so much for me.

When I looked back through the window this time, Finch was staring right at me. Phone in his hands, like he was waiting for a call himself. I held up my hand with the cigarette and smiled. *Just out here smoking. Be in when I finish.* I needed to keep my shit together.

As I took one last, long drag, I heard a trickling sound coming from behind the house. I tilted my head toward it and closed my eyes. A creek probably, maybe even one leading to the river—the Hudson River. *Alice.* She was always there, wasn't she? In every fucked-up choice I made.

For sure since that night on the roof. One second that guy had been sitting on the edge, next second he was . . . gone. At least it seemed that way to me. I hadn't been watching that close; I'd been too busy dealing with Alice. She'd been screaming at me ever since I put my hands on that girl at the party. The girl whose name I didn't even know, who was really just another example of the things I kept doing so that Alice would break up with me. Not consciously. But that night on the roof it was finally dawning on me that maybe that's what I really wanted. I loved Alice. I was out of my head for her. But it was too much. She was too much; we were too much together.

And so there we were, passing around a bottle of cheap vodka on the roof of Main Building at 2:00 a.m. with some random guy Alice had clearly brought along to piss me off. But then he'd zeroed in on Maeve and Alice forgot all about him and remembered how pissed off she was at me.

"He fell. He fell," Derrick kept saying afterward. "He was drunk and he fell. This isn't anybody's fault. It was an accident."

Stephanie had wanted to call the police, of course. Because she was a sensible person.

"But we're up here illegally," Jonathan said as we all looked over the edge. "Keith is high. *I'm* high. We'll get arrested."

"What if he's still alive!" Stephanie shouted.

Jonathan hushed her. "And what if Vassar kicks us out? All of us will be screwed. And you can forget about ever going to law school."

Meanwhile, Alice was crouched in a ball on the ground. "Oh my God. This is all my fault. Oh my God," she said over and over again, rocking as she gripped her knees.

Maeve peered over the edge. “It—it really doesn’t look like he’s moving. And his neck . . . I don’t see how he could be alive.”

“Oh my God. This is all my fault,” Alice whispered. “He wouldn’t have even been here . . .”

Jonathan looked over the side. “He’s definitely—with his neck like that. He’s already dead.”

“We don’t know that,” Stephanie said, but she sounded defeated.

“Campus security is going to see him, anyway,” Derrick had added. “He’s in front of Main Building. Their office is right there. I think Jonathan is right; we need to go. All of us getting arrested isn’t going to help anything.”

Back inside the house, I avoided Finch and joined Derrick at the window. We stood in silence for a moment.

“It’s wrong that Finch is here, Keith,” Derrick said finally.

I laughed. And it did strike me as funny that this, of all things, would be what Derrick thought I’d done wrong.

“I’m serious.” Derrick turned to look at me, eyes all narrow like he was pissed for real. “It’s messed up.”

“Messed up?” I laughed again.

But it was a little unsettling. Derrick was the guy who usually helped you forget all the bad shit you did. He didn't call people out.

"I'm serious, Keith." Derrick's tone was stern. "This was supposed to be Jonathan's weekend. What if I'd brought Beth?"

"Beth?" I gave a mock shudder. I looked over at Finch, who was chatting away with Maeve and Jonathan now. They were both smiling. Finch could be charming when he wanted to be. "I don't know, he seems to be doing okay."

"It's a problem, Keith. This entire situation. You're too beholden to Finch, and he's—" He shot a nasty look in Finch's direction. "All he cares about is himself. Maybe this thing between the two of you has run its course. He's not worth—"

"Killing myself over?"

Derrick pressed his lips together. "Finch is *definitely* not worth killing yourself over."

"Don't worry about me, man." I clapped a hand on Derrick's back. "I've got a plan to get Finch and me into a better power equilibrium."

Derrick. *He* was the plan. It had just occurred to me at that very moment. Derrick could explain to Finch the situation with London, maybe break the news in a way that softened the blow. Finch listened to Derrick, which was fucking hilarious, considering no one else did—not even Derrick's own wife. Maybe it was because Finch had been a bit of a loser and Derrick an overachiever when they were kids.

"What's with the long faces over here?" Finch boomed as he appeared behind us. "Loosen up, fellas. This is supposed to be fun, remember? It's a bachelor party. We should be getting wasted and hooking up—"

"It's not that kind of bachelor party," Derrick cut him off. "It's more like, um, I don't know—a brunch."

Finch laughed. "Man, what the fuck are you talking about?"

"No one is going to hook up, that's what I mean," Derrick said. "Or get wasted."

"Did that wife of yours finally cut your dick off, Derrick?" Finch asked.

I laughed. I couldn't help it. Finch was a motherfucker, but he had a point: Beth was as forgiving as a razor blade.

"Shut up, Finch." Derrick shot him a look.

"Just be sure to stay away from Maeve," I said. Stirring up someone else's pot to distract from my own shit stew. "She and Derrick have a thing."

"What are you talking about?" Derrick squeaked. "We don't have a thing."

"Come on, you and Maeve have a thing, Derrick," I said, but more seriously now. They did, and Beth was making Derrick miserable. "I'm just saying: life's short, you know?"

I knew this firsthand. The mistake of thinking you had time.

"Knock it off, Keith," Derrick said as his eyes shot over to Maeve on the other side of the room. "We do not have a—"

The doorbell rang. The sound was like a fist in my gut.

"Who's that?" Maeve asked Jonathan breezily.

My palms were already damp, and all I could hear was my breathing.

"I have no idea." Jonathan gave a casual shrug.

But I saw the look on his face, the fear in his eyes. It was the same feeling that was lodged in the back of my own throat—the sick realization that something you've been trying to outrun has finally caught up with you.

Alice

Everyone is acting like there's nothing we can do now except pretend it didn't happen. But it did happen. We all know that it did. And we could still say something. There's still time for the truth.

And I know—maybe I only care so much because I'm the most to blame for what happened. I was angry at Keith when we walked into the Dutch Cabin. Not just because his hands were on some other girl at the party. But because his hands were always on some girl, at some party. Lately, I was starting to wonder if he was actually doing it on purpose. Like maybe he wanted me to break up with him.

So I decided I was going to find a guy and hurt Keith back. And if there was a kind of guy Keith cared about, it would have been the guy I spotted at the far end of the Dutch Cabin in his canvas work jacket and heavy boots. A real man who worked with his hands.

Not like Keith the artist. Keith the asshole. Because Keith is an asshole. I know that now. And with the way they're acting, I'm starting to think maybe the rest of my friends are, too.

Did I get what I wanted? Did I maybe make Keith angry enough that he pushed—I don't really think that. Other people saw it happen, anyway—Derrick, Maeve. All night the guy had been after Maeve, couldn't take his eyes off her, which was a little irritating, but also good for Maeve. She still doesn't realize how gorgeous she's become.

The sick part is that there was a tiny part of me that hoped for a second Keith had gotten jealous enough to push somebody off a roof. But no, the guy was just drunk, and he fell.

Accidents happen. What doesn't usually happen is the witnesses deciding not to call an ambulance and instead scurrying away in the dark like rats.

Days later, it's like life has just gone on for my friends. And me? Am I some saint? No, not even close. Because I've wondered more than once whether Keith will think twice now before he touches another girl.

Detective Julia Scutt

Sunday, 4:43 a.m.

"Maybe you and I should talk first, Mr. Cheung? Given that this is your house," I suggest. "Out in the other room."

"You're separating us?" Stephanie asks.

"Procedure," I say. "That a problem?"

"It's not a problem at all," Maeve says, her tone much softer. "We're just upset. And Stephanie is a lawyer. She questions everything. She can't help it." A lawyer. Of course she is.

"Understood." I look over at Jonathan and motion toward the dining room. "Maybe out there?"

"Um, yeah, sure." Jonathan rubs his hands on his

pants legs. Nervous, for sure. Could be nothing. Could be *the* thing.

I follow Jonathan out into the dining room, which has one of those absurdly long tables with plank benches, the kind people pay extra for because they look worn. Jonathan sits on the near side of the table, threading his legs through the long bench as I walk around to the other side. His shoulders are still hunched, eyes heavy under that stupid beanie.

"So when's the wedding?" I ask as I sit.

Jonathan looks up like he's got no clue what I'm talking about.

"Sorry, I thought you said this was your bachelor party? That usually suggests a wedding."

Jonathan closes his eyes. "Right, of course, yeah. This has all just been . . ." He presses his lips together. "In May or June. We haven't set an exact date."

"Your house is amazing, by the way." I gesture to the huge chandelier, an elaborate architectural formation of crystals that somehow manages to be hip and not fussy. "Looks like a real labor of love."

"Yeah, we, um—we renovated the whole place." Jonathan's face tightens as he looks up at the chandelier. "My, um, fiancé, Peter, did most of the work. He has a much better eye for those kinds of things, and a lot more patience. We bought the place six months ago. The transformation since then has been—it's unrecognizable. For months, Peter was up here a lot." He hesitates. "Days and days at a time."

Jonathan sounds tense now. Maybe he expects me to care that his fiancé is a man? I don't, but it's fair to wonder. We're only two hours from New York City, but there are some deep pockets of small-mindedness in the Catskills—homophobia, racism, sexism. Even in the department, starting at the top with Chief Seldon, who talks nonstop about the "way things used to be"—code for very male and very white and extremely heterosexual. Seldon's beloved in town, though. Chief of police for fifteen years, he's flyby charming with a booming laugh, and he's married to a gorgeous young wife with twin girls and two sons, adopted from Haiti and Uganda respectively, one of whom has special needs. Taken together, it's qualified Seldon for Kaaterskill sainthood.

"How did you end up with a house here, if you don't mind my asking? I've lived in this area most of my life, so I'm partial. But I always wonder how people from the city"—*people like you with money*—"find this area. We're not exactly the Hamptons."

"Peter and I considered the Hamptons. But that's not my speed. Peter has friends who bought a house up here."

"Is Peter here?" I ask.

Jonathan shakes his head. "No." He leans forward a little like he might elaborate. I see in his face the precise moment he decides not to. He rubs a hand over his forehead instead, pushing his hat up just enough to reveal the bottom edge of what appears to be a large bruise.

"That looks painful." I point to his head.

"Oh, yeah." Jonathan tugs the hat back down. A hat that now seems not just stupid-looking but also suspicious. "There's a cabinet above the dishwasher," he explains. "It's, you know, in the exact wrong spot."

Our eyes met. "Ouch," I say after a long beat. I'm guessing either the fiancé hits him or that bump on his head has something to do with our dead guy at the accident scene. "So the five of you were up here for the weekend?"

"Yes," Jonathan says. "Wait, I mean no."

"No?"

"There were six of us at first, but Finch left."

"His name is Finch?" These weekenders sure do know how to be hateable.

"Yeah, he's one of Keith's clients."

"Keith's a lawyer, too?"

"No, no. He owns a gallery. Finch is one of the artists he represents. *Client* is the wrong word. Keith is always telling me that. Finch kind of invited himself to come along."

"You don't sound happy about that."

"It's just that the rest of us are old friends," Jonathan says. "We went to college together. Finch is always trying to insert himself into our group. And he's just really—well, he's a big personality. Opinionated. And the rest of us are—it's not the best fit, that's all."

"When did he leave?" I ask.

"In the morning, yesterday. Early. I don't know exactly what time."

"And why did he leave?"

"I don't exactly know that either," Jonathan says. "But he and Keith were having an issue, work-related. Apparently Finch was angry about some show in London. I didn't even know that until a couple minutes ago. Stephanie told me. Honestly, we were just glad when he was gone."

"Finch a violent guy?"

"Violent?" Jonathan makes a face. "Wait, you think Finch . . ."

"I'm asking you what you think."

He looks up for a moment. Seems to be genuinely considering the question. "I—I don't know what happened, so I guess theoretically anything could have.

But I'm sure he's back in the city by now. He left almost twenty-four hours ago."

"Okay, so what was happening tonight before Derrick and Keith went missing?"

"We were just here, you know, hanging out," he says. "Maeve made us dinner. Penne arrabiata. She's a really good cook."

"So you were all here the entire night?" I ask. "No one went out?"

He nods, eyes deliberately on mine now. Maybe too deliberate. "I mean, not until Derrick and Keith left to get some cigarettes."

"What time did they do that?"

Jonathan consults the ceiling again. "Nine thirty or nine thirty-five," he says. "I'm not sure."

"Had they been drinking? Using drugs of some kind?"

"Drugs?" he asks. Like he's never heard of such a thing.

"Listen, I'm not here to bust anyone. At a minimum I'd imagine you were all drinking—this was a bachelor party, right? Some pot would be expected, too. I'm only interested to the extent that alcohol or drugs may have played a role in whatever happened. We have a pretty significant issue with opioids locally."

"Keith, I'm sure, had several drinks. But Derrick, a beer or two, max. He hardly drinks."

"Drugs?"

"No," Jonathan says, then swallows, loudly. So that's a yes on the drugs. But I'll leave it for now.

"Did you hear from them after they went out for cigarettes?"

Jonathan shakes his head as he stares down. "They just didn't come back. We called them again and again for at least an hour. Texted, too."

"Where did they go to get the cigarettes?"

"Cumberland Farms."

"And they never responded to any of your calls or texts?"

"No. When they didn't, we called the police, but they said they needed to be missing for at least twenty-four hours. It was a little while later when you found the car."

I hear the front door open then. Fields talking to someone.

Jonathan turns to listen, too. "Maybe they found something?"

I rise swiftly. "Could be."

This is a high-stakes investigation—for Kaaterskill and for me. Unexpected visitors are never good.

I pull up short as I step out into the parlor area. Standing alongside Fields in the entryway is Chief Seldon—new-looking jeans, sparkling clean boots, and carefully tucked navy-blue button-down. In his late sixties, Seldon is still an attractive, capable-looking man with thick silver hair, and that dazzling smile. Not that he's smiling now. He's frowning, and the late hour has gathered puffiness around his deep-set eyes.

Seldon doesn't usually show up on scene. It's the weekenders being involved that's gotten him out of bed. He's also here because I'm in charge. Seldon's been trying to figure out how to get rid of me ever since the lieutenant died. He doesn't like that I'm a woman, but it's my messy history that's the real issue—the fact that my sixteen-year-old sister Jane and her best friend Bethany were murdered in Kaaterskill when I was eight.

I thought Seldon would flip about *The River*, the podcast detailing every aspect of my sister's unsolved murder—it had quite a local following. Turned out he was delighted, at least when it first aired three months ago. That's because early episodes pointed the finger at an out-of-town killer, even trying to connect Jane and Bethany's death to other old, unsolved cases, like some Vassar girl who'd disappeared years later and whose death was ruled a suicide. But by episode 4 *The River* had shifted back to the old familiar suspects in Jane and Bethany's murders—ones much closer to home. Or so I gather. I haven't listened and never will. But you can learn a lot from the show notes and listener reviews.

The perfectly nice producers did reach out beforehand and invite me to participate. Two Brooklyn-based artist/writer/directors who'd grown up together in Westchester—Rachel and Rochelle. They cared about the case because Bethany and Jane's high school friendship reminded them of their own, they said. I'd politely declined to be interviewed. Admittedly, I was less polite when they showed up at the station to press their case. Luckily, Seldon wasn't there when I told them to go to hell.

They went ahead anyway with their podcast, of course. I knew they would, this wasn't my first rodeo. Over the years, there've been dozens of news shows and true-crime exposés and long-form articles about the murders. People do what they want, no matter what the families say. The case is real edge-of-your-seat stuff, too, even I have to admit—two girls, fifteen and sixteen years old, good kids walking in a high-trafficked river spot; the broad daylight; the brutality. Back then, violent crime in the Catskills was all but nonexistent. It was a shocking, shocking crime.

And, well, people have a goddamn right to be entertained.

Who cares what it feels like for me? Who cares if I worshipped my gorgeous, kind, goofy older sister Jane—that she used to sing me to sleep off-key, and had the ugliest feet, and once got frostbite on her pinkie finger teaching me to spin on ice skates? Who cares that she promised me all the time that I'd never be alone, because I'd always have her.

The truth is, I loved Jane more than I will ever love anyone. Whatever actually kills me, it will always be her loss that stopped my heart.

But I've learned to tune out anything that turns her into a sideshow, including this podcast. At least I had the good sense to move from Hudson, where everyone knows my history, opting instead for Kaaterskill, the town where the murders actually took place. To take a job that requires me to work every day a floor above Jane's case files, which still contain the rusted tent stake that was used to stab her to death.

I did comb through Jane and Bethany's files once, not long after I joined the force. Only the one time, one whole Saturday. But that was enough to see there was nothing there except a bunch of dead ends. And I refused to get sucked into pointless obsessing. It wouldn't bring Jane back. It wouldn't do anything. The best I've ever been able to hope for is to keep on keeping on. Like right now—I'm going to do my job.

And Seldon's not stupid. No matter what he thinks of me, he'll be careful not to interfere. He'll wait and hope I fumble the ball on my own. An actual misstep on a case this important, and he won't have to explain to anyone why he passed me over for lieutenant. He might even be able to get rid of me altogether.

I nod firmly in Seldon's direction. "Sir."

"What we got here?" he asks, eyes skidding away from mine.

"Just beginning interviews," I say. "Two in the car went out for cigarettes, didn't come back. The three individuals here don't know what happened. The group was up for some kind of bachelor party."

Some kind of bachelor party. I hate that I said it like that. Like it's not just a bachelor party because it's two men getting married. The worst part is that I think I put it that way to appease Seldon—he doesn't approve of gay marriage, or gays in the military. Or gay people. Seldon is a straight-down-the-line bigot. It's the only thing he has going in his favor—clarity.

"Anything more from the scene yet?"

"Wallet, phone, and car registration are all missing," I say. "Could be the motive was financial."

Property crimes are rising even faster than overdoses in Kaaterskill. Bad economy has taken its toll—layoffs, closed businesses—plus opioids leave people cash-strapped and willing to take risks.

"Early to jump to that conclusion, wouldn't you say?" Seldon says, working his jaw.

If asked, Seldon would definitely say that the Kaaterskill economy is booming, and that drugs aren't a big issue. Denial is his favorite policing strategy. Effective, too, apparently. The entire town seems to think he's doing a great job.

"There's a sixth person who left after an argument," I offer. "He's also a possibility."

"Ah, interesting." Seldon lifts his chin and peers down at me in a way that makes my skin crawl. "You got someone tracking him down?"

This is the answer Seldon wants—if this is just the weekenders killing each other, that's bad press Seldon can contain. Locals might hate weekenders, but they still want them showing up to spend money.

"Yeah, I'm on it." And I will send an officer to check the train station for this Finch character, just as soon as Seldon's gone.

"Still no sign of the driver?"

"We'll find him," I say. "State search and rescue is already there."

Seldon checks his watch. He wants back to his warm bed, his pretty wife.

"Don't talk to any reporters on this," he says. "None."

"Of course not." My cheeks feel warm. It's a dig about *The River.*

"I suppose I'll leave you to it then," Seldon says finally, an edge to his voice as he turns back to the front door. "But I want hourly updates. Earlier if anything noteworthy comes up. And find that sixth person. No way him being gone is a coincidence."

My phone rings as I start back toward Jonathan in the dining room. Dan's cell. I hate that I haven't taken him out of my contacts. But it's not that simple when you were best friends before you were a couple. I think about letting it go to voice mail. But Dan hasn't called in at least a week. And at this hour, on *this* night?

"Yeah," I answer. "What's up?"

"I'm down here at the scene," Dan says. "And I think—"

"At what scene?"

"The *crime* scene," he says, like I've forgotten I'm a police officer. Like I've forgotten he's one, too. That we're in competition for the same lieutenant's spot.

Dan's eight years older, but he joined the force after a stint as an actuary. He loves facts and figures. "You know, where *the car* is?"

"What the hell are you doing down there?"

"Whoa, calm down," he says—using that exact phrase and in that exact goddamn tone that had been the final nail in our coffin a month ago.

But in Dan's case it's probably not even on purpose. He's not the passive-aggressive type. He's opinionated, though—doesn't know when to let things go. Especially when he thinks he's helping. He grew up in Hudson—same class as Jane at Hudson High. But we didn't meet until the academy. We hit it off instantly, half flirting, half razzing nonstop. Dan was married at the time, and the line was always crystal clear for both of us. We didn't sleep together till three weeks after his divorce was finalized.

Apart from having sex, we never did really make the transition past friends, which is why we broke up a month ago. At least, *I* think that's why we broke up. Dan would probably claim we were totally in love for a while—five, maybe six perfect months. Right up until *The River* aired. Dan would probably also say we broke up because I didn't like him being honest with me. That I don't understand that being in love means telling the truth.

Whatever. Dan can think what he wants. That won't make him any less wrong. Or us any less broken up.

"I am fucking calm," I snap back at him, then turn toward the wall and try to lower my voice. I can feel Officer Fields's eyes on me. "Why are you down there?"

"Seldon called me," Dan says. "Told me you could use a hand."

Unbelievable. The worst part is that it *is* helpful having a detective I can trust down there at the accident scene. The state team is good, but they can get perfunctory when they're parachuted in. And, annoyingly, Dan is a very good detective. His attention to detail serves him well.

"Fine," I say, though I still sound pissed. "What do you want?"

"You should probably come down here," he says.

"They find something?"

Jonathan appears in the doorway to the dining room, staring at me expectantly. A beat later Maeve and Stephanie are there, too, in the opening to the living room. I should have chosen my words more carefully.

"Still no driver, if that's what you're thinking," he says.

"Then what?"

"Well, there's no way this was any accident."

Jonathan

Friday, 8:05 p.m.

The last thing I wanted to do was answer that door. Actually, I felt overwhelmed by dread. I'd been feeling uneasy ever since I'd seen the text on Peter's phone: See you tonight. From some random, anonymous number. Could have been anything, obviously. But the key under the mat wasn't helping. Peter was always reminding me that we needed to be vigilant about security and setting the alarm, that the escalating drug issue in Kaaterskill meant an uptick in petty crime. And here he was leaving the key to our front door under the mat?

But Peter was not there to ask. I'd invited him to come, of course, but he said no immediately. Peter grew up in Tampa, moved to New York state to attend Buffalo State. He thought my Vassar friends were stuck up. He thought most of the people I knew were stuck up, including my family. Definitely my dad was not warm and accepting, as evidenced by the fact that he was always threatening to cut me off if I did this or that thing he didn't like. And he didn't just mean he'd cut me off from the money. He meant cut me off completely from my entire family, including my mom and sisters. I knew, deep down, that my dad loved me. I think he was even trying to help—in his own way. Ever since I headed off to "artsy, aimless" Vassar over my father's objections, he'd been convinced I was dangerously lost.

That's what I'd been thinking about when I said we shouldn't call the police that night on the roof all those years ago. And I *was* the one who'd said it first, even if everyone did eventually agree. Even Stephanie, with a little help from me. She and I shared the same sick obsession with pleasing our unpleasable parents—I knew which of her buttons to push. Alice did eventually make it very clear she wanted to go to the police. But that wasn't until hours later and while I'd cared about Alice's feelings, I'd cared more about my dad's.

I know what you did. Alice's mother's most recent email popped into my head. She'd contacted us before. And she would again. As usual, I deleted the email immediately. Unlike some of my friends, I never had any interest in discussing her messages. Some situations just mandated denial.

The doorbell rang again. "You gonna get that or what, man?" Finch leaned forward on the couch, *my* couch, like if I didn't get it, he would.

I bared my teeth at him in that polite yet menacing way I'd perfected from watching my father. "Thank you, but I'm all set."

I swung the door open to find two men standing under the porch light. The guy in front was younger, maybe in his early-thirties, bright blue eyes glowing under his red baseball hat: ACE CONSTRUCTION. He was good-looking, solidly built, the same height as the older fireplug of a man behind him but all muscle and without the gut. The older man looked to be in his sixties, with white hair and enormous arms popping out from beneath his red-and-yellow T-shirt. ACE CONSTRUCTION was printed across the front of that, too.

Oh, yes, Ace Construction. I'd written lots of checks to them.

"You must be the contractors. I'm Jonathan." I reached out a hand, which the younger one glared down at for a long beat before finally shaking it, too hard. "Peter's not here. Can I help with something?"

Did they know that Peter and I were a couple? In Kaaterskill, some surprising people couldn't care less that we were gay. The skinny old drug addict who worked the pumps at the Cumberland Farms hadn't batted an eye when he'd come upon Peter and me kissing. But that sweet old lady with the rosy cheeks who ran the farm stand had once snatched a cherry pie right back from my hands. Hate was such an unpredictable thing.

Peter hadn't told me the contractors were coming by. At least I didn't think so. He was such a big talker, though. I did tune him out sometimes.

"Yeah, you can help us, *Jonathan.*" The younger one waved a piece of paper in my face. "With this."

I didn't flinch. You couldn't with a guy like that. Instead I looked steadily at the page: an invoice with four bright-red PAST DUE stamps at the top.

"Peter handles all the renovation details," I said with an unfortunately dismissive wave of my hand. "Including payments."

The man's blue eyes narrowed. He wanted to hit me. I could feel it. And, fine, I shouldn't have said it like that, or waved my hand. As if the details—this man's details—were beneath me. I didn't actually think that—though I had grown up in a five-bedroom co-op off Fifth Avenue with live-in staff. My father had emigrated from China to the U.S. forty years ago, with nothing but his acceptance to Columbia University in hand. Seven years later he graduated with a BA, MBA, and JD and, after a brief stint at Bridgewater, soon started his own hedge fund—Cheung Capital—now worth more than ten billion dollars. But no matter how much money we had, my father had raised us all to value hard work and to respect the people who did it. Was I being a jerk on purpose?

"Seems like he's not handling the payments well enough," the older man said, pointing a crooked finger toward the wrinkled invoice that still hovered inches from my face. "You owe us eleven thousand six hundred thirty-seven dollars and forty-two cents. We need to get paid. Right now."

"A misunderstanding, I'm sure. We certainly want you fairly compensated," I said. "I can take the invoice and ask—"

"Nope," the younger man said. "Tonight, you'll pay us. We're not leaving until you do."

"Let me see that, please." Keith was at my shoulder now. He reached out and snatched the invoice from the younger guy.

Then Derrick came out into the foyer, followed by Stephanie. They formed a kind of protective half circle behind me, and I swallowed back a lump in my throat.

Finch was watching from his perch on my couch, drink in hand. My whisky, from my crystal decanter.

"He can't just pay you if he doesn't know what it's for," Derrick offered, almost pleasantly, like this was a simple fact on which we could all agree. "As soon as he talks to Peter, he could, like, Venmo you or something. Why don't you leave the invoice and—"

"Venmo?" the older guy spat out, shaking his head. "Eleven thousand dollars?"

"Yeah, I don't think so," the younger guy sneered. With more light on his face, I could see that he was older than I realized, mid-thirties.

"I will pay you," I said. "That's all he means. I have the money."

But there was a knot in my stomach, and my head was starting to spin. Lately, Peter had been paying all the contracting bills—directly from my account. Thousands and thousands of dollars. And I trusted him to do it all correctly, even though it was a fact that Peter was not exceptionally good with details. Had he lost track of something?

"It's wrong. You have my guys come here and do honest work. We pay up front for all the materials. And then you don't pay us?" The older man's cheeks went pink as he motioned back toward the driveway. That stupid car Peter had talked me into. "It's stealing."

"Stealing?" My heart had picked up speed. But if they really hadn't been paid, that wouldn't be a totally unfair way to see it.

"Damn right. Stealing from my men, that's the worst part. You take from me, it's taking from them. How are they supposed to feed their kids, huh?" The old man seemed enraged. "Like you said, you've got the money."

"Pop, that's enough," the young man growled. He looked me up and down, lip curled. I stood taller. "Don't give this asshole the satisfaction of groveling."

"Asshole?" Stephanie raised an eyebrow. "That's a nice way to talk to a customer."

"Customer?" the young guy shot back. "Customers pay their bills."

"Listen, I should be hearing back from Peter any minute," I said, hoping we could still defuse the situation. "I just texted him about . . . something else." At this point, I certainly wasn't mentioning the abandoned boards in the side yard. "Is your address on the invoice? Because as soon as I confirm there hasn't been some kind of bank mix-up, I can drive a check right over."

Not that I had my checkbook with me. And you couldn't just withdraw $11,000 from an ATM. But these were details I would sort out as soon as I spoke to Peter.

"Yeah, our address is on the invoice." The younger man took a full step closer. We were only inches apart now. I was taller than him, and I could hold my own in a fight, but the rage in his eyes was extremely unsettling. "If I don't hear from you by tomorrow morning, I'll be back." Now he looked past me to my friends. "And none of you will like what happens."

"Hey," Finch called from the living room. "Maybe he didn't pay you because y'all are shitty contractors. You ever consider that?"

Finch sounded drunk, but almost certainly was not. Finch was always pretending something.

I held up a hand. "Seriously, Finch. I'm handling it."

"Man, if you left all those uncovered boards and shit on *my* grass, I sure as hell wouldn't pay," he went on. Because when had a polite request ever stopped Finch? "I've worked construction. You pick. Shit. Up. That's 101. The grass underneath those boards has got to be all fucked. You're the ones who probably owe *them* money."

"And who the fuck are you?" The young guy stepped to the side so he could address Finch directly.

"Finch," he called back and took another sip of his drink. "That's who the fuck I am, and I'll tell you what—that mess of wood you set up out there looks to me like you're planning on lighting the house on fire or some shit. Add a little gasoline and boom. Lift off. Maybe it just scares the shit out of everyone sleeping here with some smoke. Maybe it jumps to the house and does a whole lot fucking worse." Finch got up and sauntered closer, leaned back against the wall. He was enjoying this. "Is that the plan? Set the house on fire maybe and make it look like some drugged-out degenerates did it?"

The younger man smirked and shook his head.

"Come on, Luke," the old man said. "We've said our piece."

Luke pinned me again with his alarming blue eyes. "You've got until tomorrow."

And with that, they turned and headed down the steps and toward their car. Stephanie nudged me out of the open doorway.

"It's freezing." She slammed the door and deadbolted it. Then she leaned in close and whispered, "What the fuck is going on here, Jonathan?"

But what was I going to say? Especially to Stephanie, of all people. The best-case scenario was that Peter had made an honest error, trying to execute a very simple task. Worst case? He was siphoning off our renovation budget. I did know that was possible.

"Actually, Peter mentioned he was having an issue with the contractors. I completely forgot until they were standing right there."

"Uh-huh," Stephanie said, eyeing me skeptically.

"He's withholding a payment until they fix some shoddy work," I went on, more quietly. "They probably saw the cars, knew it was me and not Peter, and decided to try and shake me down. It's nothing. I'll deal with it. I just didn't want to get into it right then."

Stephanie looked a tiny bit hurt that I wasn't coming clean. Once upon a time, I told her all my secrets.

"Okay, whatever you say." She was letting me off the hook. Stephanie could be harsh, but she always knew exactly how much you could take. She turned to the group, smiled, and clapped her hands together like a camp counselor. "Who's hungry? Because I, for one, am starving."

Detective Julia Scutt

Sunday, 5:32 a.m.

It's pouring as I drive toward the scene, roads empty, houses all quiet. Almost dawn, the sky is breaking a pale gray at the edges. I try to take a deep breath, but my lungs feel stiff.

Is it helpful that Ace Construction is involved, even peripherally? I mean, not especially.

According to Maeve, there are issues between Jonathan and Ace Construction, some dispute over money that Jonathan conveniently neglected to share. Maeve only mentioned it offhand at the very end of our brief interview. After that call from Dan, I'd been mainly focused on wrapping things up so I could get down to the scene.

"You think this conflict with Ace Construction is related to what happened, Ms. Travis?" I asked Maeve.

"Oh, I don't know." She looked taken aback at the suggestion, though what had been the point of bringing it up otherwise? "But they did seem very angry. The younger one especially. Luke, I think his name was. It was him and an older guy."

"Mike Gaffney?" I hated the feel of his name in my mouth.

"He didn't give his name. But Luke called him Dad, I think."

A fancy weekend house—no surprise Ace Construction had been the ones renovating. These days, they're the biggest and best contractor in the area. Back in the day, when Luke was a teenager, Mike Gaffney did mostly small jobs like renovating our bathroom. I still remembered my mother yelling at Jane and Bethany—always inseparable—to stop deliberately huffing the paint. They'd be dead within days. The smell of drying paint still makes me nauseous.

According to the show notes, *The River* had spent a whole episode on Mike Gaffney. But he'd been interviewed at the time of the murders and, in the end, there'd been nothing to connect him except that work on our bathroom. Plus, he'd had an alibi.

I wonder what else this group might have "inadvertently" left out, aside from this problem with Ace Construction. Their descriptions of the night were suspiciously similar, right down to the pasta Maeve made: penne arrabiata. They'd all called it exactly that. And gave the *exact* same time window that Keith and Derrick had gone out for cigarettes, "nine thirty to nine thirty-five." Drugs—I suspect that's what they're keeping from me. Could be they were all so high earlier they're not exactly sure what happened. No matter how many times you tell people you don't care about the drugs—you're a cop. They'll still believe you do.

Drugs could also be the reason we've got a dead body in a car. Could be a buy went south. The local dealers have a habit of getting unreasonably greedy.

As I round the next corner, I see the woods lit up in the distance like a sports field. There are more than a dozen vehicles lining the road, mostly cruisers, plus a larger crime scene vehicle up ahead, a shiny metal box with NEW YORK STATE FORENSIC INVESTIGATION UNIT written on its side. I drive past the line of cars until I spot an officer up ahead with a flashlight.

I roll down my window as I pull to a stop. Charles—Chuck something—I'm pretty sure.

"Park up on the right," he says, pointing with his flashlight. "It's flooded. Watch your step."

Past the RV, I can see the news crews. I'm not a fan of reporters. They surrounded our house for weeks after Jane disappeared, hungrily consuming our grief and spitting out our bones. In the end, I'd given them exactly what they wanted, racing out of our front door screaming my head off when they finally found Jane. Six days of searching in rain that would not let up, and finally my sixteen-year-old sister's decimated body had been located, her pretty face so badly smashed they had to rely on dental records to identify her. The photos of eight-year-old me running barefoot in the dark had been splashed across the front page of every local paper, and inside many of the national ones.

Or so I'd been told. It's not just the Ace Construction renovation that's faded from my memory. Jane's murder erased whole swaths of my childhood, my memories of everyone and everything hopelessly blurry—my parents, my friends, Bethany. Only Jane is still painfully crystal clear.

But despite what Dan thinks, my refusal to listen to *The River* isn't proof of anything, except me being a rational human. One of the biggest arguments we ever had was about him listening to it. I'd have considered it in bad taste even if he didn't know me or Jane. Dan and Jane weren't friends in school—Jane was in the cool crowd, Dan the nerdy kid looming in the shadows, keeping tabs on everybody. But they did know each other.

"If you don't want me to check it out, I won't, obviously," Dan said at the time. "But, I mean, I do think . . . shouldn't somebody? Just in case?"

"What? You going to find the murderer, Mr. Supersleuth?"

Dan's gaze was unwavering. "That wasn't what I meant, and you know it."

"Listen if you want. If that's your kind of thing," I'd said as I pulled my shirt off over my head. The quickest way to end this conversation was to have sex. Dan was nothing if not linear in his thinking. "I don't care."

I did suspect that Dan meant well. That he was trying to help. He'd offered on many previous occasions to go back through Jane and Bethany's files with me. I'd always refused. Because what if I finally tried to solve Jane's case—really tried, instead of just rushing through—and I still failed? As it was, I could still pretend Jane was mine to save.

As I pull past the reporters to park, I feel their eyes on me. I turn off the car and put a hand to the ring hanging on the chain at my neck, tucked as usual safely out of sight under my shirt. I press the ring against my skin until I feel the reassuring sting. I'd love a way out of my car and into the scene without walking past the reporters. But the woods look too thick in that spot, not to mention too wet to cut through. I have on lace-up boots, but they're not very tall, and it swamps quickly around here.

I take a breath as I finally climb out of the car, my heel slipping instantly. I have to grab onto the side of the car like a fool to avoid hitting the ground. *Shit.* Chuck was right.

"You okay?" a young female reporter calls out, high-pitched and shrill, as she charges over. She's very thin and wearing way too much makeup, even for TV.

I raise a hand like a stop sign and look away. I am screwed if she recognizes me. "I'm good."

She closes in fast anyway. "Detective, we've heard this is now a homicide investigation. Can you confirm?"

Goddamn it. Seldon will decide it's my fault that word of that's gotten out, even if it was on Dan's watch. Unforced error number one. I won't get many more.

"No comment," I say, keeping my eyes straight ahead as I brush past her.

When I finally make it back to the smashed Audi SUV in the woods, Dan is standing a few feet away, arms crossed, boots covered in mud. He's tall and well-built—a good-looking guy, for sure. Dan is watching a crime scene tech in a zipped plastic suit dig around the back seat. The car is badly crushed on one side, headlight shattered. The two front doors are hanging open, interior of the car aglow in the lights that have been set up. The body has been removed. Dan glances my way, then points his chin in the direction of the car.

"There's arterial spray on the far side of the driver's seat and the dash. Uniforms on the scene didn't see that at first. Dark interior, light wasn't great." He uses his flashlight to point. "Anyway, that's why I called. Thought you should see for yourself."

To his credit, Dan could have kept this from me and tried to run with this case on his own. Seldon certainly wouldn't mind. But Dan isn't doing that. Because he's too decent. It's kind of aggravating.

"Yeah, thanks," I say, a little begrudgingly. "What did the ME say?"

"On a quick look, he found two neck wounds. Left side, deep, irregular shape. Not sure of the weapon, but probably not a knife. Also, he's not sure about the face."

"What do you mean, not sure?" I ask. "Isn't it from the crash?"

"Apparently the car would have to have been accelerating *a lot* to do that much damage," Dan says carefully. "And that would have completely destroyed the car, not just smashed the front. So it's possible someone did that, too, after the fact."

I keep my eyes on the car, but I can feel Dan staring at me. He knows about Jane's face. Thanks to *The River*, everyone knows that Jane was finished off with some unidentified object to the face. A signature, the podcast fans like to speculate. There was a well-known and never-caught serial killer at the time who had a similar MO. Was it theoretically possible that Jane and Bethany were among his victims? Sure. But only because anything was possible. Is it possible the smashed face here is the work of that same guy, all these years later? Seems pretty unlikely to me, especially because it's not that uncommon for a killer to disfigure a victim's face. Damn, the pod people would love that kind of sick connection.

However, the right explanation is almost always the simplest. A person in a car dead, another person missing? Missing person is the culprit. Weekender on weekender, exactly as Seldon wants.

"So what did Seldon say when he called you?" I ask.

Dan is quiet for a long minute. Finally, he exhales. "He said go down there and keep an eye on things."

"Keep an eye on me."

"Eye on *her*. I think that was the way he said it. You know, like you were a little kid or a knapsack,"

Dan says. "Come on, Seldon's a jerk. That's not news. Anyway, one of the two punctures—weapon as yet to be determined—must have hit an artery, the ME says."

"Still no sign of the driver?"

"With the rain, the dogs can't seem to catch a scent. I called in a potential armed and dangerous as soon as we saw the blood. But the wounds are on the side. Could be they came from a third party, in the back seat. Left-handed then, would be my guess."

"There was another guy with the group who supposedly went back to the city early," I say. "Some sort of conflict. Uniforms are headed down to the train station to check for him."

Dan glances at me then, like he wants to say something but isn't sure how to put it. In which case, I wish he wouldn't say it at all. Meaning well has never kept Dan from being clumsy. "Listen, I just want you to know—I'm not going to get in the way here," he says. "Seldon told me to come, so I came, because I'm not looking to get on his shit list. But this is your case. You're in charge."

I cross my arms. I'm not falling for Dan's Mr. Nice Guy routine, even if it isn't a routine. I meet his eyes. "Finally, something we can agree on."

I head back to my car, running down potential angles to use with the group back at the house. They're withholding information for sure. If there was a conflict between the driver and the passenger, I need to know about it. I need to know more about why this artist of Keith's took off. Details about the drugs. A more aggressive approach usually backfires, it just puts people on the defensive, but maybe with this group—

"Excuse me!"

When I turn, an older woman with thinning gray hair and a light pink tracksuit is hustling my way. She's panting. "Gracious me," she says, the phrase sounding awkward coming out of her mouth—stilted, too delicate. Her rough edges don't fit with the pink tracksuit either. She waves a hand, then puts it to her bony hip as she bends to catch her breath. "You move so damn fast."

"You shouldn't be here," I say. She's not a reporter, that's obvious. Not that they belong here either. "This is an official investigation."

She steps closer, then smiles like she feels sorry for me. "My, you look exactly the same."

Her words send an uncomfortable prickle down my spine. "The same as what?" My fingers have moved to my neck, pushing down so hard on the ring that it digs into my collarbone.

"Your picture in the paper, back when"—she sucks in some air—"when you were running away from your house that night. In your nightgown."

Like she owns some piece of me. Like she's entitled to talk about what I wore to sleep as a little girl. It's like the distant ringing of a very menacing bell. Blood is pounding at my temples.

I take a step toward her, imagine reaching out and giving her one quick shove. But she might break something if she went down. "You're one of them, aren't you?"

"Them?" She laughs. "What do you mean?"

Armchair sleuths have sprung up in the wake of *The River.* And they have no sense of common decency. They've got no sense, period. They email and call. One even showed up at the station to share a theory about the killer running a sex slave ring. These people think Jane and Bethany are just a puzzle to solve.

"This is an active investigation, not a game show. Get in your car right now and drive back to wherever the hell you came from."

"Oh, I live in Hudson, right behind—"

"I don't care!" The actual reporters are looking my way. And that's the last thing I need. "Just go, now."

"Okay, okay," she says, apologetic but a little excited still. "I didn't mean to—I'm sure this is upsetting. I mean, especially with the—" She grimaces, then motions to her face. "With the—you know."

"No, I don't know," I say, motioning to my own very angry face.

"Well, I mean, the smashed faces? It's like a signature, isn't it?"

I clench my fists to avoid grabbing at her. "Get the fuck out of here," I say, voice shaking. "Or I'll arrest you for obstructing."

But as I turn back to my car, she still hasn't moved.

"You know, Bob Hoff is also back," she says. I tense—I haven't heard that name in a very long time. "Working at the Cumberland Farms, just like he used to. Like nothing ever happened."

Cumberland Farms. Also the possible last stop for our victims. I don't love that coincidence. Not that I ever thought Bob Hoff had anything to do with Jane. As far as I'm concerned, he's an innocent victim, too.

Hoff reportedly told people at the time—bragged, some said—that he'd seen something the day Jane and Bethany were killed. But when the police interviewed him, he denied knowing anything. Got scared about telling whatever he knew, my parents suspected. Because he was a young, semi-employed Black man in a sea of white, the not-talking had turned him briefly into an unofficial suspect in town. Within a week, Bob

Hoff was gone from Kaaterskill, which did nothing to make him seem more innocent to his neighbors.

I can't imagine what's brought him back now. For sure he's not a big podcast listener, otherwise he'd have known better. *The River* devoted an entire episode to the search for him: "The Disappearing Man."

It isn't until I'm in the driver's seat that I look up at the woman again. Her mouth trembles, like she's fighting a smile. I glare at her as I lower my window.

"If I see you anywhere near here again . . . if I see you, period, I'll have you arrested," I say evenly. "And you'd be surprised how fucking long I can misplace a suspect. You could sit in jail for days."

Derrick

Friday, 8:22 p.m.

"Not bad," Finch said, surveying the massive bedroom Jonathan had shown us into.

It was at the front of the house, with denim-colored walls and sharp, bright white moldings. The two double beds were covered in swollen pillows and crisp pale-blue linens with a swirled white-dot pattern—like pin-pricks of light overhead at a planetarium. It reminded me of that five-star hotel Beth and I had stayed at in Rome on our honeymoon, the one we couldn't afford—and yet Beth had still been disappointed in it, because it wasn't the more expensive hotel her friends Isaac and Henry had stayed at after they got married. Beth was routinely disappointed. That's because she'd misunderstood the difference between literary novelist and Hollywood screenwriter. Even now she was perpetually straining her eyes at the horizon, waiting for our ship to come in, even though I had told her repeatedly: no ship had ever set sail.

As I sat on one of the beds, I could feel how tense I was. My whole body was stiff. Between Keith and dealing with Finch and my fight with Beth that morning, I'd been wound tight all day. Beth had been angry about the weekend away—she hated my friends, hated me doing anything for myself. She'd hurled her favorite insults, so familiar by now that they didn't really wound—pathetic, failure, weak, spineless, talentless. I'd shot an angry look her way at "talentless." That one was new, and particularly cruel.

Finch took a deep, noisy breath—dramatic and satisfied—as he sat down on the wide windowsill. He pulled out a cigarette and lit it, inhaling deeply.

"Put that out!" I jumped up and opened the window. "You can't smoke in Jonathan's house. He just renovated the whole thing."

Finch laughed. "You really do give a shit what these people think, don't you?"

"Please," I said. "You're the one who's obsessed with 'these people.' "

He pulled a face. "That's bullshit."

It was not bullshit. Finch was desperate to work his way into my Vassar group. He'd been trying for years, but they'd consistently and wisely boxed him out. My friends all thought he was insufferable. Even Keith, deep down, but he'd made his own deal with the devil. For my part, I had no choice but to tolerate Finch. He had me over a barrel, and he never let me forget it.

"Jonathan is my friend, and he cares about his house. Stop being such a dick." I felt that familiar heat rise in my chest. "Put the fucking cigarette out."

Lately, Finch seemed to be accepting that he was never going to get a seat at our table. And so this thinly veiled hostility had taken the place of his eagerness. The biggest irony was that there were literally thousands of people who would—who did—pay to spend time with Finch. Of course, he didn't want those people. He wanted *my* people. The ones he couldn't have.

"Jesus, take it easy," Finch grumbled, obediently throwing the cigarette from the window, but without putting it out. "This was supposed to be fun."

"Fun for who?" I crossed my arms and leaned back against the wall near the door. "What are you even doing here, Finch?"

He was quiet for a minute, considering. Finally, he met my eyes. "I'm here to fire Keith."

"Knock it off," I said.

"I'm serious."

"What are you talking about?" I asked, hoping this was just Finch, thinking a messed-up joke was entertaining when it was not. "Keith's been amazing to you."

"In some ways, sure." Finch stared at me, matter-of-factly.

Holy shit. He was serious.

"Please, he *made* you, Finch."

This was true. And not even in terms of money. What Keith did was more essential than that. I knew firsthand. It was only thanks to Keith's relentless encouragement—verging on harassment, really: texts, emails, haranguing over beers—that I'd had the guts to finally send my novel out to agents. It was thanks to Keith that I hadn't quit writing altogether when I wasn't accepted into Vassar's coveted creative writing seminar.

"Do you believe in your writing?" Keith asked me late the night I'd been rejected, as we sat on the floor of my room, getting high. He was squinting through the smoke, pointing a finger at me.

I'd considered the question, trying to ignore the fact that my throat still felt raw from crying. Because I had done that—actually cried when I found out about the rejection. No one had seen me, thank

God, but it was still humiliating. Faulkner probably never cried.

"Everyone believes in their own work," I said languidly as the pot worked its magic.

"No, no—I mean like really, really deep down in the base of your spine," Keith had said. "Do you know you *are* a writer?"

I took the almost-finished joint back from Keith and inhaled again, feeling the disappointing heat already at my fingertips. I turned the question around again and again in my head—probably because I was so high. But the answer was the same, no matter which way I looked at it.

"Yeah," I said finally. "I do feel that."

"See, there you go," he replied with a grin. "Because I *don't* feel that."

I'd laughed. "What the hell are you talking about?"

Keith had just won Vassar's Annual Art Prize as a junior, no small thing, for his *Family of Origin* series. And he'd deserved it. The paintings were amazing. He'd shown me as a little boy, sitting behind the wheel of a huge Cadillac, door open, legs too short to reach the pedals. The hair on the back of my neck stood up when I first saw it. I couldn't have imagined a picture of something that never happened so perfectly capturing all that had.

Keith had shaken his head. "That series was all I had. And I'm okay with that, I think. I love art, but I don't think I am an artist. Not the way you *are* a writer. It's knit into your soul. Guard that with your life, man. The world is gonna work hard to steal it from you."

Within three years of graduation, I'd sold two books. The first nearly made me a star. And in the meantime, Keith had made a happy career out of building people like Finch. It would devastate Keith if Finch—his biggest success—turned on him. He was already hanging by a thread.

"Yeah, Keith made me, and I made *him* a shitload of money," Finch went on. "It's not like he didn't get something out it."

I never should have introduced them. That had been obvious to me years before.

"Don't fire Keith, Finch," I said again. "He really cares about you. Look, he brought you up here, even though he knew we'd all be pissed at him."

"And *that's* a perfect example of why I've got to fire him. Why the fuck am I here right now?"

I glared at him. "Because you invited yourself. Like you do *all* the time. I was there, remember?"

"Keith should have drawn a line, though, with this weekend. It's Jonathan's bachelor party, right?" Finch shook his head, disgusted. "He can't be straight with me about anything. You know, he's been pretending that I have a show going up in London at the Serpentine Gallery. But it was canceled weeks ago because of money Keith hasn't paid. Money that doesn't have anything to do with me. Somebody at the gallery called me. After I found out, I told Keith I was going to make something new, too, just for that show. Wanted to see if that would make him come clean. Nope. Not a fucking word. He'd let me work my balls off, for nothing. And you're claiming he cares about me?"

Unfortunately, that did sound like something Keith might do, especially these days. "Fine, then fire him. Just not *this* weekend, okay?"

It was actually in my interest if Finch fired Keith eventually, but right now we needed to focus on getting Keith into rehab. It was the same reason we weren't talking about the latest email from Alice's mom. Who could deal with that on top of the intervention? If Finch fired Keith, the whole weekend would definitely turn into a shit show. And, yes, I was also thinking about Maeve. Whatever chance I had to finally talk to her like I planned to that weekend would also go out the window.

Finch stared at me for a long time, that glint in his eyes. "I'll take it under advisement."

There was a loud burst of laughter, then in the distance, across the hall—Stephanie and Maeve. I looked toward the closed door.

"Does the wife know?" Finch asked.

"Know what?" I asked, turning back to him.

"That you're in love with Maeve."

He was looking at me like he was actually expecting an answer. "I don't know what you're talking about."

Finch started to laugh, throwing his head back dramatically. "Come on, man. I know you in a way these people don't, remember?"

That was true. It was how we'd gotten into this complicated situation to begin with.

Finch had shown up out of nowhere at the launch of my first book. It was a perfect night at the Strand, filled with adoration and beautiful girls and me at the center—the bright and shining literary star. Finch lingered afterward, looking unwashed and desperate. I hadn't seen him in a decade, but that didn't stop him from diving right in.

"I need some cash, man, just to get me on my feet," Finch said, approaching me outside the store. His tone was sheepish, but his directness was alarming. "Just like a couple thousand. I'll pay you back."

What Finch didn't understand—what he refused to believe, even after I explained—was that I didn't have any money. He'd taken one look at the well-heeled crowd and the free wine in the fancy upstairs Reading Room, and he'd determined, incorrectly, that it meant I was wealthy. In reality, I'd signed a $40,000 contract for two books, much of which would be paid out over years to come.

"I don't have that kind of money, Finch."

"Well, I'm a starving artist, man, like literally." He held up a fistful of launch party crackers he'd stolen for emphasis. "I wouldn't be here if I wasn't desperate. There's got to be something you can do, or . . ." Finch's expression turned cold as he squared his shoulders and stood a bit taller. "If you can't help me, I'll be sure these people know who you really are."

"Wait, you're blackmailing me?" I laughed, hoping Finch would come to his senses.

Instead, he just shrugged. "You could argue they have the right to know. Take a few days to think about it. I'll be back in touch."

Sending Finch to Keith—an already legitimate, if still green, art dealer—was the only thing I could think to offer. And, surprisingly, Keith had been totally game. He was doing well enough, but he was still building his client list. What he seemed to care about most at the time was that Finch was very good-looking and extremely charismatic. Keith knew that his way to the top in the brave new digital world would be through artists who also made good celebrities—pretty faces, unique history, good on Instagram—and he loved Finch's Arkansas-trailer-park backstory. Did he care whether Finch's art was any good? Sure. But Keith had more than enough skills of his own to close any gap.

A week later, Keith was thanking me for sending Finch his way. And Finch was delighted about the stipend Keith had given him to tide him over. It hadn't taken long for Keith to sell something of Finch's, though no one ever could have predicted then just how fast or how high Finch's star would rise.

I thought back to the biggest "art incident" Finch had ever staged—all the traffic and pedestrian lights along the busiest four-block stretch of Times Square going simultaneously red for one minute and thirty seconds. For a moment, a whole neighborhood had held its breath. It had been memorable. Cell phone video taken by pedestrians was readily uploaded to a site in exchange for a small honorarium, then spliced together into a loop that—along with the companion paintings and sculptures Finch created of the scene—had been sold to a collector for over $1 million. The combined installation was still on view at MoMA.

Now Finch narrowed his eyes at me, chin lifted. "Okay, I won't fire Keith—on one condition."

"What condition?"

A sly smile spread across Finch's face. "Get me an in with Stephanie. A chance. That's all I'm asking."

"With Stephanie?" I asked. "You cannot be serious."

"Deadly," he said.

"Stephanie hates you, Finch."

"That's an exaggeration." He looked up at me with an unfortunate twinkle in his eye.

"Also, have you met Stephanie? She's not exactly easy to manipulate."

"I think she's more malleable than you realize," he said. "Just tell her how fucked up my childhood was, my dad with the drugs and all that—how much I had to overcome to get out. Make me seem, you know, sympathetic. Multidimensional. Oh, and tell her how hard I work. It's art, but I do work my balls off."

"I'm sure she'd love to hear that. And if I say no?" But I already knew. It was always the same threat, implied or explicit.

"Then not only will I fire Keith, but I'll tell your little Vassar gang how you used to beat the shit out of people on the regular. How you almost killed that kid. I mean, you can pretend you were just saving me back then. But you and I both know you enjoyed beating him half to death. I saw it in your eyes."

I shook my head and stayed quiet for some time. Finch wasn't wrong, I did go too far. And not just that one day. There had been others before. That was just the last time, because the police were called. But I'd spent all the years since becoming a different person. I *was* a different person now.

"So you're blackmailing me. *Again*?"

Finch smirked. "I'm offering incentives."

I closed my eyes. *Fuck*.

"And what if I try with Stephanie, but I still can't convince her?"

"The main thing is that I see evidence of your effort." Finch clasped a hand on my shoulder. "And if I don't, then I guess we'll see whether these friends of yours really do love you unconditionally."

I pulled away from him and stood. I needed out of that room.

In the hall, I bumped right into Maeve. Her blue-gray eyes sliced me open. Back in college Maeve and I were around each other so much that I got past being tongue-tied. But these days, every time I saw her I felt choked anew by awkwardness.

"Oh, I'm so sorry, Derrick," Maeve said, even though I was the one who bumped into her.

"No, no, that was my—how are you?" I asked. It came out rushed and also stiff. I crossed my arms, which only made it worse. "I just—I feel like we haven't had a chance to talk at all since we got here." I motioned to her. "You look great."

"Oh, um, thanks." She tucked her long, shiny blond hair behind her perfect little ear and smiled uncomfortably.

What was wrong with me, commenting on the way she looked, gesturing to her body? This was what happened when you spent an inordinate amount of time obsessing about somebody and comparatively little time actually interacting with them. You acted like a freak.

"Sorry." I shook my head and tried to recover, my hands in my pockets now. I smiled—nice, sweet, harmless. "You look happy, that's what I mean. How are things with . . . Bates?"

As much as I hated saying his name, I needed to recast our conversation—if I knew full well about the boyfriend, then there was no subtext to anything. But I wouldn't go so far as to mention Beth. That would just be depressing.

"Oh, Bates is terrific," Maeve said, smiling, but not with her eyes. "He's really wonderful."

But was he really all that wonderful? I didn't think

so. Her face had not lit up at the mention of his name. Objectively, it had not. In fact, the word that came to mind was *bereft.* There was trouble in paradise. I was about to very gently root around for details when the door swung open behind me.

"What the hell is going on out here!" Finch boomed. "I thought we were going to dinner! I'm starving."

"Yes!" Keith shouted. His eyes were glassy as he bounded out of his room. Maybe he'd just used. Or needed to. Apparently, with opioids, being too high and not high enough were both a problem. "I could use another fucking drink, too."

Stephanie appeared in the doorway opposite. She leaned against the doorframe, studying Keith, her mouth turned down. Because worrying about him was her sole priority right now. Unlike me, who really could think only of Maeve.

"I know exactly the place to get something to eat downtown," Jonathan said, coming briskly into the hall, jacket already in hand. "The Falls. It's got a nice local vibe. And they have great barbeque."

Stephanie's brow furrowed slightly. "You've never been there, have you?"

"No, but Peter has." Jonathan forced an unconvincing smile. "And there's a first time for everything."

Two Weeks (and Two Days) Earlier

I've been watching Keith for nearly an hour from inside Bessell's café, across the street from his gallery. Well, not for the entire hour. Technically, I can only see him when he's near the front window or outside, where he is rather frequently, taking phone calls, looking around. Smoking. Must have been nearly ten cigarettes in just that period. It's revolting, honestly. This is probably why he looks so thin, so gray. Well, not the only reason. There's the drugs and all. The guilt probably isn't helping either.

They all feel very guilty, too—for the bad decisions, for failing a friend.

And I mean, fair enough. The guilt should be eating them alive, as far as I'm concerned. It's actually a wonder Keith can even live with himself, given that he is the person most responsible. Were there intervening acts? Sure. But if you look deep down into the dark core of everything awful that happened—you end up eye to eye with Keith.

To be clear, it's all self-serving anyway. They carry the guilt around so they can excuse getting on with the rest of their lives, enjoying themselves, despite what they did.

And so, after all these years, there I sit, watching. Gathering my evidence, bit by tiny bit. Someone is responsible. Someone is always responsible. And sometimes you really do get the best view from a distance.

I know what you did. Genius in its brevity.

"Is somebody sitting here?" A shaggy young guy with a knit hat and headphones, a laptop in his hands and a stressed-out look on his face, is pointing to the oversize bag occupying the stool next to me.

"So sorry." I smile apologetically as I move the bag. Not that he seems to care as he dives for the seat.

Set on the ground floor of a prime piece of Chelsea real estate across the street, the Keith Lazard Gallery has an all-glass front and a polished concrete floor. There's an overly wide desk that stretches across the front, a gorgeous young blond woman perched behind it like a piece of art herself, a huge arrangement of white orchids on her right. I wonder if Keith is fucking her. I mean, presumably, right? Keith is always fucking somebody—but discreetly, irrelevantly. That's his extra way of making amends—denying himself love. Stupid, honestly. Because it benefits exactly no one.

Keith has soldiered on quite well professionally, though. The Keith Lazard Gallery is very well respected. Of course, owning a gallery isn't the same thing as succeeding as an actual artist. Keith used to paint these enormous abstract canvases—bright blues and reds. Striking, really. And then there was his *Family of Origin* series, which he worked on for years. Kind of presumptuous, if you ask me, but they were beautiful paintings. Keith was going to be the famous artist. He did have the talent. But alas, he decided to snort all his gifts up his nose.

It's not that I'm happy it didn't work out for him. I'm not petty that way. I just believe in people getting what they deserve. And maybe Keith doesn't deserve all the bad things to happen to him. But I'm not sure he deserves all the good things either.

I sound bitter. I know. And honestly, I am feeling unusually resentful right now. Everything just feels so loaded, the stakes so high. I know what I need to do: stay composed, keep my eyes on the prize. The problem is, I have way too much on the line. I can't sit around and wait for something to happen.

A box truck pulls up in front of Bessell's front window, double-parking and blocking my view. It's time to go anyway, even if once again I am leaving empty-handed.

Detective Julia Scutt

Sunday, 6:18 a.m.

As I'm getting out of the car at the Cumberland Farms, my phone buzzes with a text from Cartright. *Are you coming back? These people are getting restless.*

Back in fifteen, I type out quickly. I already know it'll be longer. *Handle it.*

I feel a guilty little tug as I turn off my ringer and tuck my phone away. Like I'm not where I should be. But that's ridiculous. In fact, it would be negligent for me *not* to check if Keith and Derrick were in the Cumberland Farms the night before, to verify the timing, ask for surveillance tapes. However, it would feel better if I'd been planning on heading here before my friend in the pink sweats mentioned Bob Hoff.

Bells jangle as I push open the door, and a damp, mossy smell, something just shy of mildew, greets me. There's a thin white kid working the counter, an Adidas baseball hat pulled low, Budweiser tank top with a big American flag. He's hunched on a stool, staring down. Not Bob Hoff. I don't want to feel disappointed, but I am. Still, there are the questions to be asked, which is why I'm here anyway.

When the guy finally lifts his eyes to mine, his face is heavily lined, papery skin loose against his bony cheeks. The little bit of hair tufted out under his hat is the same cold gray as his eyes. Much older than I thought.

I flash my badge quickly, as I always do. I don't want him reading my name. Scutt means one thing in town: the Scutt-Leigh murders. At least the podcast was called *The River*, for where Jane's body was found. Bethany's blood-soaked, shredded clothes were nearby in a gully of leaves, left behind when her body was dragged off. Black bears are all over the Catskills, too. For a long time I'd been envious of Bethany's family, envious that they'd never had to know exactly what had been done to her—the smashed face, the dozens of deep, small stab wounds. What was left of the family was long gone from Kaaterskill now, but a few years after the murders, I saw Bethany's mom in the grocery store. Once cheerful and warm, always quick with a smile and a big hug, she'd looked stunned, almost terrified, as she circled the grocery store, gripping an empty cart. Like she'd only just been told the news. Bethany's family were very poor, her parents uneducated, but always joyful and warm. They were a wonderful family. At that time, Bethany's dad hadn't yet left, but he would soon, and her oldest two brothers—there had been seven children all together—would each spend time in prison. The unknown is its own kind of horror.

"Were you working here last night?" I ask the guy behind the counter, trying to refocus.

He peers at me. "Why?"

"There was an accident, down the road."

"An accident?" He looks toward the windows. "What kind of accident?"

"Car accident. I'm wondering if maybe the occupants of the vehicle were in here beforehand."

"Where?" He blinks at me. There's a clouded look in his eyes.

"In *here*," I say more loudly, tapping a finger on the counter. "I need to know if some people were in here."

"No, no." His eyes jump to life for a minute as he shakes his head hard. "Not in here."

"How would you know?" I ask. "I haven't even showed you their pictures yet."

He squints slightly, registering his misstep. "Fine, show me."

I hold up my phone, alternating between the two images I have—one of Derrick, one of Keith. "Two white men early thirties, around ten p.m. last night."

He leans forward but still barely glances at the pictures. "Nope," he says. "Not in here."

"Take a closer look."

He grunts, but looks at the pictures again. This time his eyes meet mine more forcefully.

"They weren't in here. Like I said. And I've been on since eight p.m." He checks the time on his phone. "I'm supposed to be off by now. Fucking morning guy is late again. Anyway, I knew every person who came through that door last night except a bunch of high school girls."

"What about security footage?" I point to the video camera mounted over his head.

He snorts. "That shit's just for show."

"Great."

There's a sound then from the back—a door, footsteps. "You can ask Bob if you want." A man emerges from the chips aisle, rubbing the back of his head. In a navy-blue T-shirt and jeans, he is fit, with dark brown skin and short hair, just slightly gray at the temples. The gray is the only sign he's not in his twenties. I feel an irrational twitch of anger, seeing how well Bob Hoff has aged. All that time Jane hasn't had.

"Yo, Bob, you see these two guys in here? Maybe when I was taking a piss."

Hoff pulls up short at the sight of me. I get it—if I were him, I'd be worried about the cops around here, too. Also, I can feel myself glaring at him. Seems highly unlikely he'll recognize me as Jane's sister, though.

I hold up my phone, try to ignore how hard my heart is beating. "I've got pictures, if you don't mind taking a look?"

"Sure," Hoff says. He sounds nervous. Of course he is, after what happened the last time he said he saw something. He leans in, eyes creasing. "Didn't see them."

"Okay," I say. And then to myself: *Leave it.* But I can't. "Are you Bob Hoff?"

He exhales and shakes his head slightly as he stares down at the floor. "Listen, my mom is sick, cancer. She needed someone to take care of her during chemo. Otherwise, I'd never have come back. I don't want any trouble with the cops. I don't want any trouble with anyone. And for the ten thousandth time, I did not have anything to do with any dead girls."

Dead girls. Like they were some stolen stereo equipment.

"One of those dead girls was my sister, you know." It's shot out of my mouth before I've thought it through. And I sound pissed. I feel pissed.

"You're kidding me," Bob Hoff whispers. "This is never going to fucking stop."

"I just want to know what you saw that night," I say, dialing back my tone. "I've looked through the file—you never made a statement."

"Oh, I made a statement," he says.

"It's not in the file, Mr. Hoff."

"I made a statement," he repeats, eyes flashing.

"Then why isn't it there?" I ask.

Already he's shaking his head. "No way," he says. "I gave my statement back then. You can't find it, that's your problem. I didn't have anything to do with those girls. And I didn't see those two men in here."

Hoff does seem awfully sure about the statement. I wonder if I overlooked it, going through Jane's file so quickly. The Gaffneys' interviews were there—they had nothing to do with anything, and didn't know anything either—as well as the statements of their alibi witnesses.

"Now can I go?" Hoff asks. "Or are you going to arrest me for telling the truth?"

My jaw tightens as I gesture toward the door. "Be my guest."

My hands are trembling slightly as I make my way back out to the car. I shouldn't have asked Bob Hoff about Jane. Can't believe I let myself get sucked in.

"What's wrong?"

When I glance up, Dan's leaning against my car.

"Nothing."

"Right." Dan looks wounded. It's as irritating now as it was when we were dating.

I swat him away from the driver's side door. "Excuse me."

"Seldon's been looking for you." He steps aside. "I told him you were headed down to the ME's office, reminded him there's no signal there so he wouldn't be able to reach you. Because *I* haven't been able to reach you. I've called and texted like ten times."

"I was conducting interviews."

He folds his arms as he peers at me. "Well, anyway, I think you're covered for a little bit with Seldon."

"I don't need your *coverage*, but thanks."

Dan's face has tightened. "Okay, so to be clear, you would have been okay if I'd told Seldon you were down here talking to Bob Hoff?"

"Bob Hoff?" I say with impressive nonchalance.

"This is where Keith Lazard and Derrick Chism were before the accident. I'm here running down that lead."

"Well, whatever you were doing here, it's—"

"*That's* what I was doing. Checking to see if our driver or passenger were here before the accident, because supposedly they were. How did you find me, anyway?"

"Some woman in a pink tracksuit busted through the crime tape up at the accident scene," he says. "She was going on and on about how she was sure this case was connected to your sister's case. She mentioned Bob Hoff and Cumberland Farms, and what did I think about you working the case if the two were related? Wasn't that a conflict of interest and whatever."

"Great," I say. "Maybe she'll tell Seldon, because that would be perfect."

"Nah, I think she'll steer clear from now on," Dan says. "I had a uniform put her in handcuffs and drive her home. Scare some sense into her. Susan Paretsky. Her kid died years ago. I think it messed with her head. Anyway, I think she's sorted." I try to ignore the way my chest feels warm. Dan looks across the street to a decrepit boarded-up building. "Hey, remember when that place was a comic book store? Eddie Freeman worked there. He was always drinking those Big Gulps of Mountain Dew."

Like Jane, Eddie Freeman had been one of the cool kids.

"Were you close with Eddie Freeman?" I poke.

"No, not really," Dan says, oblivious. "Oh, I do have something to show you. They found it at the scene." He holds out his phone to show me a photo of something resting in the leaves, something red.

"A baseball hat," I say, straining to make it out. "And?"

He flips forward a couple more photos until he finds one where I can see the words stitched on the front: ACE CONSTRUCTION.

"Where'd they find that?"

"Ten yards from the car," he says, a little regretfully. "Looks like there could be a smudge of blood on it, too."

"Shit." Ace Construction is the exact opposite of the direction that Seldon is going to want this thing to head. I don't love it either.

"Yeah, I know," he says. "But there is a house near there that Ace is working on. Plus, there was other stuff dumped out there, a bedsheet and crap. And the hat was wet when we found it."

"So who knows how long it was out there," I say.

Dan nods. "The smudge could also be paint or something else, too. Still, I thought you should know." He gestures at the Cumberland Farms. "You get anything here?"

"No," I say. "Neither our passenger nor the driver were seen, according to the guy working the counter, who I'm pretty sure is high. No tapes."

"Shit indeed," Dan says, then a long pause. "Did you see Hoff?"

I nod. "His mom's sick. That's why he's back."

"Coincidence, huh?"

"No reason to think otherwise." I feel less convinced, saying it out loud. "Claims he didn't see our guys in there either." Dan and I are quiet for a moment before I add, "And he doesn't know anything about any dead girls." It lands hard the way I say it, and Dan looks at me, concerned. I'm signaling that I need something from him, and he'll want to give it to me. It's like an involuntary tic, this need for Dan's attention. "Hoff claims he gave an official statement, but I don't think it was in the file. I need to look again."

"Let me know if you want any help," Dan offers casually, like it's for the first time. "And you sure you're okay? This is . . . a lot." He knows better than to be too explicit.

"Listen, there's some unfortunate overlap here, no doubt. But I do think it's a coincidence." I put my sunglasses on as I get into the car. "Besides, you know me—I'm good at seeing only what I want to see."

Alice

I don't know how long I'll be able to go without telling my mom. I always tell her everything and my mom is always there for me, no matter what. My friends don't understand that because they all have these fucked-up relationships with their families. I don't—my mom is my best friend.

But my friends and I have a pact about the roof. Absolute secrecy. Forever. My mom wouldn't like the sound of that. She's never really loved my Vassar group. Worries about their influence on me. Maybe she's right. They've already convinced me to pretend that guy never existed. Because who cares about some random blue-collar townie, right?

Okay, that's not fair. That's definitely not how my friends feel. They're not bad people (not even

Keith, no matter how hurt I am). They're scared, that's all.

We were all terrified—that's why we didn't call the police. It was chaos on the roof. All of us so freaked out and wasted—it's hard to remember who said what when. And then, all of a sudden, we were running down the steps and back to our dorms.

I almost called the police when I was back in my room. "But it's too late now," Maeve said before she headed up to her senior-year single on the floor above. "You can't just make that choice for everyone."

So I called my mom instead. I only told her that something bad had happened, not what. Right away she demanded to know whether I'd been sexually assaulted. She thinks people are getting raped left and right at Vassar.

I told her that I was okay, that I would be—but that I couldn't tell her what had happened, not yet. And she said exactly what I needed her to: "When you're ready, then. But I hope you know you can tell me anything. I'm always here to help."

Maeve

Friday, 8:54 p.m.

By the time we got to downtown Kaaterskill it was nearly 9:00 p.m. The storefronts were all dark except for the little "gourmet" market with the smudged windows at the top of the block. Cars were clustered in front of the Falls at the far end, the glow from the huge front window lighting up both sides of the street.

I could already imagine the damp heat inside, the yellow light, warped floor, and sticky tables. The beer would be cheap, the liquor bottles dusty. The drunk white men—and they would all be white—would be wearing graphic T-shirts, their body odor mixed with too much Polo Ralph Lauren. And that look in their eye like they already knew exactly how they'd fuck you—bent over and from behind.

What a disgusting thought. I shook my head, quickly willing it away. Dark thoughts like that had a way of multiplying. I needed to be back in Manhattan with Bates.

But my only option at the moment was to focus on making it through this weekend and staying positive, for everyone's sake. Especially for Jonathan, who was not only Bates's best friend but also—let's face it—kind of my boss. I smiled as I got out of the car, then followed him across the street.

"Hey," I said, jogging to catch up.

"Hey," Jonathan said, not even looking at me. Stress was emanating off him. He pointed his chin toward Finch and Keith. "We are screwed with Finch here."

"I think it'll be fine. We'll just have to be a little more careful." I put a hand on Jonathan's back. "Don't worry."

"Yeah, sure." Jonathan did not sound convinced.

That was the problem with being everyone's eternal optimist: they always thought you were putting an unrealistic spin on things.

"Hey, have you heard from Bates tonight?" I asked.

"Oh, uh, no, why?"

Bringing up Bates in the midst of everything else was a little self-involved—maybe more than a little. But I couldn't help it. Two of my texts had gone unanswered now: Miss you already, from the car, and then after we got here, You okay?

"I just—I texted him and didn't hear back," I said. "I want to be sure he's okay."

"You know Bates, he's the worst about responding," Jonathan said. "I'm sure he's fine."

But Bates was not the worst about responding to me. And Jonathan's tone was so careful. Was Bates *deliberately* not answering me, and Jonathan knew why?

"Right, yeah," I said, trying to sound curious, not concerned. "I've just—Bates has been kind of distant lately in general. I thought you might know something."

"Listen, Bates is a good friend. But he's weird with women. I did tell you that at the beginning." Jonathan turned to look at me. "He always finds a fatal flaw in every girl he's dating. Or he manufactures one. And then he uses it as an excuse to break up with them just as things are getting serious."

"Oh," I said, feeling ill. "So what's my fatal flaw?"

"It's not *your* flaw. That's my point," Jonathan says. "It's Bates."

"But, Jonathan, what is—"

"Maeve, come on," he pleaded.

I tried not to feel irritated. Jonathan was in a tough spot, caught between two friends. Still, if he knew something, he should be telling me.

"Please, Jonathan."

He sighed. "Bates told me last week that he thought you weren't always being yourself with him."

"What does that mean?" I asked.

"I have no idea. I didn't ask. The way he said it was just totally—abstract. Like he meant it on some kind of metaphysical level. Which is so Bates. Anyway, I told him he was being an idiot and was going to ruin a good thing." When Jonathan turned to look at me, his eyes were soft, which made my own start to burn. "Come on, don't get upset. The good news is that I think he actually heard me this time when I said he was the one with a problem." Jonathan squeezed my arm. "He'll come around. And if he doesn't, then it's definitely his loss."

"Thank you, Jonathan," I said, smiling at him, trying not to panic.

I took a deep breath and tried to collect myself as we reached the door. Okay. This was going to be okay. I eyed the bar window as Keith and Finch led the way inside. The big beefy backs of men were clustered around a dartboard that looked recklessly close to the front door. I could already hear "Sweet Caroline" playing inside. Of course it was.

"I'm sorry about before," Derrick said from behind me.

"Oh?" I turned around. I had no idea what he was talking about.

"I mean back at the house," Derrick went on, moving his hands around in his pockets like he was looking for loose change. "I feel like I made you uncomfortable."

Except we'd barely spoken. But I didn't want to hurt Derrick's feelings by seeming oblivious. I knew he had romantic feelings for me—a crush based on some idea of me he had in his head. We'd never spoken about it, but ever since we'd gotten to Jonathan's house, I'd had the sense that Derrick was finally—after all this time—working up the nerve to say something.

"That's okay," I said, looking him in the eye, hoping to head the discussion off at the pass. "Really."

Derrick looked so genuinely relieved as he held open the door for me that it filled me with dread. He was going to try again. I could tell.

Inside, the smells were just as I had imagined them—beer and damp wood and a dash of cigarette smoke, mixed with the tang of sweat. *It smells like men.*

Alice had said that to me at our first dorm party freshman year, crinkling her perfect nose as she gripped a big red Solo cup. *It smells like men in here.* Not that Alice was nearly as delicate as she seemed. Despite her fancy upbringing and her tiny ballerina's frame, she was surprisingly strong. Watching her rip across the floor in her pink satin toe shoes had always been like watching a spectacular act of violence.

Maybe standing up to her terrifying mother—once a principal dancer with the New York City Ballet—had toughened her. Alice didn't think her mother was scary, though. She adored her. They were best friends, apparently. But their relationship had always seemed, to me, unnaturally close. Not that I was an expert in such things.

I followed Derrick through the crowd, squeezing past a small dance floor, where two couples were gripping each other and a dozen or so single women were now swaying to "American Pie" as men eyeballed them from the perimeter. Finally we reached a free table against the back wall, where there was a little more breathing room. Derrick and I each grabbed some empty chairs. Jonathan and Stephanie were still some distance behind, fighting their way through to join us. I didn't see Keith and Finch anywhere, but then even with contacts, my eyesight is poor.

Derrick pressed his lips together and shook his head, staring across the room as he sat down. "Do you ever feel like you have no idea how you got somewhere?"

Oh, no, here he went again. I willed Stephanie and Jonathan to hurry up.

"Everybody feels that way sometimes," I said casually. "I think they call it being an adult."

Though, for my part, the honest answer was: No. I did not feel lost or disappointed or confused. I was where I'd always wanted to be. And I'd worked really hard to get here.

Derrick turned and looked at me, smiled. "Yeah. Maybe that's it."

I did feel sorry for Derrick. Things for him really hadn't turned out the way they should have. His first book got some well-deserved attention. But then his second barely made it into bookstores. He finished his third book two years ago, but it was never published at all. I did believe things were turning around for him, though. He'd started work on a new book, and now all he needed was to leave Beth and find the right girl, a doting student perhaps. I'd have told him so if I wasn't so afraid he might say *I* was that girl.

"Where did Finch and Keith go?" When I looked around, I clocked an unshaven man watching us. We'd drawn attention when we came in, of course we had—

our clothes, our money. And there was nothing good about standing out.

"God only knows where they went," Derrick said.

Finally, Stephanie and Jonathan were spit out of the crowd, looking put off.

"They don't serve food here, of any kind," Stephanie declared when they reached our table. "So if you're keeping score, we just started off our intervention at a bar, on an empty stomach."

Jonathan looked around a little sheepishly. "Peter told me they had barbeque. I'm sure that he did."

Stephanie dropped herself down into a chair. "Maybe we should be a little more careful about blindly following Peter."

"What's that supposed to mean?" Jonathan shot back.

Stephanie held up her hands. "Nothing, sorry. I'm just hungry."

"Did you guys see where Finch and Keith went?" Derrick asked.

"They're up at the bar getting shots, naturally," Jonathan said. "I'm sorry, you guys—I really did think they served food."

"Maybe we could order something to be delivered here?" I offered.

"Sure, how about pad Thai or macrobiotic beets?" Jonathan said.

Stephanie turned to Derrick. "Do you think you could get Finch to leave? It would make this situation a lot easier if we didn't also have to worry about navigating around him."

"I did start that conversation," Derrick said. "But I have to be careful. If Finch sniffs out that he's got something we want, we'll be screwed."

"Keith seemed extra jumpy on the drive over," I said. "What if he tries to buy drugs in here, right now?"

"Well, that would be unfortunate." Jonathan looked around the room suspiciously. "If he gets arrested especially. I got a speeding ticket once, and I can tell you the local authorities do not like weekenders."

Dealing with the police up here would be worse than unfortunate, though. It would be a disaster.

"Maybe we should just get Keith checked into that rehab now," I suggested. "I mean, why wait until Monday? Some kind of drug deal with strangers—that could be really dangerous."

"Apparently Bright Horizons only takes new admissions on Sunday afternoons," Jonathan said. "They have a lot of rules. I guess you have to when you're dealing with addicts."

"I see Keith and Finch," Derrick said. "They're coming."

Finch was snaking his way through the crowd, a cluster of shot glasses pinched in his fingers. Keith was hustling to keep up, more little glasses in his hands, chattering earnestly. But Finch seemed to be focused only on us as he got closer—actually, on Stephanie. Oh, I hoped not. Because nothing about that would end well.

"How about pizza?" Stephanie pulled out her phone and stood abruptly. "I'll be right back. I'm going to go call outside."

She headed toward the door, brushing past Finch and Keith without a word.

"Shots!" Keith deposited his glasses on the table. "Clase Azul. I can't believe they had it."

"What's that?" Derrick asked, peering down at the glasses.

"Jesus, man, tequila!" Keith called.

"Oh, wonderful, a frat party," Jonathan said.

"Come on," Finch said, holding glasses out to me and then Jonathan. "This *is* your bachelor party. You can't have a bachelor party without at least one round of shots."

We took the small glasses reluctantly. But tequila shots were, honestly, the least of our problems.

"Congratulations, Jonathan." I raised my glass high. "May you and Peter have a wonderful life together."

I swallowed the shot, my throat seizing. I really was not a drinker. With my background, drinking and drugs had always been too much of a risk. Jonathan drank his shot without flinching, but he looked troubled now, about Keith probably.

"Come on, Derrick, what are you waiting for!" Finch shouted, so loud people looked our way. "Always so slow on the uptake."

"Fuck you, Finch." Derrick was gripping his shot glass so tight I worried it might shatter in his palm. Finally he sucked in some air and dutifully kicked back the tequila. He set down his glass and stood. "I'm going to go get myself a beer. Anyone want anything?"

More drinks? That wasn't like Derrick. When no one answered, he started toward the bar.

"Debutantes aren't usually known for holding their liquor," Finch said.

And when I looked up, he was staring at me. "Oh, no," I said, looking past him to Keith, who was staring at the bathrooms, his forehead shiny with sweat. Suddenly, he stood. "Keith, what's up?"

"I'll be right back," he said, still focused on the bathroom.

"Hey, wait. Where are you going?" Jonathan reached out to grab Keith by the arm as he stepped away.

Keith slipped through his grasp. "Christ, I'm just going to piss," he called back, moving quickly toward the bathroom.

Jonathan looked relieved when his phone buzzed in his pocket. "Oh, it's Peter. I've got to take this," he said, looking down at his phone. "I don't have a signal. I'm just going to go to the . . ."

He was already headed away from the table, phone to his ear. Leaving me very unfortunately alone with Finch.

"So I've heard things about you," Finch said, leaning in like he was sharing a secret of his own instead of prying into one of mine. He put his phone down on the table—the phone that had been in his hand nonstop, like he was waiting for a pressing call. "Like that you've got a penchant for taking what doesn't belong to you."

"Oh yeah?" I asked in a monotone. Finch was just making crap up, baiting me.

"And a little bird also told me your dad is a real piece of work."

Unfortunately *that* was probably something Finch had actually heard. From Keith, I imagined, maybe Derrick.

"You should tell that little bird to mind their own fucking business."

"Whoa!" Finch's eyes went wide with delight. "Look at the mouth on you, debutante! Your daddy teach you to talk dirty like that?"

"Finch!" Derrick shouted, appearing from nowhere, beer in hand, tendons in his neck straining. "Don't talk to Maeve like that!"

"Come on, we're all friends here."

"No, we're not." Derrick looked furious. "You're not friends with any of us."

"Derrick, you and I are absolutely friends," Finch said icily. "I know you better than anybody, remember?"

"Oh, I remember." Derrick leaned toward Finch in an alarmingly threatening fashion. "I'm just not sure I care anymore."

"Hey, guys, stop." I snapped my fingers between them, then grabbed up the shot glasses in my fingers and shoved them toward Finch. We did not need a bar fight. "Get some more shots, Finch. You're right. It's a party. We could all stand to loosen up a bit."

Finch kept his eyes on Derrick for a long moment before finally taking the glasses from me. "Sure thing."

Derrick dropped himself down into his chair once Finch was gone. "I'm sorry about him," he said, then stayed quiet for a minute. "What do you think Alice would say about all this ridiculousness if she was still here?"

"If Alice was still here, none of this would be happening."

This was probably true, strictly speaking. Not that Alice was exactly a steadying influence. Keith and Alice's relationship had always been stormy, partly because Alice was intense about everything and everyone. She'd been that way from the second we'd met as freshman-year roommates. I'd already been unpacked when she arrived, huge duffel bag slung over her intimidatingly sinewy arm.

"I am so excited that we're sharing a room!" she'd said, pulling me into one of her fierce, bony hugs. When she released me, she eyed my pricey pink shift dress and matching pink headband. I braced myself for some kind of dig. I'd saved ages for that outfit, only to immediately regret it the second I stepped on Vassar's campus and saw that everyone was dressed in black. "Oh I love that dress. It's so retro chic. We should put our clothes in one closet and share everything!"

I'd always felt both flattered and overwhelmed by Alice's attention. That was her specialty—keeping you off balance. She was rarely intentionally manipulative, though. I'd had friends like that—dangling you on a string so they could be the smart one or the pretty one or the thin one. Wanting you around only so that they could be *more* compared to your *less*. But Alice wasn't like that. She was a good person. She really was.

"You're right," Derrick said. "If Alice was here, I guess we'd all be different. I probably wouldn't even be with Beth." He stayed quiet then, waiting for me to inquire. But there was no way I was touching his marriage. "So, you and Bates . . ."

"Things are good," I said. And they *were* good. "We'll see."

"And—just to confirm—Bates is his actual name?"

I laughed. Derrick's delivery had been priceless—a little bit jealous, but not too much. "Well, he *is* a friend of Jonathan's, so . . ."

"Ah, right." Derrick nodded knowingly. "That does explain it. Well, I'm glad you're with someone who makes you happy, that you've been able to move on. Much better than the rest of us have, anyway."

"That sounds a little like a criticism."

"No, no. That wasn't what I meant." Derrick shifted in his chair. "The rest of us are just so paralyzed by guilt or something—you've made healthier choices. That's all I meant."

Even if it was a swipe, Derrick was entitled maybe. He was allowed to have hurt feelings.

I sighed. "What's the good of drowning in guilt, all these years later?" I asked. "I mean, life . . . it's short."

Derrick looked at me pointedly. "Right."

"Obviously, it was a mistake what we did after—not calling the police."

Derrick looked at me again, like he was going to say something else. Or like he was waiting for me to add something more. But then he shook his head and put a hand over mine. It was unexpectedly warm and comforting. "You're right," he said. "You're definitely right."

"Well, well!" Finch bellowed as he cracked a set of full shot glasses down on the table, spraying most of their contents into the air.

I jerked my hand back from under Derrick's and wiped at my damp arm. "Was that necessary?"

"Sorry, I was just distracted by the fact that I leave for one second and come back, and here you two are holding hands," he said. "You don't waste any time."

"We weren't holding hands," I said. Except we had been, hadn't we?

Finch kicked back one of the shots, grimaced, then picked up another. "You tell yourself whatever you need to, debutante," he said. "And I'll keep on calling it like it is."

Detective Julia Scutt

Sunday, 6:50 a.m.

"Jesus," Cartright snaps, charging at me the second I step inside. He must have been waiting in the foyer, staring at the door. He checks his watch dramatically. "You said you'd be right back. That was like two hours ago."

I'd taken longer than I said, but not that long.

"Having a hard time babysitting, huh?" I glare at him. "I'll be sure to let Seldon know."

"You think it's so easy, you do it. They've been squawking about heading back to the city for the past forty-five minutes. I was about to let them go because of the fucking headache they're giving me."

"That's ridiculous," I say. "They can't leave."

"Tell them that," Cartright says.

"I plan to," I say, breezing past him. "When the uniforms get here, you can go."

It's dead quiet out in the living room. The lights are all still on, unnecessary now with the daylight. Jonathan and Stephanie have fallen asleep, leaning against opposite ends of the couch. Maeve is awake, sitting upright between them. She crosses her arms tight when she sees me, her eyes going glassy.

"Is there news?" she asks.

"Can you wake them?" I ask. "I have some more questions."

Maeve elbows first Jonathan, then Stephanie.

"Oh, did you find . . . whoever is missing?" Stephanie asks sleepily, wiping at her mouth with the back of her hand.

"We haven't found the driver yet, and the passenger is still unidentified," I say. "But we do have reason to believe now that it wasn't an accident."

"What do you mean?" Jonathan asks.

"I can't get into specifics because—"

"What—we're suspects?" Stephanie asks. "Because that would be absurd."

I smile, surely not pleasantly. "That wasn't what I was going to say. I was *going* to say that because this is an ongoing investigation, we need to keep certain details confidential. That way we don't unintentionally taint future interviews. But I will say, I don't believe you have all been completely forthcoming."

"Based on what?" Jonathan asks.

"A feeling," I say. "That and the fact that Keith and Derrick were never in the Cumberland Farms. I checked with the clerk."

"What does that prove? We told you we didn't know what happened after they left here," Stephanie says. "Only what they said they were doing. And, just to clarify, we are free to leave anytime. This isn't a custodial interrogation, right?"

A lawyer, definitely. "You are free to go, yes," I say. "I mean, I'd assume you'd want to stay and help find out what happened to your friends."

"Of course we do," Jonathan says.

"Well, maybe we just need to start at the beginning. Like with the tire tracks I just noticed—on the lawn, going around the side of the house." I point to where I saw them on my way in. "Any idea where those came from?"

Maeve is already shaking her head. "No." She looks over at Stephanie and Jonathan. "Do you guys?"

Stephanie and Jonathan shake their heads too. "No," Jonathan says, but it's not especially decisive. "I didn't even see them."

"Well, they're out there." I nod my head again in that direction. "Deep tracks all the way around the side of the house."

Jonathan frowns. "Maybe something having to do with the renovation?"

"Can you at least tell us what you *think* happened to Derrick and Keith?" Stephanie asks. "You must have some theories by now."

"Honestly, the most likely scenario under the circumstances is that there was some kind of conflict between the two of them. Any idea what that might have been about?"

"What about Finch?" Maeve offers quietly, looking at the others again.

"The client who left early?" I ask.

"There were issues between Keith and Finch," Stephanie says. "It's possible Derrick got in the middle. He and Finch grew up together, and he introduced Finch to Keith initially. The three of them have a complicated relationship."

"But Finch left," Jonathan points out.

"Supposedly," Maeve says. "But we don't know that for sure, do we?"

"Finch does like to cause problems," Stephanie says.

"Conflict. For the fun of it," Jonathan adds.

"Not sure anyone intended fun here," I say. "What we've confirmed is that the passenger didn't die in the accident. He was stabbed."

"Oh my God," Stephanie says, her eyes flooding with tears as she covers her mouth with a hand. "That's just . . ." When she blinks, an actual tear makes it out onto her cheek. She brushes it quickly away.

I feel a pang of regret for being so matter-of-fact. Murder is utterly and uniquely traumatizing.

"What about those pictures you were going to bring us?" Jonathan asks. "To try to identify them?"

I regret even mentioning that as a possibility. Because that is not happening either until I rule them out as suspects. And, yes, it will be helpful to make the ID, but not if that means damaging the investigation. "I will do that as soon as I have an opportunity."

"And you ran the fingerprints?" Maeve asks. She looks over meaningfully at Jonathan and Stephanie. "I mean, if it's Derrick . . ."

"But we don't know if that was even true," Jonathan says.

"Somebody care to fill me in?" I say.

Maeve clasps her small, pale hands together. "Derrick apparently assaulted somebody back in Arkansas.

When he was a kid. Or that's what Finch said. We never knew about it before this weekend. It sounded like Derrick was arrested."

"But Finch *is* an asshole, like we said," Jonathan says. "He could have been making that up."

"Except Derrick didn't deny it," Maeve says.

Jonathan looks up at me. "That's true. Derrick didn't deny it."

"Okay," I say, letting myself sound as annoyed as I feel. "Derrick having a juvenile criminal history in another state would have been helpful for me to know about earlier."

"Criminal history sounds so . . ." Jonathan doesn't finish.

"Accurate?" I ask. "Listen, I'm trying to stay patient here. I get that you're upset. But I need to know *everything*. And I mean all of it, right now. Let me decide what's relevant. Maeve, you mentioned earlier something about the contractors?"

Jonathan shoots Maeve a look. So much for full transparency.

"I wasn't trying to—they did come here asking to be paid, and they weren't happy," she says to Jonathan, defensive. "I thought we wanted her to know everything that might be relevant."

"Maeve is right," Stephanie says smoothly. "It could be relevant, in theory. But Jonathan was making sure they got paid."

The response is practiced, lawyerly. Stephanie has stepped in to cover something up. Maybe Jonathan doesn't have as much money as he's pretending to?

"The contractors showed up Friday night and demanded money. I wanted to pay them whatever they were owed. I know that a lot of people think the weekenders are rich, entitled assholes, but . . ." He avoids my eyes, shrugs like it's no big thing. Except tension is written all over his face. "First, I needed to at least be sure there hadn't been some sort of misunderstanding. Or a bank error. Also, you can't just take eleven thousand dollars out of an ATM."

"And so what happened?" I ask.

"They agreed I could pay them later, and then they left."

"And did you?"

Jonathan blinks at me like a stunned deer. "Did I what?"

"Pay them later?"

Jonathan rubs his hands on his thighs. "Yes, yes," he says. "I gave them money."

"Keith's also an addict," Maeve blurts out. Jonathan winces, while Stephanie stares stonily straight ahead.

Maeve's gone off script again. "I mean, it's a problem. Derrick would have been trying to get Keith to come home, trying to keep him safe. But if Keith was really determined to buy drugs . . ."

"What are you saying, Maeve?" Stephanie demands. "Now you think Keith did something to Derrick? Because that's insane."

"It is the most logical explanation under the circumstances. Victims and perpetrators are rarely strangers," I say. "And, as you've pointed out, you weren't in the car, so you don't actually know."

"Okay, fine." Stephanie glares at me. "Finch, maybe. But not Derrick or Keith. I just refuse to believe that. You don't understand, they're like brothers."

"Keith *was* out of control, Stephanie," Jonathan says gently. "And if they were buying drugs, it could have been somebody they, I don't know, picked up or something . . ."

Stephanie looks for a moment like she's going to argue, but then her mouth quivers. When she looks down, Jonathan wraps an arm around her shoulders.

"Do you know what Keith was using?" I ask. "What kind of drugs?"

"He hid it mostly," Jonathan says. "But for sure it wasn't just weed or something. Some kind of pills."

I stand. "I'd like to take a look at his things."

"Oh, sure, of course," Jonathan says. "They're upstairs."

The stairs creak softly as we head up. Just the right amount to make the house seem lived in, but not enough to make it feel run-down. I follow Jonathan, with Maeve and Stephanie close behind. The upstairs of the house is as nice as the downstairs. Standing in that pretty hall, with all those lovely guest bedrooms in every direction, I wonder about the choices I've made—to live in Kaaterskill, to be a cop. Things that'll never get me a home anywhere near as nice as Jonathan's. Jane would have wanted a different life for me.

But then, she'd always had grander plans. She was going to attend Vassar, double major in studio art and French, and be a fashion designer, living in Paris and drinking espressos on the Champs-Elysées. She had a poster of the Eiffel Tower hanging on the wall across from her bed, and another one—Coco Chanel draped in pearls—over her desk. She'd been talented, too—sewing, knitting, designing. I still have the dozen or so things she made me, all sized for a little girl except for the matching pair of sweaters she knitted us that last Christmas: grass green and cropped, with a cable-knit pattern and a dramatic cowl-neck. Mine was too big for me back then, but Jane wore hers all the time. She was wearing it the day she died, though she was found only in her bra.

"Um, Keith was staying back here," Jonathan says, pointing as he walks ahead down the upstairs hall. "In this bedroom."

We turn into a big room with two large windows overlooking the Hudson. The day is gray, the water like steel in the distance. Two of the walls are covered in a bold black-and-white wallpaper, like some kind of abstract painting. The wall opposite the windows is painted an actual matte black, something I'd have said would be absurd, but actually doesn't look half bad. I notice that the unmade bed has a twisted white comforter and a bunch of pillows, but no sheets. Dan had mentioned something about a sheet, hadn't he?

Jonathan hovers near the windows with his arms crossed. Stephanie is on the opposite side of the room, staring at the bed like something happened there. I wonder if she and Keith were sleeping together.

"His bag is over here," Maeve offers, now seeming the most relaxed of the bunch as she walks across the room toward it.

"Don't touch anything, please," I say, heading her off. "I need to preserve the chain of custody."

Maeve's hands shoot up as she takes a step back. "Oh, sorry."

I pull out some plastic gloves and put them on before picking through Keith's duffel. Expensive clothes jammed in the bag like he was making a run for it. At the very bottom I find a glass tube wrapped in tissues. I hold it up.

"What's that for?" Jonathan asks.

"Snorting something," I say. "Cocaine, crushed pills, heroin. Could be anything."

"Heroin?" Stephanie sounds genuinely appalled.

I'm still looking in the bag when I notice the nightstand drawer ajar. When I open it, there's a small fabric pouch inside. Partially unzipped. I lift the top with a finger, and sure enough, there are needles, a spoon. A cooking kit.

"Looks like maybe he was using needles, too," I say. "I'll have the medical examiner check for evidence of intravenous drug use. Might help us make an ID."

"Jesus," Maeve whispers.

"Keith's been having a hard time for a long time. We didn't know it had gone that far." Jonathan sounds stricken. "Maybe we should have. But we didn't."

"His girlfriend, a friend of ours, Alice, killed herself when we were at Vassar," Maeve says. "Keith never got over it."

"Could they have been headed to the Farm instead of the Cumberland Farms?" I ask.

"The Farm?" Jonathan asks. Hard to believe that as

a weekender, he hasn't heard of it. They've been leading the charge to get the place torn down.

"Yeah, you know, the falling-down barn on Route 32?" I say. "It's the main place around here to buy opioids. The guy who runs it kind of has a lock on the market."

And Seldon's made no concerted effort to shut him down. Claims he's planning a coordinated effort with the state. Seems to me some effort might be better than no effort at all.

I see something shiny then, on the floor between the nightstand and the bedframe. I pick it up—a driver's license, the photograph of a pretty, smiling blonde. She looks like somebody's favorite babysitter. Crystal Finnegan. Twenty-three now. But the license was issued seven years earlier when, from the photo, Crystal was a fresh-faced, young-looking sixteen.

"Who's Crystal Finnegan?" I ask, holding up the license.

There's a long delay before Stephanie finally steps forward to look at the picture. Maeve and Jonathan quickly follow suit.

"I don't know," Jonathan says, giving one palm a quick rub across his leg. "Do you guys?"

The others shake their heads.

I nod. "So you have no idea how her driver's license ended up on Keith's floor?"

More head shaking. "No," Jonathan says. "I mean, there are cleaning crews and maintenance in when we're not here. Maybe she works for one of them?"

"Sure," I say, slipping the license into a plastic bag and tucking it in my pocket. Though I'm guessing the answer is way more complicated than that.

We stop to take a look in Finch and Derrick's room next. The beds are clearly slept in. On the floor on the other side is another small duffel bag. I head over, check the name tag: DERRICK CHISM in flawless penmanship.

I kneel down, grabbing a fresh pair of gloves from my pocket and sliding them on before I open it. I move my hands carefully through the pristine contents, underwear and T-shirts rolled with unnerving military precision. I set them next to the bag.

"Beth probably packed for him," Jonathan says, regret in his voice. "She's a control freak."

The rest—jeans, socks—is totally unremarkable. But there is a plastic grocery bag tucked into a corner, and inside that are a pair of fitted cotton boxer shorts and a very soft T-shirt. Expensive, you can tell from the touch. In the bag there's a receipt for a deodorant stick and a toothbrush.

"Finch came last minute," Stephanie says as I look

at the receipt. "They probably stopped on the way to get things for him. Except that's one of Finch's T-shirts, I think. A little weird that he had a change of shirt with him."

At the very bottom of it all is an 8 ½ x 11 unsealed manila envelope. I lift it out and open it. Inside are a stack of handwritten pages. Actually, photocopies of handwritten pages. I pull them out a couple inches to look more closely.

"What is that?" Maeve asks, coming over. Her tone is protective, and fair enough. I am looking through her—possibly dead—friend's things.

"Some kind of writing," I say, extending it in her general direction. But I'd like to get a handle on what it is before I let her look too close.

"Derrick's a novelist," Maeve offers. "I know he was working on a new book. Maybe that's it."

"Or some kind of research," I say. What do I know about writing a novel?

"Can we have it?" Maeve reaches out. "We'd like to read it whatever it is. Or I know that I would."

"Sorry, but for the moment this is going to have to stay where it is. It's too early to know what might need to be collected as evidence."

"But they're the victims," Maeve says, her voice wavering.

"We don't actually know that yet about both of them, do we?" I say. "Unless you know something definitive that you *still* haven't told me, all options are on the table."

"We're trying to tell you anything that might be important," Jonathan says, which sure is a particular choice of words.

"How about you let me be the judge of what's important." My tone is sharp. I'm running out of patience with these people. But snapping at them probably isn't going to make them any more cooperative. "Listen, I'm sure your hearts are in the right place, but sometimes in trying to protect a friend, you can actually put them in harm's way."

They are all avoiding eye contact as I head for the door. Something in the garbage can—white and balled up, with big brown blotches—catches my attention. I tilt my head for a closer look, then crouch down, putting on a new set of gloves to fish it out. Crumpled tissues stained a dark red-brown.

"What is that?" Stephanie asks, close behind me.

"Looks to me like blood." I look up at her unblinking eyes. "And let me guess—you all have no idea where it came from?"

Stephanie

Friday, 9:12 p.m.

Four pizza places. That's how many I called while standing on the sidewalk in front of the Falls. Only one of them—Pepi's—even answered.

"But the Falls is a bar and not a house," the woman said. "We can't deliver to a bar."

"Could we come pick it up?"

"Yes, but we close in five minutes. You'd have to be here by then. And we're at least fifteen minutes from the Falls."

After I hung up, I squeezed my phone and leaned my head back against the brick building. Absurdly, I felt like I wanted to cry. I was also freezing, even in the sweater and jeans I'd changed into before we left the house. I closed my eyes and tried to think warm thoughts. Freezing or not, I'd still rather be out here than inside the bar. Inside, there was a clock ticking down. All those unreturned calls—I'd known it wasn't the most mature way to handle things. But when the calls finally stopped, I'd convinced myself it was behind me.

"Hey, I know you." I opened my eyes to a pair of blue ones glowing back at me. "You owe me eleven thousand dollars."

The contractor and two friends—a huge blond guy with a fleshy pink baby's face and a slight weaselly guy with a creepy grin and hideous oversize teeth—were approaching the door to the Falls. Out of his hat and in a well-fitted linen button-down, the contractor—Luke, right?—was even better-looking than I'd realized. His eyes were especially hypnotic. The two far-less-attractive guys in back wearing khakis and Ralph Lauren polo shirts—one red, one white—looked like his misfit security detail.

Luke was glaring at me. He was pissed, and he wanted his money—nothing complicated about that. It was the way the other guys were eyeing me that was making my skin crawl. Hungry, that was the look. With a side of disgust. They wanted the pretty black girl they'd just stumbled upon and were pretending to hate themselves for it. Awesome.

Push back. That would be the tactic I'd use as a litigator—always go on the offensive. Forceful, but confident. Like you already know you've won. Of course, we were far from a Manhattan courtroom right now. Out on that sidewalk, in the middle of nowhere, deflection was my only safe option.

"I'm up here staying with a friend. If you have some situation with *him*, that's between the two of you." I continued to watch Luke evenly, ignoring the other two. "Anyway, Jonathan doesn't actually owe you anything. You're just trying to shake him down. You and I both know it."

In fact, I did not know it. With Peter involved, anything was possible.

"Oh, he owes me," Luke said, with an easy smile. So easy it was unsettling. "And he'll pay, one way or another. You can be sure of that."

Luke walked past me then toward the door, but his weaselly friend stepped boldly into his place. The six inches I had on him did not seem to be deterring him in the slightest.

"What's your name, sweetheart?" he asked, voice rising at the end like he was talking to a child.

Fuck off. That's what I wanted to say. But I also wanted to stay alive. So I clenched my teeth, took a step back. I bumped right into his fat friend who'd closed in behind me. I could hear his breathing.

Luke turned back at the door, like maybe he was going to tell his friends to knock it off. Instead he just shook his head and disappeared inside. Watching him go, the sweat on the back of my neck turned cold. The little one stepped closer, lifted his chin. I could smell mints on his breath.

"At least tell me your name," the weasel said, staring conspicuously at my breasts. "We're all friends here."

The fat guy laughed like a hyena.

I could dart between them, run away from the bar. But alone in the dark was where they wanted me. I could fight, knee the short guy in the groin, throw a punch. Except getting physical first was even more of a risk. Yell for help, then pray. It was all I had left. I was about to when the door to the Falls flew open.

"Are you out of your fucking mind?" Finch bellowed, grabbing my hand and in one smooth motion pulling me clear of the men and into the bar.

Inside, I blinked, stunned—the light, the noise, all the people. A second later, the two men strolled in past me like they didn't have a care in the world.

"Motherfuckers," Finch muttered when he came in behind them. He grabbed a chair from some pissed-off guy about to sit down and held it out for me. "You need a glass of water?" He looked around like he was debating whether it was safe to leave me, then waved down a woman on her way to the bar. I desperately wanted his rescuing me not to feel good, but it did. "Hey darlin', you mind bringing me a glass of water on your way back?"

The woman smiled at Finch, then wrinkled her nose at me. "Sure thing."

Finch reached out a hand like he might touch me, then put it on the back of his head instead. "Did they, um, do anything to you?"

"No. But I think they might have." I took a breath. "Thank you for helping me."

"You want to—maybe we should call the police."

"No," I said, thinking both of Keith, probably with drugs on him by now, and the white cops who would surely come, demanding to know what crime I thought had been committed. "There's no point."

Finch still looked concerned. "You want me to go get Maeve then, or something? She was just back there talking to Derrick."

And what was Maeve going to do? Press her hands to her china white cheeks, click her Chloé flats three times, and tell me that everything was going to be fine, even though I could still smell that guy's minty breath up my nose? Better that she stay talking to Derrick. Maybe he'd get up the nerve to say something to her finally, save her from the Upper East Side and Bates.

I shook my head. "There's nothing Maeve can do."

The woman was back with the cup of water.

Once I started drinking, I couldn't stop. I wiped at my mouth with the back of my hand. When I looked up, Finch's brow was furrowed with concern. He really did seem like he'd shed some noxious shell. This new Finch was almost human, and kind. I still didn't want to talk. But better to speak first, at least try to move the narrative away from why I hadn't returned any of his dozen calls.

"It was a mistake," I said finally, looking Finch square in the eye. "Obviously."

That night I last saw Finch, a month ago, I'd left the reception in his honor at Cipriani's an hour before it ended. It was pouring rain by then, and I was standing at the curb under an umbrella, waiting for my Uber, when Finch appeared out of nowhere next to me.

"Where are you going?" he asked, no umbrella, already soaked.

"What are you doing out here?" I gestured back at the party, still going full tilt inside.

"Trying to make you stay," he said, eyes on the street in front of us. "Maybe then I'll have time before the night is over to convince you that I'm not the asshole you think I am."

"Oh, really?" I asked with a raised eyebrow, trying to will away the flutter in my belly.

"Okay, maybe I *am* an asshole," Finch said. "But I am other things, too. Some of which you might even find interesting."

"Yeah?" I gripped my umbrella tighter, my toes clenched inside my shoes. "Like what things?"

"Well, for one, all that matters to me is my work. Just like you."

I laughed despite myself. "Wait, so we'd be good together because neither of us will care?"

"Oh, I care. All those people in there, and the only thing I've been able to think about all night is what my fingers would feel like on the curve of your collarbone."

He took a step closer, so that the entire length of his body was almost touching mine. We stayed like that as my car pulled up and stopped. Silent. Motionless. And maybe it was the pressure of my patent case going to trial, or that the firm's managing partner had just berated me for something that was not my fault. Or maybe I was just fed up with doing the right thing all the time. But it was me who'd finally stepped forward and started kissing Finch on that sidewalk. There was no pretending otherwise. And while it wasn't a great decision to have sex with him, it was one I'd made fully and freely. I was an adult. I'd live with it.

The real problem started as I crept out of Finch's sprawling Dumbo loft the next morning. Some Polaroids of naked women on his coffee table caught my eye, names written in Sharpie on each one of them. A pretty girl with a nose ring named Rachel was on top. When I paused to look more closely at the pictures, I saw the representation contract next to them. It had been signed by Finch a week earlier with the Graygon Gallery.

Which meant that here we were, a month later, and Keith wasn't representing Finch anymore, and he didn't even know. I *still* hadn't said a damn thing to Keith myself because I was worried about his fragile state—yes, losing Finch was going to kill him. But I also felt guilty about how I knew. Sleeping with Keith's most important artist could easily cause problems for him—and I was embarrassed, too. So I'd decided to do the only logical thing—make my one bad decision worse by leaving Keith in the dark.

To think of all those times in college that I'd acted like I had all the answers. To think that I'd actually believed I did.

"It's like a thing I can't stop," I remember Alice saying one night junior year. She was sitting cross-legged on my bed, face tearstained as she talked on and on about Keith and how she loved him, but how he was also breaking her heart. By then the two had been on and off for more than two years. She hadn't told me the details of what had happened this time. And I hadn't asked. Their relationship was a spectator sport no one wanted to watch.

"You need to pull yourself together, Alice," I'd said. "You may be telling yourself you can't stop things with Keith or whatever. But you actually can. You're just choosing not to."

I thought now of all those times Alice had called me the night she died. All those calls I'd ignored. Because I didn't want to hear her still obsessing about what had happened on the roof. I never was good with being in the wrong.

Finch looked up at me finally. "Personally, I don't think what happened was a mistake." His voice had an edge, but a restrained one. "But I can respect that you do. Also, I was beginning to get that sense after the fifteenth unreturned message." He smiled a little, luckily. I could live with him being angry at me—I just didn't want him taking it out on Keith.

"We should get out of here," I said, getting to my feet.

Seemed best to end this conversation while I was ahead. "Before that contractor comes looking for Jonathan."

"Okay. Not sure that Keith needs an excuse to drink more, anyway."

I narrowed my eyes at him. "Weren't you the one delivering the shots earlier?"

"Never said I was perfect. But you already knew that, didn't you?" He peered up at me for a second. "Anyway, we'll need to pry Keith out of the bathroom first. Because we all know what he's doing in there."

That certainly sounded like Finch knew about the drugs already. Was that why he'd fired Keith? Because that would actually be fair. I wouldn't want Keith in his current state representing me either.

Finch's phone rang. It had been in his hand ever since we arrived. He was probably waiting for a call from his new art dealer. "Sorry, I need to take this," he said. "Will you be okay if I step out?"

"Sure, sure."

Finch pressed his lips together, then nodded before heading for the door. I could already see Jonathan coming our way.

"Jesus, there you are," Jonathan said when he finally reached me. "Keith has disappeared. He went into the bathroom and then vanished. Maeve and Derrick are still back there looking."

"By the way, the contractor is here, with some friends," I said. "I ran into them outside. It wasn't pleasant."

"Perfect," Jonathan said, then seemed to register the potential gravity. "Wait, are you okay?"

I nodded as my throat started to burn. "Yeah."

"And of course now we can't leave until we find Keith." Jonathan shook his head, put a hand to his mouth. "This is—I mean, are we about to get into a bar brawl because Keith's somewhere getting high?"

"Also, I think Finch already knows about the drugs."

Jonathan raised his eyebrows and sighed. "Well, I suppose that at least takes some of the pressure off."

Maeve appeared then, smiling a little maniacally. "We found Keith," she breathed. "Derrick's just grabbing him now."

Out of the corner of my eye, I spotted Luke. He was watching us. "Let's go wait in the car," I said. "Like right now."

"Shouldn't we wait for Derrick and Keith?" Maeve asked.

Jonathan glanced Luke's way, too. "No," he said. "Stephanie's right: we should go."

Maeve darted ahead obediently, making her way through the crowd with surprising speed. She was a couple steps ahead when Luke's weaselly friend appeared out of nowhere, heading her off. Maeve nearly bumped into him.

"Oh, excuse me," I heard her say.

She tried to move around him to the door, but he blocked her way.

"What's your name, sweetheart?"

She went to step around him again, but he suddenly cocked his head and clamped a hand around her forearm.

"I know you," he leered drunkenly. "You gave me, you know—" He mouthed a blow-job motion. "You look hot as fu—"

Maeve pulled her free arm back and gave him a whack to his sternum. The guy stumbled back and released her, and Maeve rushed ahead and out the door.

"Asshole," I spat at him as we headed past.

None of us looked back until we were across the street at the car. Maeve was pale and clearly shaken. I grasped her hand and squeezed it.

"Are you okay?" I asked.

She nodded unconvincingly as we watched Derrick come out of the bar alone.

"Where's Keith?" I called to him.

"He's coming. He's coming," Derrick said as he crossed over to us, but he seemed troubled. "Let's just get in the car."

We piled back into Derrick's SUV, all taking the same seats we had before. This time Finch seemed to be much closer to me in the back seat, our legs almost touching. I could feel the heat of him as we sat there and waited. I tried to inch closer to the window to put a little space between us.

"Oh, here he comes," Maeve said, turning around to look behind us.

"Good," I said without looking myself. "Now we can leave."

"He's, um—there's somebody with him."

"What?" Jonathan asked, looking for himself from the front passenger seat. "Who?"

I turned, too, and sure enough, there was Keith crossing the street and he was, indeed, not alone. Some distance behind there was a woman—blond hair with a reddish tinge, wearing a tiny camel-colored leather skirt and short black booties. She was giggling and wobbling as she walked. From the flat expression on Keith's face as he approached the car, I thought maybe she'd followed him, and he was trying to get rid of her. But then he slowed down and laughed at something she'd said. After that, they walked in lockstep.

"Oh, this is wonderful," Jonathan said. "Just wonderful."

Detective Julia Scutt

Sunday, 8:45 a.m.

I turn into Luke Gaffney's driveway—a short three-mile drive from Jonathan's—and turn off the car. For a second, I wonder if I've got the address wrong. I'll admit, I'd imagined something garish, one of those new McMansions that stick out like ugly sore thumbs between the classy historic remodels. But Luke Gaffney's house is every bit as elegant as Jonathan's. Not as grand, maybe—no porches or curved towers or romantic flair. This house is a clean rectangle of white stone with sharp black shutters, but all of it is just as meticulously restored. Even the grounds, filled with well-tended shrubbery and mature trees, are pristine. I probably shouldn't be so surprised by the sophistication. Like me, Luke Gaffney did eventually leave Kaaterskill for college, a SUNY somewhere upstate, I think.

But then, Mike Gaffney's totally lovely old farmhouse was also far nicer than I'd expected. I'd gone there first. If there'd been a dispute about payments, as the boss at Ace Construction, the elder Gaffney would probably be the one in charge of collecting. But according to the nervous young guy mowing the acres of grounds, he'd left early Saturday morning for a fishing trip, not returning until Sunday late. Another good alibi.

"I've gotta get back to it." The young guy looked like he regretted even saying that much, before rumbling off on his big mower.

He was wise to be nervous about Mike Gaffney and his short fuse. He'd cornered me once while he was working on our bathroom all those years ago, demanding to know if I'd taken some shirt of his. Like a little girl would ever have wanted some smelly old man's plaid shirt. But he'd gotten right in my eight-year-old face as I shook my head and tried to disappear into the wall.

I head toward Luke Gaffney's front steps now, past a brand-new Yukon parked in the driveway. Sparkling black, the SUV has tinted windows and a shiny silver grille. The tires would probably sparkle, too, if they weren't completely caked in mud—like a car that had maybe been driving across Jonathan's rain-soaked lawn.

I ring the doorbell. After a long stretch of silence, the polished black door finally swings open, and there's Luke in the doorway, blue eyes aglow. He glances back toward my unmarked, but unmistakable, sedan. "Yeah, what?"

I flash my badge, then tuck it away. "I have a few questions, Mr. Gaffney."

"Questions about what?"

"Do you know a Derrick Chism or Keith Lazard?"

Luke frowns as he digs out a crushed pack of Parliaments. He grips one between his fingers without lighting it. He has the door resting against his body so I can't see inside.

"Nope," he says.

He isn't going to make this easy. Of course he isn't.

"What about Jonathan Cheung?"

He peers at the ceiling. "Wait, now *that* guy I do know," he says. "He owes me eleven thousand dollars. Typical. Those fuckers come up here, and fine, it's a free country. They want to spend a shit-ton of money renovating, who am I to complain? But then they try to steal from us like we're a bunch of dumb hicks? We're running a business. We're *business*men." He gestures to his nice house. "Successful businessmen."

"You seem angry," I say.

"Fuck, yes, I'm angry," he says. "We're just trying to take care of our employees. And our employees are just trying to take care of their families."

When Luke shakes his head, I see them for the first time: two long, angry scratches on his neck. Luke sees me see the scratches.

"Fucking cat," he offers casually.

"Cat?"

"*Fucking* cat," Luke Gaffney repeats, coolly. Like he's glimpsed the future, and in it he's already come out clean.

"I hate cats," I say. This is true. I do hate cats. But we both know the scratches aren't from a cat. Could be fingers, or branches. *Dammit.* I'd been writing off this visit as just a box to check, nothing more. "You been in the woods over by the Hemlock place lately?"

The Hemlock place is the closest landmark to the accident scene. Everybody who grew up anywhere in a twenty-mile radius knows the house by name because every Halloween the old couple who used to live there gave out full-size candy bars. It wasn't until years later that Mr. Hemlock got in trouble for putting his hands somewhere he wasn't supposed to on one little vampire.

"Why would I be over there?" Luke asks, like I'm suggesting he might have been exchanging favors for a Milky Way. And notably not mentioning those other construction projects they've supposedly got nearby.

"I don't know," I say. "That's why I'm asking."

He looks past me again toward the car. Shakes his head. He knows I'm on a fishing expedition. Could be he's also on the defensive because of *The River.* Surely those armchair detectives have come around asking both Gaffneys questions they don't want to answer. Luke had only been fifteen at the time of Jane's murder. The police checked into him anyway because he'd helped out a couple days at our house. But he'd had after-school detention the day of the murders.

"No," he says finally, eyes squarely back on me. "I haven't been near the Hemlock place."

"Well, we've got an incident in the woods near there."

"Incident?" Luke asks. "What does that mean?"

"An accident with a fatality," I say. "We found something belonging to you near the scene."

"Belonging to me?" He laughs. "What the fuck are you—nope. Doesn't belong to me, whatever it is you supposedly found. No way. Because I haven't been over there."

"It's an item of clothing," I say, trying to stay vague,

while dangling enough to keep him worried. Of course, all I've got is an Ace Construction hat that could belong to just about anybody. And a smudge of something that could theoretically be blood. But those scratches on Luke's neck do lend a different sheen to things. And a little exaggeration never hurt. "It's yours, Mr. Gaffney. We know that it is."

Anger flashes across Luke's face, but he does a decent job of reining it back in. He's smart enough to know that losing it with a cop is not in his interest.

"Nope. Not mine. Wasn't there." He grips the door handle. "Now I think we're done, unless maybe you want to help me get my eleven thousand fucking dollars back from those people. You ask me, that's the real crime here."

"I'd be happy to look into the money you're owed. In fact, Mr. Cheung is with officers at his house right now, so inquiring wouldn't be a problem," I say, though the story of whatever is owed to Ace Construction is surely not that simple. My guess is there's plenty of fault to go around.

"Hmm." Luke grunts noncommittally. "Okay, what is it that you found?"

"A hat," I say, knowing how this is going to play out. But I don't have much choice. "An Ace Construction hat."

Luke bursts out laughing, as I imagined he might. "You know how many of those fucking hats are floating around? We give them away at every job we work on. Plus, all our guys wear them."

"Fair enough. We could clear the whole thing up if you'd come down to the station. We could take a quick DNA swab, get you ruled out completely."

"Ha," he says—less of a laugh than a statement. "You don't have an actual warrant or anything like that, do you?"

Luke Gaffney knows to ask that question. He's not stupid.

"You're not under arrest, and, no, I don't have a search warrant. But as you said, you're not involved. So if you voluntarily—"

"I'm not volunteering shit. Let me guess, you'd want to take some pictures of how my cat scratched me, too? And, bam, that'll somehow prove that I'm the guy who did whatever the hell to whoever the hell. How stupid do you think I am?"

He's right about the pictures—that is exactly what I'd hoped to do. Take pictures of those scratches that are suspicious as hell. Right after I call the ME and tell him to scrape extra careful under the victim's fingernails.

"Then how about you tell me where you were last night," I say. "I know your dad is out of town. If you can account for your whereabouts, I won't have to bother either of you again."

"My dad." He shakes his head in disgust. "Your boss know you're here?"

"My boss?" I laugh angrily. But this isn't a good direction—neither is the way Luke is starting to get to me.

"Yeah, you know, Chief Seldon."

"Chief Seldon wants me to find out what happened to the man we found dead in a car out by the Hemlock place."

And that is true, provided the answers I find are the ones that Seldon is hoping for. Or at least aren't the ones he really *doesn't* want—like drugs, or robbery, or some other cause rooted in his inability to keep a handle on crime in Kaaterskill.

Luke Gaffney rolls his tongue along the inside of his cheek. "Sure he does."

"Where were you last night, Mr. Gaffney?" I press.

"At the bar downtown," he says finally, his voice now surprisingly devoid of hostility. "Check it out if you want."

"Which bar?" I ask.

"The Falls," he says. "There some other bar in downtown Kaaterskill you know about?"

"What time did you get to the Falls?"

"Nine maybe, I don't know exactly. But I was there all night."

"Were you with anybody who can confirm that?"

"Yeah, I was with people. Bartender saw me, too. I was there until two a.m., then I came home to fuck my girlfriend."

Male suspects love to do this with female officers—talk about sex. Like we are fragile flowers who will wilt at the mere mention of a penis. I make a point of keeping my eyes locked on his. I can feel my irritation about to flame into something a whole lot worse.

"What's your girlfriend's name?"

"Crystal," he says.

Luke Gaffney's girlfriend was in Keith Lazard's bedroom? Luke doesn't strike me as somebody who would take kindly to sharing a girl with a weekender.

"And what's Crystal's last name?"

"How would I know?"

"You don't know your girlfriend's last name?"

"I was being polite," he says. "Girl that I'm fucking, okay? She's a junkie. I wouldn't have a junkie as a girlfriend."

"But you would fuck one?"

Luke almost smiles. "Didn't say I was proud of it."

"Is she still here?" I ask, motioning to the house. "Can I speak with her?"

He shakes his head. "I never found her. I said I came home *to* fuck her, not that I actually *did* fuck her." For sure, he's enjoying this. "Last I heard, she was at the Farm. Now if you don't mind, it's only nine a.m. and I'd like to go back to sleep. I think I'm still drunk."

"Okay, Mr. Gaffney," I say. "But if you're not going to voluntarily come down to the station, you know that I'll have to come back with that warrant."

"You do what you have to do," he says. "And so will I."

Luke Gaffney is about to slam the door in my face when a calico cat appears, threading itself through his legs, then sitting protectively on his foot. She eyes me, then hisses.

"See: fucking cat," Luke says. "I'd go now if I were you. She's the real jealous type."

Dan calls as I'm getting back into the car.

"Dogs finally picked up a blood trail. Back in the woods, hundred yards from the road," he says. "Looks like whoever it is could be headed back toward the house. Uniforms are on their way there just in case."

Dan's genuinely worried about my safety. I can hear it in his voice.

"Okay." I try to ignore the tightness in my chest. I don't miss Dan, but I do maybe miss that feeling. "Thanks. But I'm not there at the moment."

"Oh, good. Good. Also, word just came in that there's a guy at Hudson Hospital who's pretty beat up and trying to leave against medical advice."

Word just came in, he's trying to breeze past that like it's not relevant—but people are calling him and not me with critical information. Already they're acting like he's in charge, probably because Seldon suggested as much. I can't imagine Dan wants to be the one letting me know, but someone needs to.

"Is he our missing driver?" I ask.

"I don't think so. He's six foot three. Our two missing friends are both under six feet. But he is refusing to give his name, so—I said you'd be down."

"Okay, yeah," I say. "No luck on the ID yet, huh?"

"ME won't even venture a guess from the pictures," Dan says. "Guys don't look different enough and with the rain and the facial damage . . ."

"Friends are getting antsy for an ID."

"I'm sure," Dan says.

"Could you do me a favor and ask the ME to look for track marks on our John Doe?"

Track marks would point in Keith's direction, although the absence of track marks won't prove it's not him. I don't know for sure that it was even his kit. After all, it's Jonathan's house.

"Weekenders with track marks, huh?"

"Could be," I say. "And thanks, by the way. I know you could have just gone down to the hospital yourself. I'm sure that's what Seldon would prefer."

"I'm here to do what's best for the case, not what Seldon wants," he says. "Besides, we're still friends, right?"

"We are," I say, and it feels, unexpectedly, like the truth. "I'll see you later."

I quickly google Crystal Finnegan before starting up the car. I'll have them run her license back at the station, pull any record. But for the moment some basic information, even just from social media, would help. Results pop up immediately. Turns out Crystal Finnegan was a straight-A biology major and track star at Syracuse. That is, up until two years ago, when she got into a car accident. Drunk driver left her with a knee injury that ended her running career. And, I'm guessing, also turned her into a junkie.

Alice

They're saying now that he was there to burglarize dorm rooms. There've been break-ins—a laptop and some cash stolen from Main Building. Campus security jumped at the chance to blame him—poor Evan—whose only crime was coming home with me.

What's done is done. Everyone is right about that. But we could at least make sure people know he wasn't a criminal.

Stephanie was, of course, immediately all about "the how." How was I going to do that without accidentally revealing what really happened? It made me angry that she was right—I didn't have any guarantees that we'd stay out of trouble.

Derrick and Jonathan pretty much had the same questions. Each in their own way, of course—Jonathan worried most about his dad, Derrick worried most about all of us getting arrested. And Keith—well, him I'm avoiding. I have this feeling he's going to break up with me, which would just be perfect.

Maeve was the most open to the idea. She was kind, mostly concerned with how I've been feeling lately. Maeve knows way too much about me and my meds—the roommate always knows. But I know her secrets, too. I love Maeve, but she is kind of self-centered and also a klepto. I've cut her extra slack because she's had a hard life—but still.

Whatever. I'll think about it some more. Like everyone wants me to. Maybe I'll even think about catching up on my pills.

But, really, I can't imagine a scenario where I'm just going to be able to leave this situation like it is. Not forever, at least.

Keith

Friday, 9:55 p.m.

No one was happy I'd brought along a girl. Even with every muscle in my body shrieking, I could feel the real clear vibe of me having fucked up massively the whole drive back to Jonathan's house. Meanwhile, there was the girl sliding her hand up and down my thigh, chewing down hard on her Juicy Fruit. Juicy Fruit and gin—that's what she smelled like. I could smell her, but I could barely feel her hand over the ache in my bones. Everything was starting to look blurry, too, like I was seeing it in one of those warped subway mirrors where you can only make out the fact that *something* bad is coming, but not exactly what.

To be honest, I wasn't entirely sure how she'd ended up in the car with me. We were talking inside the bar—no, I was talking. Crystal, yeah, that was her name. Crystal was asking me where I was from, teasing me about modern art. She was cute and funny and sharp, but I'd kept the conversation going mostly because I'd hoped she was holding. The one guy selling in the bathroom wasn't interested in taking my watch as collateral.

Turned out she wasn't holding, but she had cash. Bathroom guy was pissed at her about something, so she was avoiding him. But she said if I bought from him with her money, she'd cut me in. So here we were. I did feel bad that she was there on Jonathan's bachelor party weekend, but I felt more good that I was about to get high. I'd do just about anything to avoid the horror that would be headed my way if I didn't use soon.

My phone buzzed in my pocket then. Took some effort to tug it out. You're running out of time, the message read. Then a second later, another: Your friend Maeve will be first. I squinted at the screen. But no matter how narrow I made my eyes, the words were the same. Maeve would be such an easy target, too. You have until 10:00 a.m. tomorrow.

I put my phone face down on my leg and turned toward the window. Hadn't they said twenty-four hours only a few hours ago? Not that I was in a position to object to their telescoping timeline.

"Why is everybody so fucking down?" Finch called out to no one in particular. "Is this a fucking bachelor party or a funeral?"

"Be quiet, Finch," Derrick said from the driver's seat, keeping his attention on the road.

"We're tired, Finch," Jonathan said. "We are all exhausted."

Exhausted by me. By this. By the nice but still random, probably high girl I'd invited to join our private party. By the asshole client I'd let tag along. By me and all my bullshit. Fair enough. I was tired of me, too.

"Do you have any food at your house, Jonathan?" Stephanie asked.

"I could make something for all of you! I'm a great cook!" Crystal called out, gripping Stephanie's shoulder in an overfamiliar way. "I'd just need some garlic, a tomato, a few other spices and some chilies or even some chili flakes. I can make this delicious penne arrabiata."

"Sounds great," Maeve said politely. Maeve would probably be polite to my friends from Staten Island, too, right up until they blew her face away.

It was insane that I'd allowed myself to get mixed up with them. But it had seemed so logical at the time.

I could still remember the way Frank's heavy Scotch tumbler had felt in my one hand, the fat cigar gripped in the other. We'd been standing on his Todt Hill patio, surveying the Manhattan skyline and the huge, gaudy stone houses in every direction. Frank had been hilariously talking casual shit about his various neighbors for at least an hour, and I'd been loving every crazy second of it.

"But, you know, most of them are good people," he'd said. "Nonjudgmental."

Frank Gardello was a big Italian man with a curvy, blond, heavily Botoxed wife named Griselda. Frank had a guy who drove him around in a huge Cadillac Escalade to "business meetings," the meaning of which was obvious. I'd liked Frank the second I met him at the gallery, though—coming in off the street, browsing for art like Griselda probably browsed at Prada. After twelve minutes, they'd bought a $26,000 Luca Baglio painting.

"Nonjudgmental is good," I'd said that evening on Frank's deck, and I'd meant it.

"That's what I like about you," he'd said. "People in all those other fucking galleries treat us like garbage. All of them except you. That was a big deal to Griselda. Hope it goes without saying: you ever need anything, you let me know."

No rational person would have taken Frank Gardello up on this offer. But I'd been flying pretty high that night on Frank's porch, expensive Scotch on my tongue, the sinking sun setting the sky aflame. And everything had felt like a sign.

"Well," I'd said, "there is one thing."

Eighty thousand dollars—enough to pay back the Serpentine Gallery and get Finch's show up and running. Of course, one thing had led to another, and pretty soon the $80,000 had disappeared, some out the door to keep the lights on, and then there was Jace, who'd been fronting me for months. I couldn't have him cutting me off for good.

For a while, I even thought—after one glass of Scotch and one painting on his wall—that Frank and I were close enough that he might overlook the debt. That's what too much Oxy will do—make you believe fucked-up shit that'll get you killed.

One day late on my first payment, and Frank had already passed me off to his people, the ones texting me now. People for whom I was nothing more than a job that needed to get done.

"This house is so *fancy*," Crystal said to me once we were inside Jonathan's, spinning around the living room, grinning. I felt sad for her. And also for me. "But cozy, too."

"It is," I said, trying to smile. I couldn't really.

Crystal was in worse shape than I'd noticed in the dim bar. Her skin had a grayish tinge, and her bare legs were covered with small bruises. Like an overripe banana rocketing toward rotten. She smiled back at me warmly, though, as she moved on to chat with Stephanie. You could see in Crystal's smile the girl she used to be. I wondered whether, if you looked hard enough, you could still see me.

Stephanie smiled at Crystal stiffly, then shot a look my way. Stephanie wasn't nearly as polite as Maeve, especially when she was pissed. And she was pretty obviously pissed at me. What the hell was I—wait, was I actually surprised that I'd brought some random girl home to Jonathan's house during his bachelor party so that I could use with her? After everything else I'd done, *this* was the surprising thing?

"Hello?" Jonathan snapped his fingers close to my face. "Keith, are you in there? Who is she?"

"Oh, sorry," I said, looking around Jonathan's living room, wondering how long he'd been standing there. But nothing else came—no answers for Jonathan. Inside my mind there was just a screaming blank. So

I said the only thing I could think of, my go-to answer for everything: "I don't know. I'm sorry."

God, I was so fucking sick of being sorry.

Crystal danced into the room then, gone and back from wherever she'd been—she had a bag of chips in one hand, a beer in the other, red baseball hat on.

Jonathan was staring at her. "Wait, where did you get that hat?"

"Oh, I'm sorry," Crystal said, taking it off her head and holding it out to him. "I was just messing around. It was in your kitchen."

"An Ace Construction hat was in my kitchen?" Jonathan asked, stepping closer but not reaching out for it. "Where?"

"Right on the counter," Crystal said nervously. "I'm sorry. You want to wear it?"

"No, no," Jonathan said, forcing a smile. "That's okay—I just didn't see it in there before."

I looked across the room to Finch. He was on the couch now, eyes black and bottomless as he stared at me. I felt an uncomfortable twitch in my spine. Why was Finch looking at me like he wanted me dead?

"Truth or dare!" he called out suddenly, eyes still locked on mine.

"Yeah, I don't think so," Jonathan said immediately. "Collective hard pass."

"Oh, wow," Maeve said. "I'm sorry, but that does sound very unwise."

"Idiotic," Derrick added, already headed for the staircase. "I think we should all go to bed."

"On the other hand," Stephanie called after Derrick, "a game would at least keep everyone down here and, you know, otherwise occupied."

She was talking about me—I did have occasional moments of clarity. And Stephanie was right that Crystal and I couldn't get down to using until we were alone.

"I think a game sounds fun," Crystal said, taking a sip of her beer as she sat down on the couch opposite Keith.

Jonathan closed his eyes and dropped his head. "Right, occupied."

Maeve's eyes got wide. "Okay, right, let's do it."

"So that's a yes from Keith and Stephanie and Maeve," Finch called.

"That wasn't a yes from me," I said.

"You don't have to actually say yes, Keith," Finch said, looking at me again with those black eyes. "Your answer is always yes where I'm concerned. Derrick, I know you're in, too. Because you'd never let me down, right?"

Derrick's shoulders sagged as he shook his head and backed away from the stairs.

"Truth or dare, Maeve?" Finch asked.

Stephanie laughed, but in a way that sounded like she was being strangled. "God, we're not seriously doing this, are we?"

Jonathan turned. "You were the one who said we should, remember?"

"I know. I know I did. In a universe of fucked-up options . . ."

"Um," Maeve answered finally. "Truth?"

"Great—so what's this secret you all have from college?" Finch motioned to me and Derrick, like one of us had told him. *No, not me.* I hadn't told him anything.

"I don't know what you mean," Maeve said.

"Come on, the secret," Finch said. "I know something happened. It's got a hold on all of you."

"Our friend Alice killed herself," Jonathan said.

"No, not that," Finch said. "That's not a secret. This is something only all of you know about. Or that you *hope* only all of you know about."

He pointed at each one of us in turn. The vise around my head clicked tighter, sending sparks of pain shooting across my scalp. I looked around at everyone. *I didn't tell him about the roof.* They needed to know that. Because Finch was making it seem like I had. And

I was afraid people would start adding on, thinking he already knew.

"Oh my God, *what* is the secret?" Crystal asked like it was a fucking Christmas gift.

"We don't know what you're talking about, Finch. There's no secret," Derrick said. "Move on."

Finch stared at Derrick. "You all know exactly what I'm talking about. But, okay, I'll move on to you, Derrick. Truth or dare?"

"Wait, you can't go twice in a row!" Crystal cried, flapping a hand in Finch's direction. "That's against the rules."

But everybody ignored her. Because this was Finch's game. Everyone else was only playing along because they were trying to save me from myself.

Derrick sighed. "Dare."

"Perfect," Finch said with a sly grin. "I've got just the thing."

Finch moved his hand behind him, for something tucked in his waistband. Then there it was, held high in the air. Something silver. I thought it was his phone at first. But no, too big and the wrong shape.

"You have a gun?" Crystal laughed nervously.

And sure enough, it was an actual fucking gun in Finch's hand. Held above his head.

"What the—" Stephanie scrambled to her feet. "Finch, where did you get that?"

"It's mine." He waved it around. "I brought it from home. Colt single-action revolver. I've had it forever, don't usually carry it on me. But these days you can't be too careful. You never know who's going to turn on you." He looked dead at me. "Right, Keith?"

Fuck. He already knew about the Serpentine, didn't he? I'd known word might get out. But was this—was Finch *this* angry?

"Put the gun away, Finch," I said. My words sounded garbled.

"You're freaked out now. But I want to be clear, this gun has been with me this whole fucking time. Safe and sound. I bet you'll be glad I have it if those contractors come back. Big-city liberals, y'all are a bunch of hypocrites. You hate country folks with guns until there's somebody you want to shoot with one." Finch laughed. "So, here's the dare, Derrick. Take this, go outside and shoot it into the air. Just one time. That's it."

Derrick's jaw clenched.

"Knock it off, Finch," I said. This was too much, too far. All of this. Somebody was going to get hurt. What the fuck had I done, bringing Finch up here, angry and with a gun?

Derrick stepped forward confidently and held out his hand. "Give it to me."

Finch made a face. "You sure? Because, honestly, I'm starting to doubt your dedication to the task at hand." Finch glanced Stephanie's way, then turned back to Derrick. "If you gather my drift."

Derrick motioned again. "I'll do it, Finch."

"We'll see." Finch spun the gun expertly and delivered it butt-end to Derrick.

"Derrick," Maeve called after him. "Don't—just don't."

If something happened to Derrick, it would also be my fault. Like the guy on the roof. Like Alice. So many bodies laid out like spokes on a wheel. And there I was, spinning round at the center. I pressed my fingertips against the wall to stay upright.

"Don't worry, everybody," Finch said. "Only real risk here is that you won't look at Derrick quite the same once you see how comfortable he is holding a gun."

Derrick headed for the door, indeed gripping the polished silver like he was born with a gun in his hand. "I'll be right back," he said, before the door slammed shut behind him.

The door was barely closed when there were four loud pops in a row.

"What the fuck?" Stephanie gasped. "It was supposed to be once."

She was right. We all stared at the door, waiting for Derrick to come back in. But there was nothing. Not another sound. *Holy. Fucking. Shit.*

"Where is he?" Jonathan asked.

"I think we should check on him," Crystal whispered.

"Come on, he's fine," Finch said. "Trust me. Derrick can take care of himself."

Unless that hadn't been Derrick firing the gun. What if it was Frank's men, just seizing the opportunity? Who said they had to keep their word on Maeve being first?

"Where are you going?" Stephanie called after me as I walked toward the door.

"To check on Derrick."

"Hold on," Jonathan said reluctantly. "I'll go with you."

Outside, there was just the quiet and the dark. No crumpled body on the porch, no pool of blood.

"What the fuck?" I said quietly. "Where is he?"

I listened for Derrick, for something, anything—but all I could hear was the distant sound of that fucking river.

"Derrick!" Jonathan called as he headed toward the far end of the porch. He turned back and shook his head. "Nothing down there."

"Shit," I said, on my way down the steps to the driveway, looking right and then left. Adrenaline had cleared my head a little, but the world still looked tilted and frayed.

"Do you think the contractors came back?" Jonathan was standing next to me now. "That Luke guy saw us at the Falls."

"I doubt it," I managed. There was no point in both of us feeling guilty. "Come on, let's go around back."

Derrick wasn't behind the house either. There was nothing, no one, anywhere in sight.

"Derrick!" Jonathan shouted again. "Derrick!"

Silence. But then, suddenly, another loud crack, like the others, but this one in the distance beyond the trees at the edge of the property. We started toward the sound. Jonathan was next to me as we crashed into the woods, branches slashing at our faces. We slowed as we got deeper in, the trees thicker, the ground more uneven. No more gunshots, though. Only the sound of snapping sticks and the crunching leaves as we ran on, the light from Jonathan's phone glowing white against the trees.

We were hit with a cool breeze when we finally burst through the other side, the sudden emptiness giving me vertigo. We slid to a stop on the damp ground to avoid the sharp cliff not more than fifteen feet ahead.

"Holy shit," Jonathan gasped, grabbing my arm to keep me from falling.

In the glow of the moon, the Hudson River was visible thirty, maybe forty feet below. The sound echoed up, the river a quiet roar. As we inched closer to the cliff's edge and peered over, I felt a sick split-second urge to take a running leap. Just to be done with it. Alice—it was like she was tugging me, telling me to come along. Head first. Feet first. What difference did it make anymore?

Like that guy falling off the edge of Main Building. Some poor random guy who would still just be living his life if it wasn't for us—for me. That wasn't guilt talking, either. Alice had told me straight out that night on the roof: it was my fault.

"Are you happy now?" she'd asked.

"Happy about what?" I kept my eyes on the stars.

She'd been yelling at me on and off for at least two hours. Ever since we left the party. The only respite had been when she was talking to the guy in the Dutch Cabin—that guy who was still with us.

"Happy that I'm going to fuck this random guy tonight? All because you had to dance with that—"

Somebody had screamed. "Oh my God! He just—"

Everyone was shouting then. And rushing. The guy was gone. Over the edge. He was all the way down on the ground with his neck all wrong.

And now here we were, all these years later, along the same river where Alice had killed herself a few days later. If I jumped, too, at least Frank and his friends would disappear. There'd be no point in going after anyone else without me around—blameless themselves, my friends would just go straight to the police. I took a step closer to the edge.

"Derrick!" Jonathan shouted.

When I looked up, Jonathan was already running toward Derrick, who was standing some distance away, also alongside the cliff.

"It's fine," Derrick shouted back, raising a hand. "I'm fine."

But he did not seem fine. And then, just like that, I was away from the water's edge, running toward Derrick, too.

"What happened?" Jonathan asked when we'd reached him.

"I tossed the gun," Derrick said, pointing toward the river, a confused look on his face. "But I only shot off four rounds in the air. A gun like that—you don't need to cock the hammer back for the fifth round to discharge. I should have known better than to throw it. Knocking against the side of the cliff did the trick."

"Well, as long as you're okay," Jonathan said. "You are okay, right?"

"Yeah, *I'm* fine. But hopefully that stray bullet didn't hit some random person around here."

"That seems unlikely," Jonathan said, putting a hand on Derrick's shoulder. "There's never anyone around here."

"Who does something that fucking stupid, though?" Derrick asked.

All three of us stayed quiet then, staring down at the dark water rushing below.

"Me," I said finally. "I do things that are that fucking stupid, constantly."

"Good point," Derrick said.

"Agreed," Jonathan added.

I don't know who started laughing first, but soon we all were. Laughing hard and for real. It made me feel more lightheaded and I sat down on a boulder as our laughter drifted off into silence.

"I have to say I was shocked when you took that gun so nonchalantly," Jonathan said to Derrick. "It was disturbing, but also weirdly satisfying."

"Yeah, well, you grow up in the South . . . ," Derrick offered. "Anyway, I think I was showing off for Maeve. Which is so stupid on so many levels."

"Do you have any cigarettes, Keith?" Jonathan asked. "I need a cigarette."

"You don't smoke," I said, digging them out.

"Just give me a fucking cigarette."

"I'll take one, too," Derrick said.

Soon we were all exhaling into the darkness. And for a second, I wondered if this moment with my friends was the beginning of my salvation. If I could just claw my way back to a place where we were all fucked up to the same degree, everything might be okay. I didn't need to be perfect for my friends. I just needed to be less of a complete and total disaster.

"Why did it sound like Finch knows about the roof?" Derrick asked me.

"I thought maybe you'd told him."

"You can't be serious?" he said. "I know better than to trust Finch."

"So do I," I said, feeling more bothered about the comment now. What the hell had Finch been talking about?

"Maybe it was a lucky guess?" Jonathan offered.

"Yeah, right," I said, and then took a long drag.

Derrick frowned. "I don't know, with that last email—"

There was a sudden bright flash through the trees, like a lightning strike.

"What the hell was that?" Jonathan said. A second later, there was a much larger flash and more light in the distance, steady and growing. "Holy shit. I think the house is on fire."

Bright orange flames were still licking up toward the second-floor windows from the pile of boards when we reached the house. Stephanie was spraying at the bottom with a garden hose, shielding her face with an arm. It shouldn't have been working—the flames too tall, the fire too hot. But it was, as she inched closer with the confidence of someone who'd put out a thousand fires before.

This was definitely the guys from Staten Island. Professional. Scary. But precise. No one hurt because they didn't want us to be—yet.

"Here, let me help," I said, taking the hose from Stephanie. Gripping it sent pins and needles shooting down my hands, but it was the least I could do. Like everything else, this was my fault. If I wasn't such a coward, I would have told my friends about Frank, would have admitted the danger I'd already put them in.

"Hey." Jonathan pointed at Finch who was standing next to Crystal some distance back, watching the show with a little smile on his face, beer in hand. "Did you set my fucking house on fire, Finch?"

"Ha!" Finch took a big swallow of beer.

"I'm serious." Jonathan took a step closer. "Did you?"

"So between me and the guys you owe eleven thousand dollars to, who set up those boards like that and showed up here threatening you—you're going with *me*?"

"He was inside with us when the fire happened, Jonathan," Maeve offered delicately. "It wasn't him. I don't see how it could have been."

"I think we should call the police," Stephanie said.

Jonathan nodded, but did not look convinced. "Yeah, maybe. I mean, I'd rather not get the police involved if possible."

"The last thing I want is to be dealing with the cops in this town, trust me," Stephanie said. "But this is getting out of control."

"I think it's out," I said. The wood was still smoldering, but only slightly.

Finch started a loud, slow clap. "Thank you, Keith," he sang. "Our. Hero."

"Enough, Finch," Derrick said. "We're all tired of your bullshit."

Finch smiled—so satisfied. "What if I say it's not enough, Derrick? What are you going to do? Beat me up?"

"Finch, come on," I said. Least I could do was try to redirect him. "Let's go inside and get a drink."

But Derrick had taken a step closer. "Shut the fuck up, Finch. I'm serious."

Finch took a step back, then looked around at all of us. "Y'all don't know this, but Derrick *loves* getting mean with his hands. Used to beat the shit out of people. Almost killed a kid back when we were little." Finch turned back to Derrick, whose face was flushed. His hands were balled into fists. "Gave him permanent brain damage. To this day, his parents have to feed him. Kid was a bully, sure, but Derrick had laid him out with one punch. Could have stopped there. But no, he kept on wailing on him because he *liked* it. Got arrested for it and everything. Lucky for him he was only twelve at the time."

"Twelve?" Maeve whispered.

Derrick hung his head, but didn't object. Didn't deny. He just looked devastated. For my part, I did feel weirdly unsurprised. It explained a whole lot about Derrick and Finch's relationship.

"I'm going to go back inside." Crystal was at my ear. "Want to come?"

And for a beat I did consider saying no. But who was I kidding? I needed that screwdriver to stop working at my joints, needed to stop the vise before it crushed my skull. I just needed it all to stop.

"Yeah," I said. "I'm coming."

But in the morning I would finally call an end to all of it. The drugs and the bad choices and all the fucking risks. Maybe I'd call the police or the FBI or whoever you called when you had people like Frank pissed at you. I'd tell them everything, and then I'd live with the consequences. No one else was getting hurt, not on my account. Not anymore. From now on, it would just be me footing the bill.

But first, I was going to get high one last time. And who knows, maybe it would finally be the time I didn't survive.

Detective Julia Scutt

Sunday, 10:10 a.m.

I'm waiting for the nurse behind the Hudson Hospital reception desk to get me a room number for the John Doe. Feels like she's been tapping away at her keyboard for twenty minutes, but it's probably been more like two. The clock is ticking, though, and this entire visit to the hospital could be a dead end.

There are plenty of reasons an assault victim might try to leave against medical advice that have nothing to do with our murder—a domestic situation, debt, some minor outstanding warrant. And Seldon's already got my team turning to Dan. The only thing that's going to head that off at the pass is me having a solid suspect, one who's got nothing to do with Kaaterskill.

"Any luck yet?" I ask, trying to hustle the nurse.

She glares at me—I did hit a little too hard on the *yet*.

"Does it look like it?" she asks, then goes back to her hunting and pecking.

At least I've had Jonathan, Stephanie, and Maeve moved down to the station for safekeeping. It was mostly for their protection. Whoever is our perpetrator could decide to show up at the house and finish what they started. But there are also way too many holes in their story, holes big enough for them to disappear through.

The doors at the end of the hall swing open then, and a man in a white coat and a rubber apron comes through. A morgue guy. My mind flashes back to the night we came down here with Jane's dental records. With her face smashed, it was the only way to identify her. I'd sat there on the bench between my parents, trying not to fidget with Jane's ring, already secreted on a chain at my neck. The special one that looked like braided twigs with the teeny sapphire set in between. As soon as we realized she was missing, I'd taken it from Jane's jewelry box without asking my mom, too afraid she might say no.

I shouldn't have even been there at the hospital at that age, but ever since Jane disappeared, I hadn't wanted to let either of my parents out of my sight. We'd be ripped apart before long anyway. Within weeks my dad had switched from the occasional beer with the game to a nightly Johnnie Walker. Soon it would be two Scotches then three, bigger and bigger pours each time. In the years that followed, the man I knew as my father—loving, kind, attentive, and so funny—was replaced by a mean and unpredictable drunk. He died when I was in eighth grade, his car wrapped around a telephone pole on his way back from a client meeting in the city. My mother's health declined rapidly after that, patchy memory turning into full-blown dementia by the time I was in my second year on the force. The last time I visited before she died, she kept calling me Jane. I didn't have the heart to correct her.

"The Aftermath." That was what they'd called the episode of *The River* about what became of my family and Bethany's in the wake of the murders. Drugs, arrests, divorces, alcoholism—surely not all of it could be blamed on Jane and Bethany's deaths. Judging from the riveted listener reviews, the episode had been full of salacious details, which probably explained the sickly fascinated look on that woman's pretty round face when she approached me at Home Depot, asking if I would autograph her receipt.

I asked her twice to please go away. When she didn't, something in me just broke, and I shoved her. Not nearly hard enough for her to fall the way she had, loudly knocking over the rack of specialty paint samples as she hit the ground. She'd wanted to make a scene. That's what these people always wanted—to become part of the story.

"Maybe you should, you know, talk to somebody about it?" Dan had suggested in the car on the way home. He'd managed to beat the patrol officers to the scene and talked the woman out of pressing charges. Luckily, there was no record that any of it had ever happened. He'd said we'd come back later for my car.

"Talk to somebody about the fact that there are sick people in the world who want my autograph because my sister is dead?" I asked, pouncing. "How is talking to anyone going to change that?"

"That's not what I meant," Dan snapped right back, at long last annoyed.

"Then what did you mean?"

"I'm just saying—sometimes, Julia, you only see what you want to see."

"So this is me in denial?" My face was hot, my voice loud. I'd been gunning for this fight—the big one—and I was ready.

"Maybe counseling could help you process things. So you don't have to feel so angry."

"Stop the damn car!" I shouted, already reaching for the door.

"Whoa, calm down!" Dan jerked the car onto the shoulder. "Julia, wait . . ."

I don't remember exactly what I said next, only the rage I'd felt. And how it had ended: with me getting out of Dan's car on the side of Route 32 and walking the four miles home.

"Room 304," the nurse says finally, waving a printed visitor's badge at me. "They had him in the system wrong. Elevator at the back."

I see the sleepy uniform on the door as I step off the elevator. Mark, I think. A young guy, clean-cut and too small for his uniform. He pushes himself off the wall when he sees me coming.

"Where's the treating physician?" I ask.

People admit surprising things to doctors, a lot of it unrelated to their medical treatment and hence not privileged. The trick is getting the doctor to tell you any of it. Their ethics tend to go beyond the letter of the law.

The officer points a short index finger toward a young South Asian woman standing a couple doors down, hair pulled back in a low ponytail. Even tired-looking and in her scrubs, she's quite pretty. I wonder how many patients ask for someone less attractive and more male.

"Doctor?" I ask, flashing my badge.

"Yes," she says briskly, glancing in my direction before looking back down at the chart in her hands. "What can I do for you, Officer?"

I point behind me. "The AMA who wouldn't identify himself?"

She nods, then frowns. "Ordinarily I wouldn't have called the police. As far as I'm concerned, people have the right to their own medical decisions and their privacy." Great, a doctor and a libertarian. "But we were informed to be on the lookout for an injured individual related to a homicide. And there's no doubt this patient was assaulted."

"Serious injuries?"

"Moderate. He has some minor internal bleeding," she says, eyes still on the chart. "That's why they brought him in. He was found passed out in the train station. But it seems as though it's resolving itself."

"Could the injuries have been caused by a car accident, and not an assault?"

"I'm not a forensics expert, but the pattern and size of the bruising appears more consistent with fists.

Also, there's hardly any damage to his face. If it was an accident of some kind, you wouldn't expect injuries that are so well contained." She looks up at me. "Not that the internal injuries to John Doe's torso would be easy to cause with your bare hands, mind you. Whoever beat him up was efficient and effective. Professional, you could say."

When I finally enter room 304, a tall, white man is sitting on the edge of the hospital bed. He is good-looking and well-built, longish hair pulled back in a ponytail, a little bit of a beard. He still has an IV lead in his arm, the tube detached, and he's got jeans on under his hospital gown. There's a balled-up T-shirt in his hands, like he managed to get the jeans on and then was overwhelmed by exhaustion. His lower lip is swollen, but otherwise he has no visible injuries to his face or arms. Strange—the doctor was right. John Doe is bracing himself, hand on his knee, like it's painful to stay upright.

"Who the fuck are you?" he breathes. His voice is hoarse.

I flash my badge. "Detective Julia Scutt. I'd like to ask you a few questions."

"Don't think so." I hear a touch of a southern accent. "I already told your friend out in the hall I wasn't talking. But I'll happily repeat myself: I'm not answering any fucking questions. I don't have to. Not unless it's a crime up here to get the shit kicked out of you."

I hold up my hands and smile, as warm and flirty as I can stomach. He strikes me as the kind of guy who will respond to fawning. "Hey, come on, take it easy, Mr. . . ."

"Take it easy? You can't just keep me here. I will sue the fucking shit out of you for violating my civil rights. I'll own this whole town by the time I'm done."

But buried underneath that anger is fear. A decent amount of it. He's scared of whoever did this to him. Maybe the same person who's responsible for what happened in that car.

"We're holding you here because there's been an incident."

"What kind of incident?"

"Why don't we start with your name? And then I can tell you what I know."

He glares at me for an impressive length of time. Not that I care. We can do this all day if he wants.

"Finch Hendrix," he answers finally. "What incident?"

Ah, Finch, the elusive missing sixth person in my weekend party. I was hoping it might be him.

"Something has happened to your friends," I begin, watching for a guilty tell. But he looks only confused and concerned.

"What friends?"

"Keith Lazard and Derrick Chism. One of them is dead, the other missing."

"What the fuck are you talking about?" His alarm seems genuine—eyes wide, face flushed. "Who's dead?"

"The deceased hasn't been identified. But we know it's either Derrick or Keith. The other is missing."

"What the fuck?" He leans forward, then winces.

"There was a car accident," I say, treading carefully. "The death does look suspicious, maybe not caused by the accident. A positive ID has been difficult because of the condition of the body."

His puffy mouth contorts. "What the—where did this even happen?"

"Mr. Hendrix, I'm afraid I'm going to need you to fill in some gaps for me before I can share any more details. This is an ongoing investigation."

Hendrix glares at me. He's not stupid. He knows he's got a choice to make.

"What do you want to know?" I see his body tense.

"Admission records say that you were brought in here from the train station at four this morning. Can you tell me where you were before that?"

"I fell asleep there, waiting for my train," he says.

Passed out, as the result of a beating, not fell asleep—I already know that much.

"But you left Jonathan's house early yesterday," I say. "That's nearly twenty-four hours unaccounted for."

Hendrix shakes his head, a flicker of sadness passing across his face.

"I've known Derrick since we were kids," he says, ignoring my question about the gap in his timeline. "I'm going to be—it better not be him."

"What about Keith? I thought he was your agent."

"Art dealer. And that isn't the same thing as a friend," he says. "Keith and I have been having problems lately anyway. Or rather *he's* been having problems that have been causing *me* problems."

"What kind of problems?" I ask, playing dumb.

"He's a fucking addict." Hendrix sounds disgusted. "An addict without enough money to support his habit. Without enough money, period. Fucking pathetic. Not exactly the kind of person you want having a hand in your finances."

"That sounds bad."

"Yeah, it is bad. Totally unprofessional, verging on illegal, actually. Keith cost me one important show already. In London. Obviously, I don't wish him dead, but . . ."

"You wouldn't be sorry if he is?"

His eyes flash. "I didn't say that."

"So you don't know what happened in that car, Mr. Hendrix?"

"How could I? I left yesterday, remember?"

"What about a local girl named Crystal?" I ask. "She was at the house. Did you see her?"

"No, ma'am," he says instantly. "Not that I'm aware of."

"Any chance Keith or Derrick is responsible for these injuries of yours?"

"Nope," he says, eyes still on me.

"I've heard Derrick Chism has a history of violence, one that you, specifically, disclosed this weekend. And then here you turn up the victim of an assault. That seems like a big coincidence."

"Coincidence is all you've got?" With a grimace he pushes himself off the bed, grunting as his feet hit the floor. "You can't fucking hold me on coincidence, you and I both know that. Besides, I'm the fucking victim here."

"Victim of what, Mr. Hendrix?" I ask. "That's all I want to know."

But Finch Hendrix just shakes his head as he takes off his hospital gown. His well-defined chest and abdomen are covered in the beginnings of spectacular bruises, his left side taped along his ribs. He makes one attempt to put on his T-shirt, then pauses to take a deep breath. The second time he gets it over his head, but has to stop again and rest, before finally managing to tug it all the way down.

"You know what I think?" I say.

"What's that?"

"I think maybe you and Keith Lazard finally had it out in Derrick Chism's car. Lazard got physical, and you took the upper hand. Derrick intervenes on Keith's behalf. Eventually you picked up a weapon to defend yourself. And accidentally, someone got killed. It was two against one—you have a great case for self-defense."

"Uh-huh," he says, squinting at me. "Except none of that happened. I was never in Derrick's car. Keith Lazard never laid a hand on me. And I sure as hell didn't kill anybody."

"Well, you weren't passed out in the train station for twenty-four hours either, not without anyone noticing. That much I know for sure."

Hendrix shrugs, gestures vaguely into the air. "All I can tell you is what I can tell you," he says. "And I don't know what happened in that car. You want me to guess, I bet it's some drug thing. Keith probably wanted to buy. Derrick probably tried to talk him out of it, but took him anyway. Derrick can be easy to lean on. They probably ran into the wrong people. That's why you shouldn't fucking do drugs."

He pats his pockets as he looks around for something. Finally he spots a set of keys on a small table near the door, and stiffly makes his way over to pick them up. I watch him reach for them with his left hand.

"Mr. Hendrix, why don't you just tell me where you were for the nearly twenty-four hours between when you left the house and when you were found passed out and bleeding internally at the train station? Tell me that, and then you can go."

"How about I just go now? How about I just walk right out that door without telling you anything?"

"There's an armed officer on the door who will stop you, Mr. Hendrix."

This is a lie. I can't stop Hendrix from leaving. There's definitely more to his story, but nothing that a judge would believe constitutes probable cause to hold him. And so I watch as Hendrix makes his way somehow both arrogantly and gingerly toward the door, taking with him my best chance to make Seldon happy—a real live suspect who doesn't have a damn thing to do with Kaaterskill.

"Mr. Hendrix," I call after him as he pulls open the door. "This isn't over."

"It is for me," he calls back over his shoulder. "If you have any other questions, you can call my lawyers. I've got lots of them."

Two Weeks (and Four Days) Earlier

I'm sitting on a bench across the street from Stephanie's office building on the edge of Madison Square Park, watching the lawyers march in and out, gazing at the stately stone facade. Of course Stephanie's office is convenient and impressive. Nothing for her but the very best.

So much hostility—I know it's unsavory, not to mention misplaced. My anger has always been like that, with a mind of its own. It can move in so suddenly, too, like a summer storm blackening the sky. Soon it's impossible to see anything clearly. But never for long. My anger recedes just as quickly, sometimes leaving terrible things in its wake.

It's hard not to feel bitter about how judgmental Stephanie has been. Even if it is her way of dealing with her own insecurities—to look down on everyone else. Maybe I want revenge for that. But then—that does sound pathetic. And I am many things, but I am not pathetic.

It's possible Stephanie can't help lording her perfection over everyone—stunning Stephanie, smart Stephanie, successful Stephanie. Always so unattainable. Always so controlled and focused on her goals. From day one, I found it nauseating, quite honestly. No one is really that perfect anyway. No one is that above everything. In fact, it's usually those people who are secretly nosing their way through the deepest sewage. You just need to stick around long enough to see their baseness revealed.

Like, for instance, the fact that Stephanie always puts herself and her ambition first—and look at the cost. Who knows what would have happened if she'd been there to answer those calls that last tragic night?

Maybe I'm justified in being most angry at Stephanie. I'm hoping that just by looking at her, I'll know—in my gut. I have very, very good instincts about people. And right now, everyone remains a possibility. *I know what you did.* It was perfect, really—so vague and yet so precise. So many different ways to be interpreted.

Finally I see Stephanie coming back from her meeting, dressed in a dark pantsuit, looking elegant and powerful as she strides alongside two older men. Men who seem to be hanging on her every word. Of course they are. Everyone is always hanging on Stephanie's every word. At the door, she stops abruptly, digging for her ringing phone. I know that's what she's doing. Because I'm the one who's calling her.

When she can't seem to find her phone, she gestures for the men to go inside. She drops her bag and crouches. Finally she manages to pull out her phone and looks down at the screen. A blocked number, of course. She jerks to her feet, throws her phone back into her bag but misses. It lands on the cement. She retrieves it, examining the screen—cracked, no doubt, in her temper tantrum.

She drops her face into her hands then. Wait—is Stephanie crying?

Huh. I don't think I've ever seen Stephanie cry. Not once. Stunning Stephanie, smart Stephanie, successful Stephanie—maybe she's not so perfect after all.

Jonathan

Saturday, 6:42 a.m.

I opened my eyes to the rising sun, squinting at the light, sparkling gold over the Hudson, as I turned to my clock. Only 6:42 a.m. So early. And all I wanted was to sleep through the rest of this disastrous weekend. Things had already unraveled, between Finch and the fire and the contractors, not to mention Keith's new friend, who he'd disappeared off to bed with, surely to get high. So far, this was an A-plus intervention.

And unfortunately, the stakes were even higher than I'd let on: my dad wasn't just planning to call in his loan, he was planning to have Keith arrested for fraud. If Keith was in rehab, I thought maybe I'd be able to change my dad's mind. Because my dad believed in people working hard, and in making amends, which was why our relationship was so complicated. My dad wasn't a bad person. He was just rigid about things that—yes, thanks to his hard work and success—I had the freedom not to care about.

Occasionally, I could appeal to my dad's softer side. After all, he dealt with me coming out even though it wasn't easy for him. But if he found out about me going ahead and purchasing the Kaaterskill house six months ago, over his strong objections (he thought it was a reckless investment), not to mention proposing to Peter (who he really did not like), all bets were probably off. He might put Keith in jail just to make a point.

"You're awake." A voice right behind me.

I whipped around and there was Peter sitting on the edge of the bed, gray eyes glowing in the sun. He reached out to grip my calf in one of his strong hands and squeezed it affectionately.

"Sorry," he said. "I didn't mean to scare you."

"What are you doing here?" I asked, flooded with relief. Peter had explaining to do, of course he did. But I was still happy to see him.

"I should have come to begin with." Peter shook his head.

Then he stood, tossed his jacket on the chair, and worked his way out of his shoes. Soon he was standing there naked at the end of the bed. I loved that Peter was warm and funny and full of life—that most of all. But it was his beauty I had been drawn to first, that night at the Waverly Inn, after he brought me my gin and tonic as I waited for Keith to arrive.

Peter crawled across the bed. "I missed you," he said, pushing his weight hard against me, his mouth over mine. All of it, exactly the way I liked.

I woke up with Peter still curved around me, damp chest pressed up against my back, heavy leg slung over my thigh. I felt at ease for the first time since we'd left the city. Peter was distractible. And immature, though he was actually a couple years older than me. But whatever was going on, we could work through it.

The sun was higher now, no longer glinting off the water. Peter was snoring lightly, in that sweet way he always did after we made love: like a little boy, or a small dog.

I did wonder how close he really was to finishing up his book. And, yes, an agent had compared Peter to David Foster Wallace, but she'd only read the first chapter. I'd read the first two, and they were very good—I think. Honestly, they didn't make that much sense to me, but what did I know? The problem was,

Peter's idea of "finished" and actually being finished weren't always the same. This was the reason my dad didn't like him. He believed, above all else, in finishing things. I should have considered this before: that attention to detail wasn't Peter's strong suit. This thing with the contractors could be a real problem.

I nudged Peter with an elbow. He stirred, breath catching before snuggling closer to me. I lay still, pretending he'd just woken on his own.

"So, the contractors?" I began.

I don't know anything about any boards, Peter had responded to my first text last night. After my second set of texts about the money the contractors were owed, he'd called. We were at the Falls by then. He said that he had no idea what they were talking about, that he'd paid everything that was owed. I might have believed it more if he hadn't sounded so nervous, or if I hadn't heard the sounds of a crowded bar in the background after he'd told me he was staying home.

"Peter?" I asked. "Hello? The contractors? Is there something you're not telling me?"

When I pulled away, Peter rolled onto his back, an arm covering his eyes.

"I'm sorry," he said finally. "I just—" He lowered his arm and looked at me so sincerely and so sadly. "I want you to know that I love you—very much. You have to at least promise—before I tell you—that you believe me on that. You do, don't you?"

My stomach was somersaulting as I hastily slid out of bed. Suddenly, I wasn't sure that I wanted to know the truth. I stepped toward the windows and looked out over the river. It was perfect—the house, my life with Peter. Or it could be. Maybe even still.

"What happened, Peter?" I asked, crossing my arms as I turned back from the windows. Peter had to know that this was serious. I wasn't some fool. "Tell me the truth, now. All of it."

Peter leaned back against the headboard.

"Remember how I told you Liam was starting a juice bar?" he began, tentatively.

Did I remember that? Maybe. I knew a Liam.

"Yeah," I lied.

"Well, Liam needed some cash to cover the security deposit for his lease. It was this perfect little spot in SoHo. Right near Balthazar, off Lafayette. You know, one of those slivers of a store, almost like a closet?"

"Okay," I said. "And?"

"Well, anyway, if that spot didn't work, Liam was going to have to go with like a truck or something, but then you always have to be worrying about where to park and that's pretty hard to—"

"Peter."

"Liam was supposed to get the money right back to me. He'd calculated exactly what he'd pull in that first week, more than twenty thousand, conservatively. He was going to have it back to me in plenty of time to pay the contractors . . ." Peter put his arm back over his eyes.

I turned back to the window, looking again at the view that Peter had selected specially because, he thought, with all the stress of working for my dad, I could benefit from some nature and peace in my life.

"Let me guess. Something didn't work out?"

"The juice bar got shut down by the Department of Health on the first day," Peter said quietly. "Some glitch with the refrigerator thermometer. I'm so sorry, Jonathan. It was your money. I had no right to—"

"It was my money."

But the money doesn't matter. That was also right there on the tip of my tongue. But I could *not* write off $11,000, even if Peter had taken the money to help someone. Not if we really were going to get married. We couldn't have a life where Peter did things like that without discussing them with me first, a life where he lied to me.

"As soon as Liam told me he couldn't pay me back, I called the contractors and told them to stop work on the deck," Peter said. "But they said I'd still need to pay them the full eleven thousand because they were already out for materials. And they were not at all happy."

"I'm getting that sense," I said. "They tried to burn down the house last night."

"What?" Peter jumped out of bed and came over. He looked so worried. "Are you okay?"

"Yeah, yes—I'm fine. They just lit the boards for the deck on fire." I motioned to the side of the yard. "Luckily, it didn't spread to the house. I think they were only trying to scare us."

Peter wrapped his arms around me. "This is all my fault."

"It is your fault," I said into his shoulder. Then I forced myself to step out of his embrace. "You should have told me everything from the start. And you shouldn't be lending your friends that kind of money."

Though that part did make me feel like a hypocrite. I'd given Keith a lot of money over the years, over and above that loan for the gallery. And Keith was a *drug addict.* I was also the one who'd given Alice the money to track down the family of the guy from the roof. Not that anyone else knew that. Not that I knew what she'd used the money for. Bribing people for information, I'd supposed. I hadn't wanted to know. That was me—hand money over first, be an actual good friend later.

"You're right," Peter said. "You're absolutely right."

And now I needed to leave the room. Otherwise I was going to cave too quickly. I grabbed my robe and started for the door without looking at Peter again.

"Wait, Jonathan, where are you going?" he called after me. "Aren't you going to say anything?"

I paused in the doorway, but without turning back. "Do you want some coffee?"

A peace offering.

"Yes." Peter sounded relieved. "Thank you, Jonathan."

The house was silent as I made my way down the steps, softly creaking in that way I loved. My parents believed in pristine and new, with the exception of our Hamptons estate, whose antique vintage was acceptable only because it was constructed entirely of stone.

The newly remodeled kitchen was filled with pretty stainless steel and lots of white marble and cool gray cabinets stocked with cooking items only Peter knew how to use. He might have been bad with money, but he was an excellent cook. And he liked taking care of me in that way. With the sun still low and the lights off, the kitchen had a cool glow. I stood there for a moment, drinking in the stillness. It *was* nice, this life Peter and I had built for ourselves.

I left the lights off as I made my way over to the large, shiny espresso machine. It wasn't until I was standing in front of it, coffee cups in hand, that I remembered I had absolutely no idea how to operate it. Peter always made the coffee.

I was still staring at the coffee machine when the door swung open.

"Good morning," Keith said, looking sheepish, but cleaned up, and fully dressed.

His eyes had also lost some of their manic sheen. Of course, that probably meant he'd gotten high.

"Feeling better?" I asked.

"Not sure *better* is exactly the right word," Keith said. "But it doesn't feel like my bone marrow has been replaced with battery acid anymore or like I need to claw my skin off. So, sure, I guess that's progress."

And suddenly, there we were, talking about it—Keith and the drugs. We were always talking around it with Keith, the same way we were always talking around what had happened to Alice. That was what we did with the things we felt bad about, circled them endlessly, never close enough to actually make contact.

"Is that really what it's like if you're not high?"

"Yup," Keith said. "If I wait too long, my intestines feel like they're being twisted in a fist. Eventually the stomach pain is so bad you're essentially incapacitated. And then I start throwing up. Don't get me wrong, I liked being high in the beginning. That's what started all of this. But using these days is mostly a way to avoid getting sick. And the more you use, the worse it all gets."

"Jesus, Keith."

"Yeah, well, don't do drugs, man," he said mildly, then looked me up and down, as I stood helplessly in front of the coffee machine. "Here, give it." He motioned for a mug.

I handed it over. Keith grabbed a tea towel and tossed it over his shoulder, setting about filling the espresso handle with coffee and locking it back into place. As the coffee brewed, he took a carton of milk from the refrigerator, filled the small metal container, and turned on the steam with a loud hiss.

"Where did you learn how to do that?" I asked.

"Um, in the world." Keith raised an eyebrow. "You should check it out sometime—it's this place where all the regular people have to do stuff for themselves."

"Fuck you," I said, rolling my eyes.

Keith smiled as he handed me the coffee, and for a second I saw in his face the old him. A little wild, sure—he was an artist, after all—but wild with heart, and hope. And then Alice killed herself, and that 10,000-watt bulb inside Keith popped. Ever since, his center had been nothing but a dark and infinite void.

Keith looked down at the second mug. The one I'd already had in my hand when he walked in. "This wasn't for me, was it?"

I shook my head. "Peter is here."

"Ah, I see." Keith nodded slowly, stepping forward to start making the second coffee. "So I suppose you'll be wanting this coffee for him?"

I nodded, trying not to feel embarrassed. Was it obvious there was some issue with Peter not paying the contractors? But Keith was hardly one to judge. "Maybe you should bring your friend Crystal some coffee?"

Keith shook his head. "Touché, my friend. Touché," he said. "I'm sorry that—actually, I don't think I can apologize any more. At a certain point, you feel like *more* of a dick saying you're sorry. When did Peter get here?"

"Early this morning," I said. "Looks like we *do* owe the contractors money. It was a mistake—Peter was trying to help a friend, things got complicated."

"Eleven thousand dollars kind of misplaced. Makes sense."

Keith was right that I was understating the problem. Also, the contractors had tried to burn down the house *after* I agreed that I'd pay them, which suggested something even worse than Peter had told me. Whatever it was, it would be better to sort it all out from the safety of our Tribeca apartment, with its protective doormen and many alarms. And, yes, Bright Horizons was very strict about logistics, and they had said Sunday afternoon was the only check-in, but all manner of flexibility could be purchased for a price. All I needed to do now was talk Keith into going.

"Why don't you drink that coffee?" I said. "We could sit outside for a minute. There's a table out there. It's really nice."

Or so Peter had told me. I'd never sat out there myself.

"Okay," Keith said. "But I probably shouldn't leave Crystal up there alone too long. Last night she was weirdly open about being on the lookout for something to pocket."

It was nice outside; Peter was right. He'd placed a little café table and two metal chairs under the overhang, framing a view of a couple large maple trees and the bush with a bluebird's nest Peter had told me about. Sure enough, there were a bunch of small birds flying around, though they looked more brown than blue.

"This is nice," Keith said, after we'd sat in silence for a while. "Guess Peter isn't entirely useless."

I felt a flash of anger. "Seriously?"

"Come on, that was a joke." Keith laughed. "Whatever, so Peter didn't pay some bill. Still nice that he did all this with the house for you. It's good for you to have someone like that. I feel like after your dad, you need that kind of devotion. Everybody does."

I didn't want to talk about my dad. "Listen, I think—we all think that—"

"I know." Keith put his coffee down. "Rehab, right?"

I exhaled. "I got you a spot at a place, Bright Horizons. It's all set up."

"Bright Horizons?" Keith made a face. "A little on the nose with the name, don't you think?"

"It's a good place," I said. "They come very highly recommended. It wasn't easy to get you a bed. And they specialize in medically assisted treatment. I'm not saying that will make it easy or anything, but it should make it *easier.*"

Keith nodded, but his mouth had turned down. "Where is it?"

Too far away from the gallery. Too much time away from work. I could hear the excuses already.

"It's in the Finger Lakes, only a three-hour drive from here," I said, but really it was more like four and a half. And now I had to get to the point, or at least part of it. "You have to check in by Sunday, at the latest, or my dad is calling in your loan. Apparently somebody from his office went by the gallery—they said you seemed high."

Keith's brow furrowed like he was trying to remember. Finally, he grimaced. "Ah, I think I remember that. I joked about it with the guy. He was young, or whatever, so I thought he'd think it was funny." He shook his head ruefully. "That's what happens when you're high this much: you start thinking, and saying, crazy shit."

"I'll work the gallery myself if I have to," I offered. I figured that would be Keith's first stop on the excuse train.

"You'd do that, wouldn't you? You'd fucking go to my gallery every day and hand-sell paintings."

"Of course I would." I'd actually already cleared my schedule. I was an executive vice president of new development at Cheung Capital—a reasonably big job. But I was hardly critical to daily operations. And I could pretend to have good taste in art. Being smug and obnoxious was half the battle.

"Why are you always so fucking good to me?" Keith asked.

I thought for a long moment. "You remember that painting you did of me? For that family series?"

"Yeah, *Family of Origin.* I did one for each of you."

"But do you remember my painting specifically?"

"Of course," Keith said. "I remember you were pissed about it."

"It was a huge painting of just my dad. He looked like a monster, and I was like this little shadow in the corner."

"Do you want me to say that I was wrong to paint it like that? That it was an oversimplification of a complex relationship, and I did it because I was an asshole? Because I was definitely an asshole," he said. "I'm still an asshole. I thought we'd established that."

"No," I said quietly. "You were right. That painting was right. So much of my life has been defined by who I'm not—explaining or apologizing for not being the ambitious, driven son my father wants. At least I don't pretend as much anymore. But I think I forgot to figure out who I actually am instead. Anyway, if it hadn't been for me, we would have called the police that night. Alice would be alive. Maybe you'd even be—"

"Nope. Nice try. We were all there that night. We made our own choices, including Alice. She could have gone to the police afterward, any time she wanted."

"Okay, but I definitely put pressure—"

"No," Keith said resolutely. "We were *all* there." He looked away toward the bush, watching the birds come and go in silence for a moment. "I'll go to rehab, but not Bright Horizons. I need someplace farther away. Someplace where I can really disappear."

"You can disappear at this place," I said. "I've seen pictures. It's in the middle of nowhere."

"No. I mean like an airplane ride away. Somewhere no one can find me." He looked up at me, held my stare. There was something else I didn't know about, something worse than losing his gallery that he was running from. "And I need to go today. Right now."

"Okay," I said, afraid that if I hesitated, he might tell me what this other bad thing was. Honestly, I didn't want to know. "We'll find a new place."

I couldn't imagine we'd be able to. I'd try, though. I always did.

"Great," Keith said as he stood. He looked determined now, and maybe even a little hopeful. He consulted his watch, like I might be able to sort it all out within minutes. "I'll get my stuff together. And let's pay those contractors on the way. I don't want you dealing with them alone."

"Yeah, okay." I already knew none of this was going to work out the way Keith was suggesting. But still, it was progress.

Keith opened the back door. "Listen, I may be a selfish fucker, but I'm still your friend. I'm obligated to look out for you." And then he smiled. "Make sure Peter knows that, okay?"

"I will," I said. "This is going to be okay, Keith. *You* are going to be okay."

Keith nodded. And now it was his turn to lie. "I know."

Detective Julia Scutt

Sunday, 12:15 p.m.

It's dim and gray as I get out of the car at the Farm. Like the sun never fully rose. And you really want full daylight in a place like the Farm, where even an ordinary situation can turn dangerous. When people have lost everything but the need for a fix and are desperate enough to live here, in a jerry-rigged shack with no running water or electricity, all options are always on the table.

The Farm is privately owned, inherited by a developer in Manhattan with big plans for condos on the land, and no plan to waste money cleaning it up in the meantime. Activists—weekenders, all of them—have tried to challenge the owner's right to ignore the squatting, but he has enough lawyers to keep those cases stalled in the courts.

Back when Seldon was lieutenant himself, patrol officers used to go in regularly to chase some of the squatters off, round up others for petty drug possession and trespassing. But then an officer died clearing a building in the dark, a head wound in an accidental fall. Since then, the officers have steered clear of the place unless there was a specific callout.

But I've got no choice now. I need to see if Derrick and Keith were here before the accident, need to try and locate this Crystal Finnegan. Seldon doesn't want the Kaaterskill drug trade implicated in the murder of some weekender, but I've got to follow the facts where they lead. And right now, some of the facts are pointing straight to the Farm.

It's nearly silent when I get out of the car. Generally speaking, opioid addicts aren't early risers. I stop some distance in front of the ramshackle building constructed from plywood and metal scrap at the bottom of the hill. Once upon a time everyone slept in the barn, until part of it collapsed in the middle of the night, almost killing three people. That's when some of the squatters patched together the outbuilding. With its obvious tilt to the right, it doesn't seem much more secure.

I'm debating which threatening-looking door to knock on first when there's a loud crash from the barn up the hill. Loud even from thirty yards away. A thrashing sound follows. I turn and wait, listen. It's quiet for a stretch. But then another noise, louder this time, followed by more frantic rustling. Like someone inside is careening into things—high and disoriented maybe. Or injured. I don't *really* think it's one of the guys I'm looking for, but it's also not impossible.

Fuck. Slowly, I start up the hill toward the barn.

It's been quiet for a spell. But then again—bang, bang, scramble, bang.

I move my hand so that my palm is resting against my gun. No need to draw yet. The coldness of the metal against my fingers is enough. The last thing I need is Seldon pinning an improper discharge on me.

The barn looks even worse close up—bent, rusted nails, shattered glass. Like any second it's going to crash the rest of the way down. Probably the fucking second I go inside. I stop in front of a huge crack providing something of a doorway.

"Kaaterskill Police. Come out of the building. Now!"

On cue the noises start up again. Near the door. I can feel them, too, through the rickety wall. The impact.

Thud, thud. Bang. Bang. Scramble. I pull out my gun, step closer to the opening, flashlight up. I don't see any movement, but there is so much debris, whoever is in there could be hiding anywhere. I spot something at the edge of the makeshift entrance. A red-brown smear that could be dried blood.

"Last chance!" I shout over the noise. "You don't come out, you might get shot!"

The thumping gets louder. I take a deep breath, preparing to move into darkness. *Don't shoot too early. Don't shoot too late.* As soon as I turn, something smacks me hard, right in the face. The impact sends me reeling.

"What the fuck!"

Blinded, I try to get my footing. My gun is still in my hand. But I can't see a goddamn thing. I blink a few times. My eyes are still burning and watering, but at least I can see again.

Laughter then. From some distance behind me. With my eyes still tearing, I make out the outline of a woman, sitting on a rock.

"Fucking turkey vulture," she says, then laughs some more as my vision finally clears. She points to the sky. When I look up, I can see the outline of a massive bird, already soaring up near the tops of the trees. "They've been getting stuck in the barn ever since that deer died in there. Dumb things get in, and they can't get out."

My nose is throbbing. I hope it's not broken. I tuck my gun away at my back.

"Man, that thing really nailed you," the woman says, laughter still in her voice.

When I squint at her now, she finally comes into view. Painfully thin, she looks to be in her mid-forties, with long, dull brown hair and overly tanned, heavily lined skin, too much of it exposed in a thin tank top and ripped jeans.

"There's blood on that doorframe," I say, motioning to the barn, glad for the excuse to look away from her bony arms. "Any idea where it came from?"

She peers up at me like I'm the one who's high. "Um, I don't know, the fucking *deer*." She shakes her head. "Some hunter shot it, and it wandered in there. Whole place smelled like death for weeks. Still does sometimes. Fucking gross."

"Have you seen either of these guys?" I ask, coming closer to show her the pictures of Keith and Derrick on my phone.

She studies the screen, then looks up at me. "Seen them where?"

"Here," I say, pointing at the ground, straining to keep my patience. "Buying drugs maybe." *Because I know that's what's going on here, and I could arrest all of you if I wanted to*—that's the implied threat. God knows if she even notices. "But I don't care about the drugs. I'm just trying to find these men."

She looks back at the screen. "Never seen them. You should ask Crystal, though. They look like her type."

"Crystal?" I ask, playing dumb.

She waves behind her toward the outbuilding. "She likes that kind of thing."

"What kind of thing?" I ask. "Men?"

"Nah, weekenders with cash," the woman says. "Crystal fucks them for money. I mean, not like an actual prostitute. Crystal's not like that. She just picks them up, goes home and has sex with them, then lifts a few twenties on her way out." She peers up at me and smirks. "I guess that is kind of like a prostitute. But Crystal's a nice girl. Smart, sweet too."

"Which room is hers?"

"This isn't a fucking bed and breakfast. People stay where they stay. Then they go."

"Great," I mutter, looking back down the hill toward the menacing outbuilding.

"Hey, wait, I know you."

"I don't think so," I say. But when I turn back and look at her again, more closely, there is something familiar.

Suddenly she pushes herself off the rock. "Wait, yeah, I definitely do."

"Ah, no, you don't," I say starting down the hill, bracing for her to say something about Jane.

"We went to fucking Hudson High together." She points to herself. "Lauren Avery? We got drunk a few times together in Promenade Hill Park—you, me, Amy, Tim, Becca. All those people." She's looking at me now like I'm the one who's got the problem. "Remember?"

And then, all at once, I see her the way she used to be. Lauren with the shiny auburn curls, the big smile, the noisy laugh. She was a loudmouthed clown back in high school, at the center of a group that I stayed on the far periphery of. I faded out for good when I left for UCLA. Some of us are still connected on social media that I never look at, but I haven't spoken to anyone from high school in years. Most people move on from Hudson. Lauren's dream had been a job in sales and marketing with the New York Giants. She was a guy's girl and a sports fanatic. The drugs have ravaged her.

"Oh, right," I say, finally. And luckily stop myself short of *How are you?* Because the answer is obvious.

"You're a cop?" she asks. "Here?"

She knows about Jane, of course. Everyone always did. And even in her current drug-addled state, she thinks it's a weird choice for me to stay and work as a cop in the town where Jane was murdered. She's got a point.

"Yeah, I'm a cop," I say, inching backward down the hill. There is nowhere good for this conversation to go. "You shouldn't be staying here, you know. This isn't a safe place. Trust me."

Lauren shrugs and smiles sadly. "Then what are you doing here?"

"I don't have any choice," I say, turning to leave.

"Nah," Lauren calls after me. "Everyone's got choices."

Back down the hill, I rap on the first of the ramshackle doors. Move one hand to my gun, just in case. Silence. Passed out, too high to hear me—so many possibilities.

"Police, open up!" My voice sounds deep, confident.

I wait a long, long beat, then pound again, even harder this time.

"Hold the fuck on!" finally comes a muffled voice—youngish, grouchy, male.

Noises follow: shit being hidden, thrown out, evidence destroyed. Not that I care if it's only related to drugs, but there are other possibilities. I knock again. "Come on, open the damn door!"

"I said I was fucking coming!"

I take a step back as heavy footsteps approach, hand still on my gun. Finally the door snaps open.

"What the fuck?" The young guy in the doorway is shirtless, his chest concave-skinny, wearing faded boxer shorts with a sagging elastic that barely clings to his bony hips. His ribs look like they're about to tear through his pasty skin. There's something, someone, moving in the room behind him under a pile of blankets on the floor.

"Who is it?" A woman's voice.

"That Crystal?" I ask, pointing.

"What?" He asks like he's never heard the word *crystal*, much less of a person named that.

"Crystal!" comes the muffled voice again. "She wants to know if I'm Crystal."

"Crystal?" he says, kind of disgusted. "Crystal's not fucking here. Why would she be here?"

I take a deep breath. Patience. This is going to be a long conversation. "How about the last time you saw her?"

"I don't fucking know. Check the Falls. She's always hanging out there, trying to pick up weekenders so she can shake them down."

This is the second time I'm hearing this. Maybe Crystal tried to rob Keith and Derrick, and things unraveled? But even if Crystal is a thief, it seems unlikely she could have taken out two grown men on her own. With Luke Gaffney's help on the other hand?

"Have you seen either of these men?" I hold up Keith and Derrick's pictures on my phone, swiping between the two of them a couple times. When the guy leans in to peer at the screen, he reeks of cigarettes.

"Nope," he says finally.

I have to step into the room to show his girlfriend, who rises onto her elbows but otherwise stays prone on the floor, naked it seems under the blanket. She is pretty but her skin is sallow and her short, pink-streaked blond hair looks unwashed.

"Me neither," she says finally, flopping back down. "Cute, though. You find them, you can tell them where to find me. By the way, it was Thursday."

"What was?" I ask.

She waves her toothpick arms in the air like a marionette. "When we last saw Crystal?" She gestures to her boyfriend. "Remember, Tommy?"

"No, I don't remember." Tommy snorts. "How the hell do you know what day it was?"

"That guy came here and got her. And then we went to the Cumberland Farms for the Powerball. Powerball is Thursdays. We asked Crystal and the guy to give us a ride, and he said no."

"Do you remember the guy's name?" I ask.

"Oh, wait, yeah." Tommy smacks a palm against his forehead. "I remember that fucking guy. That dumb accent, talking to everybody here like they went way back. Meanwhile, did you see that huge fucking watch he had on? Fucking hate guys like that."

"His name was like a word that means something else," the girl says. "It wasn't like a regular name. Like Birch or Pine or something."

"A tree?" I ask.

"No, not that," she says. "But like that—"

"A bird!" Tommy snaps his fingers at her. "It was a fucking bird. See, I remember shit, too."

"Finch," I say. "Was his name Finch?"

"Finch! That's it!" Tommy flashes a gap-toothed grin. "Birdman, that was what I called him. I was trying to piss him off, but he didn't seem to give a shit."

"That must have been Friday or Saturday, though," I say. "It couldn't have been Thursday."

"It was Thursday!" Now it's the girl's turn to yell. "Because of the Powerball! We got the fucking tickets." She flaps her hand toward her boyfriend. "Didn't win because we never do. Tommy's got luck for shit."

Alice

I can't sleep. I can't eat. And each day the weight pressing down on my chest gets heavier. My friends are all fine, though. Only four days later, and it's like they've already moved on.

They aren't monsters, but it's just so weird to me how they can put it aside. It's not a thing that can be erased. It happened. And we did it. We are responsible.

Last night we were all together in Jonathan's room before we were going to the Mug. A little pre-party, like the good old days. Or that's the way everyone else was acting. Beers in hand, drinking, joking. Like that guy never even existed. Meanwhile, the whole time I felt myself sliding deeper into some dark hole.

I never went to the Mug with them. Instead, I went back to the Dutch Cabin. I wanted to see if the bar-

tender knew where Evan was from, or even just his last name. The news had been keeping it quiet so far. And it had seemed that night like the bartender and Evan were friends. The bartender said straight out that he'd tell me, but only if I came back with cash. Fucked up, but what could I do? So I found Jonathan and he lent me the couple hundred the bartender wanted.

I didn't tell him what I needed the money for. And, typical Jonathan, he didn't ask. My friends wouldn't like it at all that I went back to the Dutch Cabin, asking questions.

But it's okay. It's all fine. And now, I know his full name: Evan Paretsky. His family is from Hudson. All I need is to go there and talk to his mom, tell her that her son didn't steal anything, that he didn't do anything wrong—except for agreeing to come home with me.

I can't tell my friends that I'm going to Hudson. They'll completely freak. But I know what I'm doing. It's what needs to be done.

Derrick

Saturday, 7:56 a.m.

The sun was up, the light on our side of the house a filtered gray. I'd been awake for a few minutes, lying there, replaying my conversation with Maeve from the night before. I wanted to think that it had gone well. That Finch hadn't done too much damage, telling her about my past. But I didn't feel at all sure.

"Is everything okay?" I'd asked Maeve as we headed back toward the house once the fire was out. I'd gestured to her phone in her hand. She'd been checking it constantly. Better to focus on that than on what Finch had just told everyone about me beating up that kid.

"I just haven't heard back from Bates," she said. "I'm sure he's fine, but I'm getting a little worried."

That's because he's a jerk. You'd be much better off with me. I'd never make you worry.

"You know, the signal up here is weird," I offered instead. "Mine keeps going in and out."

Maeve's face softened as she turned to look at me. "That's true." She motioned back to where the boards had been burning. "This situation—maybe we should just go back to the city tonight."

"Yeah, maybe." I glanced back at Jonathan as we made our way up the front steps. He was still staring at his smoke-damaged house. No firefighters, of course. No police. Jonathan had already admitted to Maeve and me privately that we couldn't call anyone because his dad didn't even know that he'd bought the house, that he'd done it over his dad's specific objections. "But if we go back without Keith in rehab, he'll still lose the gallery."

"Then maybe he loses the gallery," Maeve said, putting a hand on my forearm for emphasis or for some different reason—one could only hope. Regardless, it set the whole side of my body aflame. "All we've been doing is enabling him."

"No, you're right." And she was, there was no doubt about that.

"I think it's because we all feel so guilty about what happened to Alice. And, well, the roof. It's like we'll do anything now to be sure that nothing else bad happens."

"That's true," I said, turning to look into her iridescent eyes.

I thought for a minute that we might exchange some kind of extra knowing look then. *The roof, the tragedy.* What had happened that night could be a bond we shared, just the two of us. And I wanted a bond with Maeve more than anything. But maybe some things were just so dark they could only drive you apart.

"And what if in trying so hard to keep Keith from losing the gallery, we make something even worse happen?" Maeve went on. "If that fire had spread—if one of us had gotten hurt or died—it wouldn't matter what became of the gallery."

Maeve was right about that, too. And while I selfishly didn't want our weekend to end, I couldn't ignore the obvious fact that we were in danger.

"I agree," I'd said once we were inside. "We should talk to Jonathan in the morning about leaving first thing."

Maeve smiled and looked so relieved. "Good," she said. "I'm glad I have one sane person on my side."

I took a breath and decided to roll the dice. "I'm glad you still think I'm sane, after what Finch had to say."

Maeve had shrugged. "We all have a past, Derrick. You're our friend. Nothing is going to change that."

A noise from the foot of the bed startled me back to the present.

"You do know she's right next door, right?" Finch was sitting on the floor next to my unzipped duffel bag.

"What are you doing?"

"Well, I was just sticking these contracts from Keith in your bag for safekeeping," he said, holding up a manila envelope. "But I got distracted when I found these."

He was thumbing through the pictures I'd brought with me. Yes, pictures of Maeve—mostly from college, but some from later—birthday parties in Brooklyn, my book launch, my wedding. Maeve alone, Maeve in groups, Maeve laughing, Maeve posing, Maeve looking away. Together, they were the story of her. My story of her. The one I'd been holding on to, hoping we might build a new story together.

"I mean, this is kind of sick, man. She's right there for you to look at."

I felt myself flush—some mix of shame and fury. "Put the pictures back, Finch," I said, as composed as I could.

Finch made a show of flipping through the pictures some more. "I mean, dude, really. You've got a problem. I think you need to tell her."

I got out of bed and moved closer. I couldn't stand him touching those pictures.

"If you don't tell her, I almost feel like maybe I have to. This fixation of yours is like a violation. Not that I get the fascination with a girl who's fucking some trust-fund dickhead like a high-priced whore."

Pain shot through my knees as I hit the floor. On top of Finch, fists flying. I could see them. I could hear the meaty thud of them making contact. But I couldn't feel them. The face I hit only once—faces were too much to explain, I'd learned that from my dad.

Finch tried to roll away, to block. But he was useless in a fight. Even back when we were kids—

Kids. When I almost killed a boy. Bam. Back in my body. Right there. On top of Finch. I froze.

What the fuck was I doing? How long had I been hitting him? My hands were on fire.

I pushed myself off, panting. Finch was completely, terribly still. After an endless second, his chest finally rose and fell. He coughed.

I leaned back against the bed, trying to catch my breath. My hands burned as I picked up the pictures scattered across the floor. I wondered if I'd broken a finger.

I looked down at the photos in my hands. There was one from freshman year, back when Maeve wasn't all that she was now—very pretty, yes, I thought even then. But much less noticeably so, with pixie hair and glasses obscuring her fuller face. Even after she got contacts and grew her hair long, she still seemed attainable to me, a stealth kind of beauty. These days, though, she was impossibly gorgeous—totally out of reach.

Maeve would never look at me the same way now, not after what I'd just done to Finch. This wasn't something in the distant past.

"You're a fucking psycho," Finch grunted as he lifted himself to a seated position. His mouth was bleeding, his lip already swollen. "I mean, you really fucking are." He winced as he stood and headed unsteadily for the door. "This shit better not look as bad as it feels."

I tucked the pictures into the envelope of contracts. It wasn't until I'd sat back on the bed that I looked down at my throbbing hands. The knuckles of two fingers were broken open and bleeding. I checked Jonathan's nice sheets. Blue, at least. I grabbed some tissues, pressing them against my hand. One after another they turned bright red. I balled them up and tossed them into the garbage can.

When Finch didn't return, I got up to look for him. For all I knew, he was showing off his wounds to Maeve.

There was no one in the hall. Maeve and Stephanie's bedroom door was closed. I crossed over and put my ear to it. I heard quiet talking. Couldn't be Finch, he was always loud. Keith's door was open, but just slightly. The bathroom door was closed, the light on inside. Maybe Finch was in there cleaning up. But then the door swung open suddenly and Peter stepped out, bare-chested in a pair of snug briefs.

"Oh, hi," he said, eyes darting away nervously. Peter was always nervous around us. He motioned to the bathroom tentatively, like this was my house and not his. "Sorry, were you waiting?"

"No," I said. "I was, um, just checking to see who was up."

"I'm not sure, except for Jonathan. Oh, and Maeve. I saw her out the window like an hour ago," he said, motioning behind him. "Leaving for a run."

"Oh, okay," I said, feeling a rush of relief. Finch couldn't have told her anything yet. But was it even safe for her to be out there, with the contractors so pissed off?

"I'm sorry for the mess with the contractors," Peter went on. "That was definitely my fault, not Jonathan's."

"Yeah, they're, uh, angry," I said, motioning to the side of the house. It didn't seem like it was my place to mention the fire. But I hoped Jonathan had.

Peter took a breath. "I know, the fire. Thank God no one was hurt. Still, I'm sure it was—"

"No! No! No!"

The screaming, growing louder and louder with each word, was coming from down the hall. Keith's voice. I ran past Peter.

When I threw open Keith's door, he was on the bed, on top of Crystal, shaking her. Her head was flopping side to side, her limbs lifeless.

"Fucking breathe!" Keith screamed as he shook her even harder.

"Keith, stop!" I shouted, rushing closer. I worried he might be hurting her.

But she was ice cold when I reached to check for a pulse.

"Oh my God, what happened?" Maeve was in the doorway in her running clothes, her skin shiny with sweat.

"I don't know. I don't know. I don't know," Keith said over and over, still on top of Crystal.

"Here, I know CPR," Maeve said. "Let me try. Move, Keith, move."

Keith climbed off Crystal, stumbling back into the wall as Maeve took over, alternating between compressions and mouth-to-mouth. On and on. She continued for five minutes at least, maybe more. It was endless.

And awful. Crystal's body was so limp and lifeless. Finally, Maeve stopped. She moved off Crystal carefully, like she was afraid of hurting her.

"I don't think . . ." She looked from me to Keith and back again. "I mean—I just learned CPR to volunteer at the Boys & Girls Club. But I think she's dead."

"Oh my God." Stephanie was in the doorway now. "What happened?"

"I have no idea!" Keith shouted, eyes locked on Crystal. "I just found her like this."

"What do you mean, you just found her?" Stephanie asked, a hand pressed to her stomach like she might be sick. "Weren't you in the room with her?"

"I was downstairs with Jonathan," Keith said. He put a hand over his mouth. "Holy fucking shit. I did a line on that fucking nightstand next to her after I got up. Maybe if I'd checked on her instead . . . I didn't—I didn't even look at her, really. . . . And she could have been lying there still—holy fuck."

Whenever she'd died exactly, Crystal's skin was an awful shade of gray now, her limbs splayed awkwardly. I leaned against the wall and swallowed back bile.

"Oh my God." Jonathan had appeared in the doorway.

"She must have OD'd," Maeve said, stepping away from the bed. "Right, Keith?"

Keith shook his head, moving his hand to his cheek. "I guess, I don't know."

"You guess?" Jonathan asked, taking a step closer to Keith. "If she didn't OD, what else could have happened to her?"

"I don't—I don't know." Keith was tugging his fingers through his hair as he stared at Crystal. "We came up here. We used . . . She was keeping up with me. I'd been crashing for hours so I almost overdid it. And I'm much bigger. Maybe it was too much for her. But we had sex after . . . I don't know what happened then. We fell asleep, I guess. I think maybe I heard her coughing once."

"I'm calling the police." Stephanie pulled her phone out of her sweatshirt pocket.

"Stephanie, wait—" Maeve turned to Keith. "You *heard* her coughing? And you didn't do anything?" Maeve looked again at Stephanie, more pointedly. "Isn't that, um, a problem? Couldn't that make Keith . . ."

"I don't think so," Stephanie said, her trembling hands clumsily tapping on her phone.

Maeve looked stricken, and I shook my head sympathetically.

"Keith, why don't you back up and tell us exactly what happened," I said. "Start from the beginning."

Peter was in the doorway now. "Jonathan, are you—" He gasped when he saw Crystal. "Oh my God." We ignored him.

"We started talking in the bar. Crystal offered to pay for the drugs if I bought them. She said she had some kind of conflict with the guy dealing at the Falls. So I bought the drugs, and—"

"Wait, what?" Stephanie interrupted, pulling her phone down from her ear. "Keith, *you* bought the drugs?"

"Yeah," Keith says. "It was her money. But I bought them. Why?" His eyes were darting around wildly now.

"What difference does it make?" I asked.

"When people OD on opioids, they've been charging the supplier with homicide," Stephanie said. "It's a new war-on-drugs thing."

"But he didn't supply them," Jonathan insisted. "All he did was—"

"Supply them," Stephanie finished his sentence. "Keith doesn't have to have charged her for them, doesn't matter that it wasn't his money. I'm not saying that he would be prosecuted, but he could be. It's at the prosecutor's discretion. They don't do it in New York City, but they do on Long Island—parts of it. It's controversial. There was this big thing about it in the *New York Times* a couple weeks ago that—"

"Yeah, I read that, too," Maeve said, biting her lip and nodding at Stephanie. "And up here—where the opioids are out of control . . . What do you think they'd do?" She turned to Jonathan, wide-eyed. "You said they don't like weekenders . . ."

Jonathan stood silent for a moment, then gave a slow shake of his head. "They don't."

"She was fine when we fell asleep." Keith stopped pacing between the bed and the window, and looked at Crystal. "She was going to go back to her parents' house next week, to try to get clean."

"I don't understand what you're debating," Peter burst out. "You need to call the police." Nobody responded. "This is *your* house, Jonathan, and these are *your* friends, but I'm not going to be a part of this." Peter shook his head in disgust and disappeared out the door.

"She was a runner at Syracuse, you know," Maeve said, staring numbly at Crystal. "She told me about it last night when I said I was going to be up early for a run. This is . . . it's just . . . tragic."

"It should have been me," Keith said.

"You're lucky it wasn't," I said sharply. "You should remember that."

We were silent again.

"We're not going to do this," Keith said finally. "Not again. Call the police, Stephanie. Maybe jail will be good for me."

"How is you going to jail going to make anything any better?" Maeve protested. She motioned to Stephanie. "Tell him! Something like this—it's not like for a few months."

Stephanie crossed her arms. "*Potentially*, it could be very, very bad, Keith. Especially if there's other evidence in your life of drug use. Something back in your apartment, people you called, maybe."

"You mean like my dealer, forty-three times yesterday?"

"Yeah, like that," Stephanie went on. "They could try to claim you're working for him."

"Sure they could. Maybe they even will," Keith said. "But you guys can't—"

"Let us decide what we can and can't do," Jonathan said. "I'm not thrilled about having the police here for my own reasons. And I can't imagine the partners in your law firm would like you being mixed up in any of this, Stephanie."

"Hey, let me worry about myself," she snapped.

"What if we just took her home?" Maeve offered gently.

"To the city?" Jonathan sounded skeptical.

"No—Maeve means to *her* home," I interjected. Maeve gave me a grateful look, and nodded as I went on. "It's where she would have OD'd if she hadn't been here. This could have happened wherever she was last night."

"Do we even know where she lives?" Jonathan asked.

"She said something about that Farm place," Keith said.

"That doesn't exactly sound like a home," Stephanie said.

We were all quiet again, looking at Crystal.

"She OD'd," I said finally, shaking off the guilt that was starting to creep up on me. "This isn't our fault. It isn't anyone's fault."

"It's never our fault, is it?" Stephanie raised her eyes to meet mine. "When are we going to stop pretending these are things that are just randomly happening *to* us. Our regret doesn't do shit for anyone."

Stephanie wasn't wrong. The way we all blamed ourselves for what happened to Alice did sometimes strike me as perversely selfish. Like the penance was actually a way to let ourselves off the hook. For sure I'd only been thinking of myself when Alice turned up in my room that night, asking to borrow my car.

"I'll explain when I get back," she'd said. "I just—I want to see if I'm right first."

I didn't like the smell of it—the way Alice's tiny body was vibrating as she stood there, her refusal to get into details. For days she'd been so upset about everything that had happened on the roof, and now suddenly she seemed almost excited? But then I remembered: if Alice was gone for the night, that would leave just Maeve and me to watch the movie the three of us had planned to see together. And so I'd said, "Yes, take my car. Take it for as long and as far as you want, Alice." In the end, Maeve had wound up having to work the information desk in Main that night anyway, so our intimate movie night had never even happened.

"Thank you, Derrick," Alice had said, the last words of hers I'd ever hear. "You're the best."

No matter how tightly I gripped the wheel as we drove toward the Farm, I could still feel the weight of Crystal's body in my hands. Keith and I had carried her downstairs, wrapped in the sheets, while Jonathan pulled my car around the side of the house up to the back door. We drove in silence until we reached the crushed farmhouse. There was no choice but to get through this as fast as we could. The sooner it was over, the faster we could get back to the business of forgetting.

I rolled down a dirt road just past the main entrance to the Farm and pulled over behind the dilapidated barn, in a place where we could park out of sight then cut through the short stretch of woods to the building, which somehow looked even more menacing in the daylight.

"Maybe we should come back when it's dark?" Jonathan suggested. "This doesn't feel especially clandestine."

"Let's just hurry up and get this over with," Maeve said. "We're so conspicuous sitting here."

I glanced Maeve's way. She looked so worried as she chewed on her lip.

Keith started to get out before the car was even off. "I've got this. I'll meet you guys back at the house."

"Wait, what are you talking about?" I asked, jumping out to follow him. "You're not doing this alone, Keith."

I walked around to the passenger side and handed my keys to Jonathan. "You guys drive back to the house, get your stuff together. We'll walk back. Half hour, hour, something like that. And then we can head back to the city together."

"Are you sure, Derrick?" Maeve asked, looking at me, I swear, like she was seeing me for the very first time.

"I'm sure."

Detective Julia Scutt

Sunday, 1:09 p.m.

Dan is waiting for me outside the Falls when I pull up. He's leaning against the building, talking on the phone, wearing a fresh shirt, light blue and long-sleeved, rolled up above his elbows. Seeing him there, waiting for me, I feel an unexpected pang of regret.

"They've got Hendrix," Dan calls to me as I cross the street, still shaking off the feeling. "They're bringing him down to the station."

"Good," I say, like I'd never doubted they would head him off.

Really I'd been bracing for the possibility I'd have to tell Seldon that I let Finch Hendrix sail out of Kaaterskill and back into the vast ocean of New York City. At least we've found him, even if the justification for holding him is thin.

"He's pissed, though," Dan goes on. "Apparently he's screaming about some art exhibit, lost opportunity costs, damages. Lawyers."

"Just keep him separate from the homeowners. Don't want them matching notes."

"I told them that downtown," he says. "Cartright's on it."

"Cartright, great." I roll my eyes. Dan shrugs. He likes Cartright. Dan likes everybody. "I ran into Lauren Avery at the Farm. You remember her?"

"No," Dan says. "I don't actually know everybody." He pauses. "Or everything."

I can feel him looking at me. I don't look back. "She looked . . . rough."

"That's too bad," Dan says, a little tentatively. He's probably worried that my voluntarily engaging him in conversation is some kind of trap.

It's a fair assumption. I know there are ways my behavior has left something to be desired. When we stay quiet for a moment longer, I think of thanking Dan for coming to get me after the incident at Home Depot. I should have before. But it feels too late for that now. It feels too late for a lot of things.

"You get any word back about Mike Gaffney's whereabouts?" I ask instead. "I haven't heard anything."

Dan shakes his head. "He's going to love being rousted, though."

"Sending a car to confirm he's been fishing is hardly rousting him," I say, though I know Dan is right. "We found an Ace Construction hat at the scene. The victims owed him money. Not confirming his alibi would be ridiculous."

"Agreed. He'll still be pissed, though. That guy's always pissed." Dan points over his shoulder toward the Falls. "What's in here?"

"Need to confirm Luke Gaffney's alibi, too," I say. "He claims he was here all last night. But he's got some nasty scratches on his neck that suggest otherwise."

Dan nods. "You want company?"

"I'll be fine."

"That wasn't what I asked."

No—that's my reflex. But for once, I choose the opposite. "Yeah, okay, sure."

At 1:00 p.m. on a Sunday there are only three older men sitting separately at the bar, and not one of them even bothers to look our way when we come in. At the far end, the bartender, a young guy, stocky and bright-eyed, is wiping down the counter with an exceptional amount of elbow grease and good cheer.

"What can I get for you guys?" He smiles up at us as we approach, but his face stiffens when I pull out my badge. "There, um, a problem, Officers?"

"Were you working last night?"

He looks down at the bar, scrubbing at an imaginary stain. Part of me just wants to arrest him for looking so fucking guilty. "Uh, yeah."

"Did you see this girl in here?" I hold up my phone with a photo of Crystal's driver's license.

He leans in. "Oh, Crystal?" He looks relieved. "She's always in here trying to pick up weekenders, get a drink, free meal, whatever. Girls like her love to hunt the weekenders." He blinks when he finally notices I'm glaring at him. "I mean, that's what people say."

I think of those pictures of Crystal as a track star—her beaming smile and healthy, confident glow. *Girls like her.* Where she is now has nothing to do with who she really is.

"And was she here last night 'hunting,' as you say?" I ask, my eyes still digging into him.

"Um, Friday, definitely." He looks away. "But I didn't see her last night, which, come to think of it, is a little weird. She's usually right up near the bar." He points to the TV screen mounted above. "But last night the McGregor fight was on, so the place was wall-to-wall. Crystal could have been here. Maybe I just didn't see her."

"What about this guy?" I ask, holding up a picture of Finch that I found on the internet. He's much better-looking when not beaten up.

"Oh, yeah. I got him and another guy a round of shots. They bought our most expensive tequila. Nobody drinks that crap." He grins. "It's twenty-five bucks a shot, and tastes like shit. They even bought more than one round. Decent tip. Some of these rich weekenders are cheap bastards. Wait, but that was Friday, not last night."

"Are you sure?"

He looks at the ceiling again. "Yeah, definitely. Because there was some room to breathe up here. Friday, for sure."

"Was the guy who bought the tequila with one of these two?" I ask, showing him pictures of Keith and Derrick.

"Yeah, that one." He points at Keith. "Definitely. Actually, I also saw Crystal talking to him."

"This one?" I hold up my phone again with the picture of Keith.

"Yeah, actually they left together. There was a big group of them—nice car. Audi SUV. I'm a car guy."

The bartender then looks past me, motions to someone. "You want another, man?"

When Dan and I turn, there's Bob Hoff. He tosses a twenty-dollar bill on the counter, avoiding eye contact with me as he starts for the exit. "No, I'm good."

"Mr. Hoff," I call after him as he heads quickly toward the door. "Can I ask you a question?"

Almost at the door, he stops and shakes his head. When he finally turns, his eyes are fiery. "This is bullshit, you know. I'm just here taking care of my mom—who's dying, by the way—and minding my own business. You actually don't have the right to keep trying to drag me into every crime that happens in this town."

"You're right," I say. Honesty is really my only option. "You're absolutely right. And I'm not trying to drag you into this situation here. But I was just a little girl when my sister Jane was killed, and I *still* don't know what happened to her. Your statement isn't in my sister's file, Mr. Hoff. All I'm asking is that you tell me what it said." Bob Hoff shakes his head again. But he's still here—and that's something. I step closer, so I can lower my voice. "You don't owe me an answer, you don't. But I'm still asking: What did you see, back when my sister was killed?"

Hoff closes his eyes, shakes his head again. "Mike

Gaffney, okay?" he says finally. "That's who I saw. Coming out of the woods near where those girls were killed. I was only driving past and I only caught a glimpse. But he was wearing one of those red Ace Construction hats, and he had on this damn ugly plaid shirt I'd seen him wearing the week before when he came into the Cumberland Farms."

When I come in, Finch Hendrix is slumped across the table in interview room 2. He's gripping his right side with one hand, the other propping up his head. He's pulled his shoulder-length hair back in a headband, which makes him look significantly less attractive.

"You do know I'm going to sue the shit out of you?" he asks, but in a tired voice, as I pull out a chair and sit. "I have a show to put on tonight. A delay costs me actual money."

"Killing one, maybe two, people does have a tendency to limit one's financial opportunities," I say. Shock value is never a bad place to start. Also, I'm hoping it might help me focus on this conversation. Because I'm fixating on Mike Gaffney and Jane—all alibis are not created equal, and I never went back to double-check Mike Gaffney's myself. He'd said he was on a remodeling job at the time, but it'd be good to confirm that again.

"I didn't fucking kill anybody," Hendrix says. "This is bullshit, and you know it."

"Where's Crystal?" I ask.

"Who?"

"The girl you picked up on Thursday night from the Farm," I say. "Before going back down to the city and pretending to come back up for the first time with everyone else on Friday."

Finch glances up from the table. "So I knew some girl? That's not a crime."

"But stabbing someone is. Was Crystal your accomplice?" This theory's half formed at best, but wild accusations can sometimes dislodge the actual truth. "If Crystal was involved, I'd get that on the record. You could be the one who makes a deal here. Because I'm betting she'll be game to talk as soon as we find her."

"Wow, you are so fucking lost," Hendrix says, with an uncomfortable amount of confidence. "It's comical."

"Help me out then," I say. "Enlighten me, Mr. Hendrix."

He is quiet, studying a spot on the wall above my head. "When I left on Saturday morning, Crystal was in bed with Keith," he says. "He brought her home from the bar Friday because he was hoping to use with her. I don't know what happened to her after that. And

I sure as hell don't know what happened in that car with Derrick and Keith. I was long gone by then."

"Who did that to you, Mr. Hendrix?" I gesture toward his swollen lip.

He's quiet for a long minute, staring now at the back of his hands, splayed out against the tabletop.

"Derrick," he says finally, looking up at me. His gaze is steady. "Okay? Derrick, that insane motherfucker, beat the shit out of me."

"Was this before or after you stabbed him?"

He shakes his head, but his stare doesn't waver. "You can keep saying that. It won't make it any more true."

"So tell me what did happen. Why did Derrick do that to you?"

Finch smooths his palms across the table, like he's wiping something away. "I found some pictures in his bag. I gave him a hard time about them, and he did not appreciate it." He points to his face. "In case you don't know, Derrick's got a temper."

"Yeah, so I've heard," I say. "And yet you were still his friend?"

Finch frowns, looks a little bewildered himself. "History. We're always trying to claw it back, aren't we?"

"I heard you were also always trying to elbow your way into this group. Sounds a little desperate."

Finch laughs arrogantly, but then winces again. "Listen, I've got whole rooms of people showing up to spend time with me. A calendar full of invitations. Why would I give a shit about these fucking people?"

"I don't know. Maybe because they didn't want you?"

He squints just the tiniest bit. I've hit the nail exactly on the head. Finch wanted in with *this* group because they didn't want him. Famous artist, arrogant, maybe even a little bit of a sociopath. Rejection could have been too much for him to take. Maybe he wanted to inflict a little pain of his own.

"And Crystal?" I press on. "You were seen at the Farm picking her up. Why?"

Finch hesitates for a long time, staring again at that same spot on the wall.

"I paid her to end up with Keith," he says finally. "Came up here a few days before, tracked down somebody who I thought would work—pretty enough, smart enough, high enough. Gave her cash for a few days in a hotel. She was supposed to have drugs on her by the time we met at the Falls and Keith was there."

"Why would you do that?"

"Because I was pissed at Keith for how he fucked my London show." He drives a finger against the tabletop. "Keith betrayed me. Letting me work my balls off for something that wasn't ever happening? It was seriously messed up."

"So you sent a drug addict to have sex with him?"

"No, I sent a drug addict to confirm that *he* was a drug addict. I suspected, but I didn't know for sure. And I've got a representation contract with Keith that I'd very much like to get out of without financial penalty. For that I need cause, like proof of a drug problem." Finch laughs. "Real question is, what's his friends' excuse for not stepping in to stop him from having sex with a drug addict? Despite what this group seems to think, standing by while your friend slits their own throat isn't some act of devotion."

"So that's what you were doing here? Being Keith's friend?"

"Fuck no," Finch says. "Like I said before, he sells my art, he's not my friend."

"What kind of pictures did you find in Derrick's bag?" I ask, then motion to Finch's face. "That led him to do that?"

"Pictures of Maeve," he says. "Fucking weird."

"I thought Derrick was married?"

Finch shakes his head. "Sure, barely."

"Meaning?"

"They don't like each other very much, Derrick and Beth."

"Does Beth know about Derrick's feelings for Maeve?" We haven't confirmed the whereabouts of the wife, though we have been trying to track her down. Angry wives do all sorts of things.

"I've got no idea what Beth knows."

"And so you confront him with these pictures, and . . ."

"He just fucking lost it on me." Finch gestures again to his face. He sounds almost . . . wounded. "And then I left. You can ask Peter, Jonathan's fiancé. I literally ran into him in the hall on my way out the door."

"Peter is here?" I ask.

"Yup," he says.

"The whole time?"

"Not the night before."

"Okay, so, bleeding internally, you get to the train station by midmorning Saturday. But you're still not on a train by four a.m. the next day?"

"I don't know what you want me to tell you—that's what happened. So can I go? I've answered your questions, and if I leave now, I'll make it to my show, and I won't have to sue the shit out of you."

"No, Mr. Hendrix," I say. "You cannot go. Because none of that makes any sense whatsoever. I might be lost right now, but I'm not stupid."

"You can't just hold me here forever."

"You're right. I can't hold you forever," I say. "But I can hold you a whole lot longer."

Twenty minutes later Dan is with me in the file room, a dark fluorescent cave down a flight of concrete steps. I asked him to come, and he did a good job of pretending it was no big deal. In the end, it takes us under a half hour to find the right box. Jane's case files are well organized at least, all the witness interviews in one place.

I flip through the stack of files on my lap twice while Dan looks through his pile. "I've got the Gaffneys' statements and their alibi witnesses," I say. They seem like reasonably credible statements from third parties—though you never really know until you confirm with a witness yourself. "But I still don't see Bob Hoff's statement."

"It's not here either," Dan says. "But things do get lost." Then I see his expression tighten, as he stares down at the contents of another folder. Finally, he holds out the page to me. "And sometimes they get lost on purpose."

The page is an inventory of the box, a list of all the interview notes that should be included. What *would* be there unless somebody removed it after the fact. Sure enough, there it is, listed four lines down: "Witness Interview: Bob Hoff."

Maeve

Saturday, 11:29 a.m.

Stephanie, Jonathan, and I sat in the living room on the uncomfortable bright-red couches, waiting for Derrick and Keith to get back from the Farm. Or Jonathan and I sat; Stephanie paced. I tried sitting upright, counting my breaths. Panicking would only make this out-of-control situation worse.

What had happened to Crystal was horrific. Of course it was. An awful twist of fate—what were the chances of Keith bringing someone home, using with her, and that being the time that finally pushed her over the edge? I'd never believed in curses before, but this sure felt like proof.

We needed to leave town; that was obvious to me. Nothing we did now could change the awful things that had already happened. Our best option—our only option—was to move on, *before* the Kaaterskill police showed up.

"We shouldn't have moved her," Stephanie mumbled as she stalked back again in front of the couch. She stopped and looked up at Jonathan and me. "But we can still make a different choice. It's not too late. We moved her, yes, and we'll have to face those consequences. If I get disbarred, I get disbarred. There are more important things than my job."

"That's true. But it's not just about you, right?" I said, my chest tight. "Keith's the one who'd go to jail—for *murder*. I mean, is that his punishment for being an addict?" This was bad, very bad. "I'm sorry, that's just wrong."

I looked over at Jonathan, but he was utterly blank. Like a cardboard Jonathan who might topple over at the slightest push. "It's not punishment for him being an addict," he said. "Of course not."

I tried to ignore my racing heart as I glared at Stephanie, then Jonathan in turn. "I'm sorry, maybe it's because I don't really have a family, but I don't think it's brave to turn on a friend like that. Whatever might happen to the rest of us, it'll be so much worse for Keith. We have to protect him."

Stephanie opened her mouth like she was about to object. But then her face fell.

"Fuck," she said quietly, dropping down into a chair. "You're right. Of course you're right."

We all stayed silent for what felt like an eternity. The adrenaline was draining out of me. Honestly, I wasn't sure how much longer I could keep this up. I was exhausted.

"Wait, where is Finch?" Jonathan suddenly asked.

It was a good question. It was one thing for all of us to keep this a secret. Finch could not be trusted.

"He left earlier," Stephanie said. Jonathan and I glanced at each other, waiting for her to elaborate. "It was before Keith—before Crystal. But he was still here when Keith screamed." Finch and Stephanie together? "But then I didn't see him after I was in the room. He might know Crystal OD'd, but not the rest of it. He was pissed off at Keith, though, about some show in London."

"And what about Peter?" I turned to Jonathan. "Where is he?"

"God knows. He sent a text saying he was going to make everything up to me. Probably means he went grocery shopping to cook for all of us or something.

That's usually what he does when we get in a fight."

We heard the front door open then.

"They're back, thank God," Jonathan gasped.

But when we ran to the foyer, it was only Peter, frozen there, face drawn.

"Peter, what's wrong?" Jonathan rushed closer, concerned.

Peter shook his head as he stared down at his expensive designer sneakers. "I am really sorry, Jonathan."

"Sorry about what?" I stepped closer.

"The contractors." Peter motioned toward the door like whatever had happened had just taken place right there.

"They were here again?" Jonathan asked.

"No, no," Peter said. "I called them. To explain that it was my fault, what happened with the money, and not yours. They asked me to come meet them. I didn't feel like I had a choice."

"Are you okay?" Jonathan asked, looking Peter up and down.

"Yes—I mean, I am a little freaked out."

Stephanie stepped closer too. "Wait, what happened, exactly?"

Peter was silent for a long time. "They know."

My stomach was tight. "They know what?"

Peter looked unsteady suddenly.

"Wait, wait, come sit out here." Jonathan guided Peter into the living room. "Start at the beginning."

Jonathan and Peter sat side by side on one of the red couches. Jonathan had an overly protective hand on Peter's back. I swallowed back my irritation.

"So I called them and said that I wanted to apologize and explain and—"

"Yeah, we got that part," I cut him off. "And then you went to see them, and then what?"

"Come on, Maeve." Jonathan flashed me an imploring look. "Give him a chance."

"I'm just—we told Derrick and Keith we were going to be packing up," I pleaded, more gently. "I think we do need to move things along."

"They didn't give me a choice about going to meet them." Peter looked up at me with his big, sad eyes—he was obviously accustomed to this working on people. "They told me if I didn't meet them at the bank, they'd come here and start doing some 'real damage.' I was trying to help. I mean, I got us into this mess. I wanted to get us out."

"That makes sense," Jonathan said reassuringly, his hand still on Peter's back. "So you met them at a bank . . ."

"I told them I didn't have access to that much money. Because it's your money." He looked at Jonathan. "Which I swear I recognize, Jonathan. And you are so generous. It's one of your most amazing qualities."

Stephanie motioned impatiently. "No offense, Peter, but Maeve is right—we need to be getting out of here. Can you just tell us what actually took place?"

"Well, I gave them everything I had in my account, only like six hundred dollars," Peter said. "But they said I had to find you, Jonathan, because they wanted the rest. And so I called and called . . ."

Jonathan pulled out his phone and glanced down at the screen. "I'm sorry, Peter, we've just been so consumed."

"It's okay," Peter said. "Really, Jonathan, this was all my fault."

Of course it's your fault!

"After I couldn't get you on the phone, they got even angrier. I thought they were going to get physical, and it was three against one," Peter continued. He looked embarrassed. "I honestly—I panicked. It just came out. I'm so sorry."

No, I thought. He couldn't possibly mean . . .

"*What* came out?" Stephanie asked.

"About the girl," Peter said quietly.

"What about the girl?" I asked, my throat so dry I barely got the words out.

"I said that a girl had OD'd in the house. I had to explain why I couldn't reach you, Jonathan. Because you were dealing with that."

"You told the contractors that we were moving the body of a dead girl?" Stephanie's voice wavered. "You have got to be fucking kidding me."

"No, no, I only told him that she died. That's all. That it was an accident, of course." Peter looked up at Jonathan. "You had to be there, Jonathan. There was just—I wasn't thinking clearly."

"Obviously!" Stephanie shouted. "And by the way, it doesn't matter if you told them we moved her or not. Because that would still mean she's dead and we haven't called anybody? It's not like that isn't also a problem."

"Stephanie, stop," Jonathan snapped. "It doesn't matter how we got here. We're here now. Yelling isn't going to help."

"They want more money," Peter went on, his voice unsteady. "Twenty thousand dollars. On top of the eleven thousand."

I lowered myself onto the couch. This was actually happening, wasn't it? How did this situation keep getting worse?

"They want thirty-one thousand dollars?" Jonathan asked. And finally, *finally*, his hand dropped from Peter's back.

Peter nodded. "Yes, but then they promised they won't say anything to anybody about the girl."

"Oh, well, as long as they gave us their word." Stephanie brought a hand to her forehead. "We are so completely and totally fucked."

Holy shit. Stephanie was right. I'd have said as much if my mouth hadn't been frozen stiff. "It's fine. We are going to be fine," Jonathan said, though even he didn't sound convinced. "I can get at least a decent chunk of it by going into a bank or a couple banks today. Probably not all of it. They don't always have that much cash on hand. I'll wire the rest to them. They just want money, right? Luckily, paying them isn't a problem."

"And if they won't take a wire?" I asked. "I mean, they *are* blackmailing us."

"If they want the money, they'll take a wire," Jonathan said. He turned back to Peter. "How are we supposed to get it to them? Are they calling you back or something?"

"The main guy, Luke, said he would text me later with a location."

"All right, let's go get the money then," Stephanie said, all business now. She checked the time on her phone. "The banks probably close early on the weekend." This was how she'd been about that night on the roof, once she finally agreed not to call the police: ruthless about getting the actual job done. It was impressive.

I did not move toward the door. "Maybe I should stay? Somebody needs to explain what's going on to Derrick and Keith when they get back."

"Good idea," Stephanie said, clasping one of my hands briefly on her way out. "So much for getting out of Dodge, huh?"

I sat on one of the chairs along the wall in the parlor, waiting and waiting for Keith and Derrick. The whole time, I worked hard to find again that hopeful place in myself. The one everyone counted on to spy the bright side in the distance. Even when none existed. Like right now. Because this situation was catapulting only one way: straight downhill.

Finally, the door opened, and Keith and Derrick stepped inside. "Are you guys okay?" I asked, jumping to my feet.

"We will be," Derrick said, closing the door quietly and carefully with two hands, like he was sealing off a memory.

Keith wrapped his hands around the back of his neck. "We're exactly as good as two people should be who just left the body of a perfectly nice girl in a disgusting barn."

"That sounds . . . traumatizing."

"It was, and probably best not to talk about it." Derrick reached over and gave my hand a quick squeeze. I managed a small smile. "Where is everybody else?"

"Yeah, there was, um, a bit of a situation with Peter," I began.

"Situation?" Keith asked. "What does that mean?"

"He seems to have told the contractors about what happened with Crystal," I said. "And now they're demanding more money or they'll go to the police."

"What?" Derrick stepped closer.

"Yeah," I said. "Only that she'd OD'd, not that we moved her. It's still definitely not great. We'll pay them and hope for the best."

Keith shook his head. "Holy shit."

"Is it crazy if the three of us go right now?" I said. "I mean, back to the city. There's no reason for all of us to stay, under the circumstances." I eyed Derrick meaningfully and motioned at Keith. "We could even, you know, make a stop on the way."

Derrick nodded, seeming to get my reference to Bright Horizons, despite the fact that it was hours in the opposite direction and the chances of a Saturday check-in were slim. "That's a good point."

"Wait, where did that come from?" Keith was pointing to the fireplace mantel as he headed over, at an empty picture frame.

"I don't know," I said. "I didn't see it there before."

Keith picked up the frame and studied it in silence before finally walking toward the staircase, the frame still in his hands. "I'm just going to, um, go take a shower."

"Shower?" I asked. "Keith, we're going to leave."

Keith shook his head. "No," he said. "I can't. Not yet."

"Sure you can," Derrick said. "Jonathan told me before that you agreed to Bright Horizons. We'll take you there. Everything is going to be fine."

Keith nodded. "Yeah, maybe," he said. "There's just something I need to—I just need a minute to figure something out."

"A minute?" Derrick asked.

"Time," Keith said, still staring at the picture frame as he started up the steps. "I'll do what you guys want, whatever you want. Just give me a little while, okay? I need to think."

"No, not okay, Keith," Derrick called after him. "You need to go to rehab. There's nothing to think about."

"No, no, not about that," Keith said with a shake of his head. He paused, looked at us. "I need to talk to

Finch first. That's all. There's been a miscommunication about something. I need to work it out with him before I go anywhere. I don't want him firing me while I'm gone."

"You're sure that's all it is?" I asked. The look on his face was just so stunned, frightened almost.

"Yeah." Keith looked first at me, then Derrick. "That's all it is. I'm sure."

And with that he disappeared up the steps, empty picture frame still in his hand.

"Maybe this is good," Derrick said.

"Good?"

Derrick shrugged. "When we were out at the Farm, it definitely seemed like maybe Keith had finally hit rock bottom."

"Rock bottom is great," I said. "As long as the rest of us don't get stuck down there with him."

It was impossible not to think of Alice. In those days right after the roof, she'd been completely manic, obsessed with figuring out who the guy from the roof was, making sure his family knew he wasn't some thief. She wanted to make amends. But some things couldn't be fixed. Sometimes your apology meant nothing, to anyone. The only option was to learn to live around the awfulness, like a river flowing over stones. I tried to explain that to Alice, but she refused to listen.

"I just want to tell his family that he wasn't stealing anything," Alice had said, sitting on the edge of my bed as I leaned back against the wall. She looked like she hadn't slept in days.

"Alice, come on," I said in my most reasonable voice. "How can you possibly tell his parents without also admitting you were on the roof with him? That we all were."

She was undeterred. "I'll figure out a way. First, I need to get to Hudson and find his family. Then I can, I don't know, leave an anonymous note or something. I'm not going to do anything that puts you all at risk, obviously. This is just something I need to do for myself."

Whatever I did in that moment, I had to do very gently. Alice did not respond well to pressure. She'd dart away and do whatever the hell she wanted anyway.

"Listen, I understand why you want to do that." I kept my tone even. "It makes complete sense. We all regret not calling the police. But you can't go to Hudson by yourself. That could be dangerous."

I wondered, looking at Alice then, how unstable she really was. She'd been off her medication for at least a week before the roof—we all knew. It was always obvious.

"You'd go with me?" Tears made her eyes shiny. Of course that was not what I'd said.

"Maybe." There was no way I was going to Hudson with her. "But only if you take your medication first."

She shook her head. "No, no, I have been. I'm—"

"Alice," I said. "You're not thinking clearly. And this is the kind of situation where you definitely need to be."

She stared at me for a good minute before her head finally dropped. "Okay." She marched over to her bureau, pulled open the top drawer, retrieved a bottle of pills, and shook it. There were plenty inside. She took one while I watched. "Happy?"

But I wasn't happy, of course. Not then. Not now.

"Don't worry," Derrick said, putting a hand on my shoulder, drawing me back to Jonathan's living room. To the mess we were in. "No matter what happens with Keith, I promise not to let him pull you down."

He meant it sweetly, of course. But it irritated me. I didn't need his protection. I needed his car to drive me back to the city. Right now.

"Thanks." I forced a smile.

But Derrick was still looking at me. In *that* way. *Shit.* He was going to do this now, wasn't he?

"Maeve, there's something I have to tell you," he began, though I willed him not to. "Something I've been meaning to tell you for a really long time."

"Are you sure now is the best time? We have so much else going—"

"I *know*, Maeve," Derrick said meaningfully. "I've known this whole time."

"You know what?" My heart felt like a drum.

"I know what happened on the roof."

My mind flashed to the anonymous email: *I know what you did.* It was Derrick who'd sent it?

"But I know it wasn't your fault," he said. "That's all I wanted to say. I hope *you* know that, too."

All I could do was stare at him. Because his tone and words were kind, but given the context—that creepy email? He was obviously threatening me. It dawned on me fully now. And how exactly did he think this was going to go? That I'd fall in love with him because he had something on me?

"I don't understand, Derrick." I must have seemed angry, too, because Derrick looked panicked.

"I would never say anything. Never," he added, quick and forceful. "That wasn't the—We're friends, Maeve. I'd do anything to protect you. I mean, I already have, all this time. I guess I just wanted you to know that."

Right. I looked up at him and smiled. "I don't know what you want me to say." And that was the absolute truth.

"You don't have to say anything," he said. "But please, stop looking at me like that."

"Like what?" I asked, trying to ignore how lightheaded I felt.

"Like I've betrayed you," Derrick said, and he sounded so sad, heartbroken really. "Because honestly I would never, ever do that."

I nodded. "That's good to know."

Except he already had betrayed me, and in such a secretive, sneaky, manipulative way.

"But I do also want to say: you deserve better," he added in a rush, as if it was hard for him to get that part out.

"What do you mean?"

"Your phone—you've seemed disappointed each time you looked at it this weekend. It's none of my business, and I don't know what's going on. But I do know you deserve not to feel bad."

"I'm not disappointed." But my cheeks were on fire now.

I had finally gotten a text back from Bates: Sorry, got caught up. See you soon. No "love" or anything. But I felt sure we could get past whatever these doubts were he had about me. I could do a better job of opening up. I would, finally.

"Okay." Derrick gestured helplessly. "Well, then, I think I should go shower," he said, heading for the stairs. He looked different to me as I watched him go, standing a little taller, stronger now that he'd unburdened himself.

"Derrick," I called after him. Because I couldn't very well leave it like that. "Um, thank you."

"For what?" he asked, brightening a little.

"For being a good friend," I said. "I—I appreciate your honesty. It's not easy, but—you've given me a lot to think about."

Derrick nodded, and smiled tentatively, hopefully. "Good."

Two Weeks (and Five Days) Earlier

Jonathan approaches Gramercy Tavern, looking handsome in his well-tailored suit. On his phone, of course, as he crosses the street—dangerously distracted as usual, stressed by some business or family call. Despite what people think, Jonathan's life is not easy. Money does not solve all problems—certainly it hasn't eased the pressure Jonathan's father puts on him. Even this lunch date for the two of them—every Friday at 1:00 p.m. in the exact same place, no exceptions or excuses—is like some sort of test. You do have to feel for Jonathan, living his life to please someone who will never be satisfied.

That's surely why Jonathan has always been excessively generous with countless friends in countless ways. Connections, jobs, money, boyfriends—even back at Vassar, Jonathan handed it all out like it was nothing. And I mean, in a way, it is nothing to Jonathan—he has so much of everything. Still, it's led to problems. Bad things happen when you expect people to be generous in return. Bad things *have* happened. People take advantage. Maybe even Jonathan has his limit.

Still, it's *very* hard to imagine that Jonathan—of all people—is the one. I feel like I'd know.

When Jonathan reaches the restaurant door, he stops. He is still on the phone, not with his father, surely not now that he's so close. Someone else then—Keith? He is definitely too generous with Keith, another example of how the best intentions really can cause the worst problems. With Keith, Jonathan's generosity is like a deluge after days of drought—anything left worth saving gets washed away in a flash flood.

Jonathan's consuming call could also be something with the fiancé, Peter. From what I've seen, Peter is up to something. Something that will be very bad for Jonathan. Part of me wants to warn him. But a bigger part of me knows that people get attached to the lies they tell themselves. The last thing they want is somebody picking at their scabs—even if it is for their own good. And I know firsthand, old wounds sometimes bleed harder the second time around.

Detective Julia Scutt

Sunday, 2:24 p.m.

I enter the interview room alone, having left Dan with Jane's files to check one more time for Hoff's statement. Jonathan is leaning back in his chair, eyes closed. Maeve's head is resting on the table, on top of her folded hands. Meanwhile, Stephanie is pacing back and forth, chewing on a fingernail.

Jane—now everything is making me think of her.

Jane did hate nail biting, though. She was always squealing at Bethany to quit it whenever she gnawed at her hands, which was almost all the time. Even Mike Gaffney commented on it once: "You'll have enough troubles getting a boy without chewing your fingers to stumps." It was true Bethany was not an attractive girl—overweight, bad complexion, limp hair, glasses—I did remember that. But then it was hard for anyone not to suffer in Jane's shadow.

And Jane had told Mike Gaffney to shut up, hadn't she? She was always so protective of Bethany, who had so much less than Jane in every way. Everyone thought they made an odd pair. Everyone except Jane that is, who never could see beyond her feelings for the people she loved.

I wonder now if it could have been something as stupid and simple as that—Jane telling off Mike Gaffney—that had gotten her and Bethany killed.

"Oh, you're back—*finally*," Stephanie says, not bothering to hide her irritation. "Listen, we want to help, but you and I both know you can't hold us here indefinitely unless we're suspects. We're tired and uncomfortable. We want to leave. Now."

"You're being held here for your safety. And so that you can help us find your friends," I say. "Which I assume you also want."

But she is right. We can't make them stay. And once Finch's lawyer shows up, I'll probably have to let him go too. I know they're all lying but I can't yet determine what it is they're covering up.

"Of course we want that," Maeve says.

"Did all of you know that Derrick beat up Finch? That's why he left."

From the look Jonathan and Maeve exchange, they didn't know. "Are you sure?" Jonathan asks. "Why would Derrick do that?"

"Hard to say," I lie. "But apparently he did."

"I did know," Stephanie says.

"You did?" Jonathan's surprise seems genuine.

Stephanie nods. "I saw Finch right before he left. His lip was obviously swollen. He said Derrick had hit him. But I didn't want details. Finch is a—Whatever happened, I'm sure he deserved it."

"Meaning what exactly?" I ask. "Because it turns out Finch didn't leave town. In fact, he's in an interview room across the hall. And he can't seem to account for a lot of the time around when Keith and Derrick disappeared."

"Wait, you think Finch did it?" Maeve asks. She looks at Jonathan and then Stephanie, like she's piecing something together. She puts a hand over her mouth. "Oh my God."

"It's a possibility," I say. "The beating Derrick delivered was bad enough that Finch ended up in the hospital."

"Really?" Now it's Stephanie who seems surprised.

I nod. "Could be Finch got his revenge."

"And he brought that gun up here." Maeve's eyes are wide. "For all we know, he could be worse than just difficult. He could actually be dangerous."

"Wait, what gun?" I take a breath to avoid laying into all of them. But a fucking gun? Seriously?

"It's gone now," Jonathan says. "Derrick tossed it into the river."

"Finch sure enjoyed freaking all of us out with it first," Maeve adds.

"It's not impossible that Finch is responsible for whatever happened," Stephanie adds after some consideration. There's a strange tightness to her tone. Like it's hard for her to admit this. "Maeve's right. He could be capable of a lot worse than we imagined."

I agree that he seems capable, not to mention defensive and evasive, and Seldon would love a suspect like Finch—an outsider. I prefer a direction that points away from Gaffney and Jane too. Still, I'm not at all convinced that Finch is the guy.

"Seems like you all have worked pretty hard *not* to know him."

"You've talked to Finch," Jonathan says. "Can you blame us? He wants everything to be about him all the time. That's why he doesn't have any actual friends."

"I'm sorry, but is there maybe another room you could move us to?" Maeve asks, gentle but insistent, rubbing her hands up and down her arms, though the room feels warm to me, not cold. "We've been up all night, and it's just not—It's really uncomfortable in here. Stephanie is right."

"We'll get you out of here as soon as we can. I just have a few more follow-up questions."

Jonathan tugs his dumb hat down a little. I haven't forgotten about that bruise, which I still don't have a good explanation for. "Following up on what?"

"Well, starting with the driver's license we found, belonging to Crystal Finnegan—you said you had no idea who she was, correct?"

"Mmm," Jonathan says, pressing his mouth together and nodding as he gives one palm a quick rub against his thigh.

"I'm sorry, is that a yes or a no, Mr. Cheung?"

"Wait, I don't understand. Not to be selfish here, but a friend of ours is still missing, maybe injured," Stephanie says. "Shouldn't we be focused on that?"

Her unruffled delivery is impressive, given what I already know.

"Crystal seems to be missing as well, and it could be related to what happened to your friends." I stare back at her evenly. "Perhaps we'd be making more efficient progress if you all weren't wasting my time by lying."

"Lying?" Maeve asks, blinking quickly. "About what?"

"You all know exactly who Crystal Finnegan is. You knew who she was when I found her license. She drove home with Keith from the Falls in Derrick's car, with *all* of you."

All three of them stare at the floor for a long quiet moment.

Finally, Maeve looks up at me. "The Crystal situation is—"

"Complicated, obviously," Stephanie jumps in. "We weren't happy Keith brought some random girl home. He was using. She was using. It was a mess."

Jonathan leans toward Stephanie, insistent and nervous. "I really don't think we should be—"

"Be what? Telling the truth about Keith? We can't keep trying to protect him, Jonathan," Stephanie snaps back. Then turns to me, eyes forceful. "Keith brought Crystal home from the Falls because, I guess, she had drugs on her and he wanted to use. That doesn't make him look very good, but it's true."

"He just appeared with her outside. The rest of us were already in the car," Jonathan adds, talking fast, like he can't get himself to stop. "We'd lost him inside.

There was this huge crowd near the bar because of something on TV, a boxing thing. We didn't even know they'd met."

Of course, the fight wasn't on Friday night. It was on Saturday night, at the exact time the entire group was supposedly at Jonathan's house, eating penne arrabiata.

"Sorry, just to go back a quick second, you were home all night last night—Saturday night. Correct?"

"Yes," Jonathan says decisively, as I study Stephanie's suddenly very stiff face.

"Listen, Keith probably did go to buy drugs last night," Maeve offers. "Convinced Derrick to do that instead of going to the Cumberland Farms. I mean, he always needs more. He's in pretty deep with his addiction, I think."

"We're just . . . Keith is our friend," Jonathan adds. "I know we should have told you about Crystal before, but there's this whole complicated situation with my family and Keith and money. He's got real problems. We didn't want him getting into more trouble."

"Withholding information can derail an investigation in ways you can't possibly anticipate, because you don't have all the relevant facts. For instance, Crystal Finnegan is also having a relationship with Luke Gaffney from Ace Construction," I say, hoping an appeal to logic will encourage them to be more forthcoming. "Could be he was angry about Crystal and Keith, and he's responsible for whatever happened in the car. These facts that you're leaving out might seem like minor details, but they can point in unexpected places, important ones."

"I really don't think Luke Gaffney's dating Crystal," Stephanie says.

"Yeah, no," Jonathan adds with an emphatic shake of his head.

I'm not sure why they're so quick to dismiss this idea. "How do you know?"

"We don't, obviously," Maeve insists, shooting a look toward Jonathan and Stephanie. "He could be."

"And to confirm—now that we're on the subject of complete disclosure—you did or didn't pay Ace Construction everything they were owed?"

Jonathan shifts in his chair, rubs a palm across his thigh. "We paid them a lot of money, but not everything they wanted," he admits. "They kept raising the price."

"And so when you told me it was all sorted out earlier . . ."

"It was sorted out to the best of our ability at that time," Stephanie offers, splicing a lawyerly hair.

"You can only withdraw so much cash in one day. I gave them everything I could get my hands on," Jonathan says. "I said that I would wire the rest."

"And when did your fiancé, Peter, get here?" I toss that in like an afterthought. But it's meant as a warning—*I already know way more than you realize.*

Jonathan meets my eyes. "I'm sorry I left that out. But I was—I *am* upset with him. It was Peter's fault we didn't pay the contractors. We got into an argument about it, and he left. But Peter doesn't have anything to do with what happened to Keith and Derrick."

"Okay, but we don't *know* that, right?" Maeve offers tentatively.

Jonathan whips his head in her direction. "Yes, we do."

"How could we, when we don't know what happened?"

Jaw clenched, Jonathan shakes his head angrily. "I know, Maeve. *I* know. Believe me."

"Okay, I think we should pause here for a second," I say. This new tension between them could be useful. As a united front, they're impenetrable. I have a feeling the only way I'm going to get the whole truth of what happened is by prying open the cracks between them. "Maybe the three of you need some breathing room."

"We can leave?" Maeve asks.

"No, no, that won't be possible quite yet." But I do plan to send Cartright back in to separate them. Rock the boat a little. My phone buzzes then with a text from Dan. I stand, lifting my phone in the air. "If you'll excuse me for one second. I need to handle this. I'll be right back."

I step out before they can object. In the hall, I read Dan's message. *There's no Hoff statement anywhere. Double-checked Mike Gaffney's alibi. Woman hates him, but still swears he was working on her kitchen at the time.*

"Scutt!" a voice bellows. When I look up from my phone, Seldon is striding down my way, face livid. "You had a patrol car show up at Mike Gaffney's fishing cabin? Have you lost your goddamn mind?"

Seldon doesn't like me, but he's not usually a yeller. And right now he looks like he's about to pop an artery.

"We found an Ace Construction hat at the accident scene," I say, trying not to sound rattled by his anger. "And there was a dispute between the victims and the Gaffneys over an unpaid bill. The officer was there and gone within minutes. All he did was confirm that Mike Gaffney was there, so we could rule him out."

"Mike Gaffney doesn't need to be ruled out!"

"Um, why?" I ask. The question is a mistake. Instantly, I know it.

"Because he's an upstanding business owner!" he roars. "A pillar of this community, not a damn criminal!"

Mike Gaffney is a successful local business owner, sure. But pillar of the community is a stretch. Still, this is not a good fight to be having.

"Simply trying to advance this investigation methodically, sir," I say, more steadily now. Because this is ridiculous. "Ruling out Mike Gaffney gives us the opportunity to focus on the more viable leads."

Seldon crosses his arms. "What leads?"

"For instance, that individual who left halfway through the weekend is being held in interview room two. He was the victim of a physical assault perpetrated by one of the individuals in the car, perhaps the deceased. And his alibi isn't credible."

Seldon narrows his eyes at me and works his jaw some more.

"Fine. Get back to it then. But be sure to stay focused, Scutt," he says, nostrils flaring. "This investigation is make-or-break for you."

Stephanie

Saturday, 4:52 p.m.

"Thank you, Stephanie," Jonathan said as we reached the top of the steps. Back at his house, finally, at nearly 5:00 p.m. "I couldn't have made it through all that without you."

"No problem," I said, like it had been no big thing. Even though I was pretty sure Jonathan, in fact, could not have done it without me, and I had a pounding headache from arguing with so many different bank employees.

We'd had to drive all the way to Albany and back—forty-five minutes each way—visiting four banks to get together the $20,000 Jonathan now had in two envelopes. He'd also arranged for a wire of the remaining

$11,000 to the contractors for Monday. All we needed now were the details on where to send it. Peter seemed concerned that the contractors weren't going to be satisfied with the delay on the balance. Unhelpful, given that we had no alternatives. Thus far, that was Peter: completely unhelpful.

"No, I mean it, really." Jonathan glanced back toward Peter, who was some distance behind. "Also, for the record, I do know this situation didn't have to be—" His voice cut out. "But Peter is a good person—he's just . . . immature."

"You don't owe me an explanation," I said. "That's the point of old friends. No excuses required."

"I know," Jonathan said. "But it is kind of excruciating, all of this happening in front of you. I just feel so ashamed."

"I'm not trying to make you feel ashamed, believe me."

"No, no. You've never made me feel bad about even my worst choices." He considered for a moment. "But somehow you also never pretended they were okay either," he said. "I've been grateful for that, even if I haven't always admitted it. I love Maeve and Derrick and Keith—but they're a little too good at pretending."

I was about to say something snarky, to joke, to deflect. Instead, I put a hand on Jonathan's back.

"Anytime," I said. "Besides, you aren't the only person who's had shitty romantic taste lately."

"Wait." Jonathan mimed shock. "*You* had a romance?"

"Ha ha," I said mildly. "Yeah, and when I fuck up, I fuck up spectacularly."

"That seems fair, actually."

I held his gaze. "Promise me one thing, though?"

"Anything."

"Work this out with Peter *before* you get married. And work it out for real. I'm sure he regrets how this played out, but that doesn't actually make it okay."

"I know that. I just need some time to process, that's all."

"And as your friend, I'm obligated to remind you that not every process has to end in forgiveness."

Inside, the house was eerily silent.

"Where is everyone?" Peter asked.

"Hello?" Jonathan called out.

"Out here," Maeve called from the living room.

"I'm going to get out of the way and give you all a minute," Peter whispered loudly as he headed for the steps, warmly squeezing Jonathan's arm.

Maeve was sitting alone at the center of one of the red couches, looking wound like a coil. "Did you pick up the money?" she asked, with a forced smile.

Jonathan nodded. “Twenty thousand,” he said. “The rest will have to get wired on Monday.”

“Great, so we can go then?” Maeve stood. “I mean, we should, right? Leave town. Considering everything that’s happened.”

“We still need to actually get the money *to* them,” Jonathan said. “They’re calling Peter soon, hopefully.”

“Oh.” Maeve brought a manicured hand to her lips. “I see.”

“Maeve, what’s wrong?” I asked. “Where *are* Derrick and Keith?”

Jonathan looked around. “They’re back, right?”

Maeve nodded, chewing on her lower lip. “Yeah, they’re back.”

“Maeve, come on,” I pressed. “You look about to crawl out of your skin.”

“Keith is trying to get out of going to rehab.”

Jonathan waved a hand. “No, no, we talked about it. He’ll go somewhere. He just doesn’t want it to be Bright Horizons.”

Maeve shook her head. “I don’t think so. I just went up to check on him, and he’s saying that he needs to go see Finch instead.”

“Back in the city?” I asked.

“Keith said that Finch texted. He’s still in Kaaterskill.”

The way my conversation with Finch had ended that morning, the possible explanations for his sticking around all seemed very bad. He'd barged into my room without knocking. Luckily, I was already up and dressed, making the bed.

"What happened?" I asked, motioning to his cut lip. But before he could even answer, I gestured for him to keep his voice down. The last thing I needed was anyone catching us having some private conversation.

"Derrick. Told you he's a psycho," Finch whispered. He waved the phone in his hand toward the door. "Anyway, I'm taking off. Let's go."

He said it so matter-of-factly as he turned back for the door. Like it was a foregone conclusion.

"What are you talking about?" I'd asked.

"Grab your stuff."

"You must be—no," I'd said. "Absolutely not. Why would I do that?"

When Finch finally looked at me, there was that familiar, mischievous gleam in his eyes. "Come, or I'll fire Keith. How about that?"

"You're extorting me?"

He winked. "Let's call it forceful courting."

"Get out, Finch," I said, and laughed, angrily. "I'm serious. Get the hell out of my room. Right now."

"Sure thing." Finch's eyes went cold. "But Keith will regret this. I'm not joking about firing him."

"Oh, please, you already fired him," I said. "I know you did. I saw your new contract. So you can drop this, whatever you think you're doing."

He didn't look surprised that I knew—like he'd already surmised as much. "Yeah, I fired Keith because he's such a fucking drug addict that his money problems derailed my show at the Serpentine Gallery in London. You know what a show like that means?" He shook his head in disgust. "But I wonder what Keith will say when he finds out you knew all this time that I'd already fired him, and you didn't tell him."

"Go to hell, Finch."

"Suit yourself," he said, as he headed for the door. "But don't say I didn't warn you. The choices you make, sometimes the fallout can be . . . far-reaching."

A minute later I heard the front door downstairs bang shut behind him.

I looked up at the ceiling now and thought of Keith upstairs, still desperately trying to keep Finch happy. I'd made it so much worse by not telling Keith right away about Finch and me, and Finch and him. But I could still come clean now.

"There's no point in Keith waiting on Finch," I said, starting for the stairs. "I'll go talk to him."

"Okay, but if you can't convince Keith to go . . ." Maeve hesitated. "Maybe the rest of us should, anyway."

"What do you mean?" Jonathan asked. "Leave Keith here?"

"We're not leaving Keith," I said sharply.

Wait, did Maeve just want to get back to Bates? After all, what would Mr. Wonderful say if he learned about this mess? I wondered if Alice had also been right about Maeve all those years ago. "You're underestimating Maeve," she'd said to me not long before that night on the roof. "Trust me, she knows how to get what she wants." But Alice had been trying to convince me that Maeve had some klepto problem, which frankly was so paranoid and ridiculous I'd dismissed the entire conversation as more Alice drama.

"Listen, I'm sure you want to get out of here and get back to the city, to Bates or whatever—"

"Bates? What does Bates have to do with anything?" Maeve asked, and then her eyes filled with tears. Maybe I wasn't being fair. I could see she was distraught. "I'm just . . . really worried, that's all. About all of us."

"The contractors still need to get paid anyway," Jonathan said, tired but matter-of-fact. "We can't go anywhere until that's taken care of."

"We're all just stressed," I said. "Let me first go talk to Keith."

When I got upstairs, Keith's door was open. He was sitting on the bed, eyes on his phone. Next to him on the bed was an empty picture frame. He looked up at me, then back down at his phone. I crossed the room and sat next to him on the bed. Picked up the frame.

"What's this?" I asked.

"A picture frame," he said lifelessly.

"Yeah, thanks, I can see that," I said. "Why do you have it?"

"It's from my apartment," he said, and there was something unsettling about his tone—a mixture of sadness and resignation. "There was a picture of all of us in it. One from college. Alice gave it to me sophomore year."

"Alice never gave me a picture," I said, looking down at the empty frame.

"That's because she loved me more," he said. "Everybody does."

Was it sweet that Keith had brought the photograph with him? Maybe, if our picture had still been in it. Or if it hadn't been Alice who had given it to him. As it was, the empty frame was disturbing. Had Keith gotten rid of the picture? Wasn't that a suicide warning sign? The drugs had always been Keith's slow-motion way of killing himself; maybe he'd finally decided to take a short cut.

"Everybody does love you more," I said, then stayed quiet for a minute. "So, what's this bullshit about not going to rehab?"

"Oh, I'll go," he said unconvincingly. "I just need to talk to Finch first. He texted and wants to work some stuff out about his London show. I have a fiduciary duty to get things in order before I'm unavailable. But then I'll go. I'm not trying to get out of it, I swear."

"No," I said. "I don't think so."

"What do you mean, no?"

"I don't think that's what happened. Maybe Finch texted, but not about London," I said. "Or if he did, he's fucking with you."

"What are you talking about?"

"Finch knows about his London show getting canceled."

Keith winced. And all I felt was awful. "He does?"

"He told me this morning," I said. "He came into my room, before everything with Crystal. Right before he left."

"Your room?" Keith looked even more confused. "And why would he tell you that and not me?"

"Finch signed on with the Graygon Gallery a month ago."

"I have no idea what the hell you're talking about."

I nodded. "I know. That's because I didn't tell you. I saw Finch's contract with the new gallery, all signed and finalized."

Keith's brow furrowed even more deeply. "How did you see one of Finch's contracts?"

"Because I had sex with him the night of the Cipriani party. I saw the contracts at his apartment."

"You what?" Keith looked stunned. I turned away.

"I know," I said, unable to bring myself to look at him again. "I don't have an excuse. But it happened. And I'm sorry—he's your most important artist. I knew that at the time, obviously."

"Wait, that reception was a month ago. You knew about that contract this whole time?"

"I didn't know how to tell you. I was just so embarrassed about the whole thing. I'm sorry, Keith," I said. "Really."

For the longest time, he didn't say a word. Finally, he took a deep breath. "I know I told you to, like, live your life and feel things and whatever. But for the record, Finch was not what I had in mind." Then he turned to me with a sly but forgiving smile, and I felt overwhelmed by relief.

We startled when Keith's phone rang. He answered it. "Hi, hold on one second," he said into the phone. He looked at me. "Sorry, I need to take this. Privately."

"Is that Finch?" I asked. I'd grab the phone if I had to. Finch could fire Keith if he wanted, but he could not kick him when he was already down. Not on my watch.

"No, it's not Finch," he said. "It's somebody else who is actually way more pissed at me than Finch, believe it or not. I've got to—I'm, um, trying to deal with it."

There was genuine fear in Keith's voice. And Keith didn't get scared of things. It was actually a problem. "What is it? Do you need help?"

He shook his head. "No," he said, smiling, but in a way that was distressing. "I've got this. You've helped enough." He waved me toward the door. "Go, go. Please."

"Okay," I said, feeling increasingly uneasy as I crossed the room.

"But, hey, Stephanie," Keith called after me. "Thank you. You're a good friend. I mean, except for the part about sleeping with my most important artist."

I raised a finger in the air at the door and forced a playful smile. "*Former* artist. That's totally different."

Detective Julia Scutt

Sunday, 5:09 p.m.

The Falls is busier when I return, but not by much. There are maybe twenty people scattered around the tables, the bar stools mostly full. It takes a minute of waiting for me to get the bartender's attention this time. He does not look happy to see me.

"I need to know if some people were in here on Saturday night."

"Didn't we already do this?" he asks, crossing his arms.

"Different people." I hold up my phone and swipe through photos of Maeve, Jonathan, and Stephanie. "Did you see any of these people in here on Saturday night? I know they were here Friday. That's when

Crystal left with them in that SUV. But were they here last night, too? While the McGregor fight was on?"

The bartender is already shaking his head. "Not that blond one. I mean, she might have been here, but I didn't see her. The other two, though . . ." He rubs a hand over his face, glances around to see if anyone is listening, then gestures toward an empty table at the back. "They were sitting over there with Luke Gaffney. They got into a thing." The bartender shakes his head. "I didn't see what happened. But there was some kind of dustup. A minute later they were gone."

Dan is waiting for me outside, standing near my car. As I get closer, I can see that his mouth is turned down. He's here to deliver bad news. I wonder if Seldon has already fired me.

"I'm guessing you're not here to tell me we lucked out with those Arkansas prints for Derrick Chism?"

Dan shakes his head. "I wouldn't get your hopes up on that. I didn't get the sense they were real well-staffed. Or motivated. The NYPD is sending officers to collect DNA from their apartments. But, as you know, that's gonna take some time. What'd you find in here?"

"Bartender remembers Stephanie and Jonathan," I say. "From *last* night."

"They sure do know how to lie, don't they?"

"Yup," I say. "Starting to look like what they're covering up is the truth about what happened to Keith and Derrick. Weekender on weekender. Seldon will be happy."

Me too, that's the honest truth.

"Or . . ." Dan holds out a paper evidence bag. There's something palm-sized and T-shaped at the bottom.

"What's that?" I lean in closer.

"I was just taking it to the station when I saw your car. It's a corkscrew," he says. "Dogs followed that scent in circles. But eventually, this was at the end of it. Or rather it was over the side of the cliff at the end of it, on the ridge right below. My guess is that somebody tossed it there in the dark, didn't realize it landed only seven feet below in plain sight, instead of forty feet down in the river."

"A corkscrew?" I can see now that it's covered in mud with maybe some blood near the handle.

"I checked with the ME—given the irregular shape and depth of the wounds, it might fit the bill. No track marks, either, by the way, and he confirmed that the facial injuries were indeed postmortem."

The same as Jane. *Dammit.*

"There's, um, engraving on it," Dan says, holding up his flashlight and shining it into the bag.

I can see now the etching on the handle: *LG.*

"Luke Gaffney?" I ask. *Fuck.* "Seriously?"

Dan shrugs. "You're looking at what I'm looking at."

"Did you also double check Luke's alibi from Jane's case?"

"Just a minute ago, yeah," Dan says. "Apparently the teacher who swore he was in detention got fired two years later for smoking pot with some students. Doesn't mean he lied about the detention, necessarily, but . . ."

"It's not outside the realm of possibility."

Dan nods. "Did you know that Luke Gaffney tried to get Jane to go out with him? Somebody talked about it in the podcast. She said no, apparently. Could be he didn't take it so well."

I had not known that. Luke was barely fifteen when Jane and Bethany died, but probably big enough, strong enough, to have killed them. Maybe what Bob Hoff saw was Mike Gaffney coming to clean up after his son. Maybe, after all these years, Luke got angry enough to kill again.

"Fuck," I say quietly.

"I already sent units to sit on Luke Gaffney's house," Dan says. "They're pretty sure he's in there."

It isn't Luke who answers the door. It's a good-looking young blond guy.

He takes a step back when I flash my badge. "Luke here?"

"He's on the phone, I think." He gestures vaguely behind him.

"Can we come in and maybe you go get him?" I ask, stepping inside without waiting for an invitation. "We have a few questions."

"Um," the man says, stumbling back and looking over his shoulder like he's hoping someone might appear to rescue him. "Okay, I guess."

"And you are?" I ask, trying to keep him occupied. It would be better for him not to warn Luke that we've talked our way inside. But he's already inching back out of the foyer.

"So, I'll just go get—"

Dan heads him off, smoothly leaning against the wall behind him in a way that is both casual and imposing. When he almost bumps into Dan, the guy looks a little panicked.

"It's okay. We can just wait," I say nonchalantly. "I'm sure Luke will be out when he's done. Sorry, I missed your name."

"Oh, me." He squints. "I'm, um, Luke's cousin. I'm just, uh, visiting."

"From where?" Dan asks.

"What?"

"Where are you visiting from?" I press, taking a step closer. The guy is so nervous, no saying what might pop if we lean into him.

"Oh, the, um, Florida."

"What the hell do you want?" Luke shouts, storming into the foyer. Before I can stop myself, I've imagined him over Jane, a rusted tent stake in his hand. "I already told you that I'm not answering any more of your questions. Now get the fuck out of my house."

My hand twitches toward my gun. *Breathe.* I just need to breathe. I try to swallow down the rage clogging my throat. "You lied to me," I manage.

"Lied to you?" Luke snorts. "Bullshit. Now, like I said, get the fuck out."

"From what I hear, you got into it with Jonathan Cheung and his friend last night at the Falls. You told me you didn't see them."

"What are you talking about?" But already he's dialed back his tone.

"Some kind of argument. Maybe you were pissed about the money you're owed," I say. "Or maybe you were pissed that Crystal was sleeping with Keith Lazard."

Luke shakes his head. "Why would I give a shit what Crystal does?"

"You told me you were sleeping with her."

"Nope." He laughs. "I figured if I said that to you, it would get back to them. I wanted to fuck with them."

"Crystal Finnegan is missing, Mr. Gaffney." I work to keep my voice steady. It's not easy. "I suggest you stop playing games."

"Have you asked those fucking people what happened to her?"

"I'm asking you."

Luke Gaffney shakes his head in disgust. "Let me guess, it wasn't even those fuckers who told you about our supposed argument?"

"We have a witness."

"A witness to what?" Luke asks. "Those people come up here for the weekend, thinking they own this place." He looks back at the blond guy. "Thinking they own everyone. You want to know what really happened?"

"Yes, Mr. Gaffney, I would love to know what really happened."

"Luke . . . ," the blond guy begins. Nervous speaking up, nervous about what Luke is about to say. Maybe both.

When Luke glares at him, he retreats.

"Crystal is dead," Luke says. "And those fuckers dumped her body at the Farm like she was garbage."

The turkey vulture, the smear of blood on the doorframe—Goddammit. At least I was right that Jonathan and his friends were hiding something.

"What happened to her?"

"How the fuck would I know?" Luke asks. "But they were willing to pay me a shitload of money to keep my mouth shut, so you do the math."

Still, none of this explains the monogrammed corkscrew, and it doesn't prove Luke isn't responsible for whatever happened in that car. Or that twenty years ago he wasn't a pissed-off teenage boy with a well-connected dad willing to do anything to protect him. I feel my hand aching again to move to my gun. My heart is hammering.

"Why don't you just account for your whereabouts between eleven p.m. last night and four a.m., Mr. Gaffney?" Dan asks when I still do not speak.

"That's none of your fucking business."

"Well, we've got a murder weapon with your initials on it that says otherwise."

"My initials?" Luke snorts again. "What the hell are you talking about?"

"A monogrammed corkscrew," Dan says.

"A corkscrew?" Luke scowls. "Who the fuck monograms a corkscrew?"

"If it's not yours, then I'm sure you won't mind the officers coming in to confirm there's not the rest of a matching set anywhere around," I say.

"Yeah, I think I'll pass on that." Luke smiles and steps confidently toward the door. He opens it and motions us out. "You can go now."

I shake my head. "Mr. Gaffney, I'm afraid that's not—"

"Wasn't your boss already pissed enough at you for bothering my dad at his cabin?" He flashes a menacing smile my way.

"My boss?" I ask.

"Yeah, you know, Chief Seldon was supposed to be up there fishing with my dad this weekend. And trust me, that bunch does *not* like to be disturbed. You have any idea how pissed Seldon's going to be if he finds out you're still hassling us?"

An officer appears in the open doorway then, holding out a folded piece of paper. I check quickly—the warrant, luckily. I show it to Luke.

"You know what, Mr. Gaffney, I think I'll take my fucking chances."

We leave uniforms at the house running the search while Dan offers to go down to the lab himself and see if he can get a manual comparison on the corkscrew prints expedited. We have at least one fingerprint card on Luke Gaffney, for a drunk driving charge last year. The connections to Jane's case are multiplying rapidly—the similarities in the murder weapon, the smashed faces, Luke Gaffney's disappearing alibis, his motive. Running the tent stake for Luke Gaffney's prints will be next. The thought does make me feel sick: all this time, Jane's murderer was so close by?

In the meantime, I storm back to the station, determined to find out what the hell happened to Crystal. I already have officers headed to the Farm to look for her body. Soon we'll know exactly what we're dealing with.

"Hey, wait!" Cartright calls as I pass him on the way to Jonathan's interview room, hopeful that I'll get him to break if he's on his own. "Hendrix wants to make a statement. Won't shut up about it."

"What exactly did he say?" I ask, skeptical.

Cartright eyes me dumbly. "That he wanted to make a statement."

I do have a witness now, who can officially poke a hole in Hendrix's alibi—a uniform found a guy who works the newspaper stand at the train station. He saw Finch Hendrix going into the hotel across the street around noon on Saturday. So much for him being at the train station all night. But none of that matters if Luke Gaffney's prints are on that corkscrew—unless Finch is responsible for what happened to Crystal. I can't rule that out. Not yet.

"Did his lawyer show up?"

Cartright shakes his head. "Not that I've seen."

It's been more than enough time now for a lawyer to get here from the city. Which means Finch has decided not to call one. That seems reason enough to see what this statement is all about.

When I come in, Finch has his head down on the table, eyes closed. For a second I worry he's bled out internally, but he shifts slightly when I close the door.

"Jesus," he grumbles into the tabletop. "Took you fucking long enough."

"I hear you have something you want to tell me?"

He lifts his head off the table. "You do know I've got a show? You heard that part, right?" He checks his watch dramatically. "Back in the city, tomorrow. I've got to set up."

"I thought it was tonight?"

"Tonight, tomorrow, I've still got to go."

"Don't you think it would be better to postpone the show—I mean, given that your agent is either missing or dead?"

"Dealer, former dealer," he says, then smirks. "Ironic, with all the drugs, that he was *my* dealer, isn't it?" He goes to lean back in his chair but winces again. "Anyway, even Keith would want the show to go on. And just to reiterate—if my show gets fucked because of this, I am going to sue the shit out of you, personally."

"So you keep telling me."

"Just want to be sure you're aware how much my art is worth—how much you could be costing me, and so how much it'll cost you."

"And just so you're aware: obstruction of justice is a crime."

"Obstruction of justice. Bullshit." Finch laughs. "How did I supposedly obstruct justice?"

"Well, it's all the things you've been leaving out, then there's also the gun you had up here. There's no permit in your name in New York State."

"What gun?" Finch raises his hands and smiles.

"We'll find it, Mr. Hendrix. And I'm sure your prints will be on it. You also weren't passed out in the train station for fourteen hours. We have a witness who saw you go into the hotel across the street. But what I'm most concerned about, at the moment, is how Crystal died."

"Died?" His eyes widen. "What do you mean?"

"Apparently she's dead, Mr. Hendrix," I say. "You know anything about that? Maybe she was even with you in that hotel room when it happened."

"I was working in that room, that's all. I'm using it as a temporary art studio. My work is a combination of video, sculptures, and paintings re-created from memory," he says, tone smooth and practiced now, like he's being interviewed for a magazine profile. It's extremely aggravating. "That's why the hotel. I have to go right back and start, while the scenes are fresh in my mind. But I can't get into too many details because there's always a lot of anticipation around my next—"

"Mr. Hendrix, I don't give a shit about you or your art." I rise. "I'm trying to find out what happened to Derrick Chism, Keith Lazard, and Crystal Finnegan. If you don't have anything useful that you'd like to share—"

"Okay, okay. Their friend from Vassar, Alice, killed herself. It's why that whole group is so fucked up."

"Yes, they mentioned their friend Alice. I don't see how that's relevant, Mr. Hendrix."

"It's *why* she killed herself that's the thing." He rubs a hand over his face, considering. "I can get into some details, but only if you *promise* not to tell anyone about my current proj—"

"Mr. Hendrix!"

He holds up his hands. "Fine, fine. There's a journal. This woman I was seeing, Rachel, she made this podcast about some other murder, and she included Alice's suicide in one of the episodes. Seemed pretty unrelated to me, but I guess they both happened near the Hudson River. Anyway, the girl's mom died, and her housekeeper was a fan of the podcast. She mailed the journal to Rachel and Rochelle and—"

"Wait, Rachel and Rochelle?"

The River. The episode with the Vassar girl. She was Alice?

"Yeah, the two of them made the podcast. Rachel told me about the journal, and she mentioned a Keith and Vassar. I knew about Keith and Alice because he'd told me. So I asked to take a look at the journal. I knew as soon as I read it that I had my next project. Well, not right then. First, Keith screwed me over, and then Stephanie, well—let's just say she let me down."

"And so you plan a big art project about these people, and one of them just happens to end up dead?"

Hendrix shrugs. "I'm not saying it's a coincidence. The project required that I press some of their buttons, raise the stakes. That's why I came up here. I saw a text to Keith about Jonathan's bachelor party a few weeks ago. Enough time to get the ball rolling. Some things I knew already, like about Derrick and his past, and that Stephanie had made some choices she regretted. From the journal I figured out that Maeve is some kind of klepto. Other things I just lucked into seeing firsthand, like those contractors. But there were things I set up beforehand—like sending along some anonymous emails. 'I know what you did'—just to ratchet up the tension." He sighs theatrically. "And so I stirred their sick little pot and then taped the blowback. It's amazing, the footage. My project is about the costs of blind loyalty and the danger of always accepting people for better and so much worse. It's about *this* group—because if there ever was a fucking example of the dark side of friendship—"

"No one's mentioned your little project. No one."

"They don't have a clue, not yet. They don't know I taped everything. All you need to do is hit record on your phone and make your screen go dark. These days no one questions a phone in somebody's hand all the time," he says. "Listen, I might have called the whole thing off if any of them had stepped up and surprised me. But these people will never change."

"I still don't see what this project of yours or this journal has to do with Crystal or that dead guy in Derrick Chism's car. Because that's all I care about, Mr. Hendrix."

"To be honest, I've been a little worried you might say I wasn't allowed to use Alice's journal in my installation, because it could be evidence of something."

"Evidence of what?"

"They killed somebody before. Maybe they did it again."

"What are you talking about?"

"You can read all about it yourself. I forgot the pages back at Jonathan's house. Supposedly, it was an accident. Guy fell off a roof. But then they just left him there to die. Alice was so upset, she killed herself. I'm telling you, that's the kind of thing these people do—bad thing after bad thing until people end up dead. I'm going to have the pages blown up, poster-size, as part of the installation." He leaned in like he was sharing a precious secret. "You want to know what the piece is called?"

"I have a feeling you're going to tell me, regardless."

"*Friends Like These.*" This time Finch smiles, a shit-eating grin. "Clever, huh?"

Keith

Saturday, 5:14 p.m.

"Yeah," I finally answered once Stephanie was gone.

I'd felt a jolt of panic when the phone rang. Especially with Stephanie sitting right there. But I had a plan, one that would keep everyone else safe, which was all that mattered.

"You get the gift?" The same voice from the night before, deep and toneless.

"Yeah, thanks," I said. "Super creative. Do I get the photograph back?"

"Sure. You have our money?"

"Yeah, I've got it." Such an easy lie.

"All eighty thousand?" Wise skepticism.

"No, twenty."

I'd heard Peter on the phone with the contractors—at least I was assuming it was them—talking about having that much. I liked that it was an amount of money that existed nearby. Made it easier to lie. Also, I'd been such a deadbeat so far, having only some of the cash was exactly the kind of thing I'd do. And it was important that they believe me. It was the best way to get them to come after me, and leave my friends alone.

"Twenty thousand? Are you fucking kidding me? How about the eighty thousand you owe?"

"Twenty thousand is what I've got for now," I said. "I'll get you the rest. If you kill me you get nothing. Consider the twenty thousand a show of good faith."

"Meet us out front," he said. "End of the driveway—ten minutes."

"No, no," I said. "Can't do that."

"Oh, no?" He sounded amused in an I-am-going-to-enjoy-killing-you-slowly kind of way.

"No," I said. "I'm going to have to grab the money off my friend. If I stay near the house, they might call the police. I'll meet you downtown."

"You think you got space to negotiate here?"

"I think Frank is going to be pissed if you come back empty-handed. If you want your money, this is the way to get it."

"Fine. Eight p.m. downtown," he said finally. "Look for a text with an address."

I waited for some rush of regret after I hung up. The return of that fear. But nothing came. Protecting my friends was the right thing to do. After everything they had done for me over the years, everything they were still doing—it needed to stop. Otherwise, I'd just keep dragging all of them down, forever. I knew that I would.

Worst of all was letting them share the blame for Alice. When what happened was all my fault, not theirs. I'd taken our fragile, broken friend, a girl I loved, and shoved her right over the edge—and I'd never owned up.

Alice had been off her medication for weeks before the roof. I could always tell. I'd told her to get back on it. The way I always did—with a lot of bravado, but without any actual follow-through. I didn't call her mom, didn't go to the health center. Didn't tell anyone. Because deep down I was too afraid they'd say I was the reason she needed medication in the first place. How fucking self-involved is that?

And then the accident on the roof happened, and Alice went from bad to so much worse. I knew that I couldn't, shouldn't, be accountable for her. Alice needed someone brave enough to actually help her, strong enough to make the right choices.

Alice saw it coming, too. Right away, she seemed defensive when I showed up outside her dance class unannounced. Tugging on one of her long reddish braids, looking strong and fragile all at once in her cropped hoodie and leggings. It was only five days after the roof. Five days for me to realize that I didn't have it in me to put Alice back together again. We needed to be apart for good.

"What's wrong?" Alice asked me, already downshifting from defensive to wounded.

Staring at her sweet, freckled face, I wanted to cave. To forget the whole thing. But what about the damage I'd do if Alice and I stayed together? And so I panicked when I felt myself wavering, all the careful things I'd planned to say going out the window. I grabbed instead for something quick and easy and so unbelievably cruel.

"I'm in love with somebody else."

"What?" Alice had laughed, sure it was some kind of joke.

"No, it's true," I lied. "That's why—that's the reason I can't be better to you. Because I'm in love with someone else."

Tears flooded her hazel eyes. "Of course you are," she said finally. "That would make sense."

"I'm not good for you, anyway," I offered feebly. And also Alice wasn't good for me—that was true, too, wasn't it?

"Right." Alice had gripped her dance bag against her strong, small body as she blinked back her tears. Already, her face was setting into stone. "Who is—you know what, I don't even want to know who she is."

"We shouldn't be together anyway, Alice," I added, still afraid I might try to take it back later. Because I did love Alice. I did.

"Okay, fine," she said with an angry, exaggerated shrug. "Whatever you want, Keith. Whatever."

And with that, she'd turned and walked away. Six hours later, thanks to me, she'd be dead. And all these years later, I was still letting my friends believe they were as much to blame as me.

I didn't leave my room at Jonathan's house until 7:30 p.m. I even pretended to be asleep when the door opened and closed a couple times. I'd found a pad of paper and a pen in the nightstand drawer (of course, only Jonathan), and I wrote a quick note: "You deserve better than Peter. Keith." There was more I thought about writing to Jonathan, more I could have thanked him for, or apologized for, or tried to explain. But it seemed like too much and not enough. And

Jonathan being worth more than Peter was the part he needed to remember.

I headed toward Jonathan's bedroom, hoping to leave the note somewhere he'd find it later. But the door swung open just as I reached it, and there was Peter, shirtless and in a pair of jeans. Peter was always shirtless.

"What do you want?" he asked—aggressive, loud. Peter was only that way with me, always out of Jonathan's earshot. Like I was a little kid he could abuse because I'd never be believed. He wasn't wrong—it had been a justifiably long time since anyone had listened to me. "Oh, wait, let me guess, you're here for our money? You sure could buy a lot of drugs with twenty thousand dollars."

"Don't you mean Jonathan's money?" I asked. I couldn't help it.

Peter smiled snidely, stepped back into the room, and slammed the door in my face. So much for my note. I crumpled it in my hand and jammed it in my pocket.

"What was that about?" Derrick asked from behind me.

"Nothing," I said, turning toward him. "But I'm glad you're here. I was about to come looking for you."

Derrick held up his palms like a traffic cop. "No. The answer is no, Keith."

"You don't even know what I'm going to ask."

"I don't need to. My answer is no, whatever it is."

"Finch called from downtown," I began. "And he—"

"Downtown?" he interrupted. "I thought Finch left."

"Guess not. Anyway, he said he really needs to tell me something."

"About what?" Derrick asked, nervous now. Probably about being in my crosshairs.

"I have no idea," I said. "That's why I need to go talk to him. I just heard he's moving to a new gallery, so maybe about that."

"Oh, right," Derrick said, like this was old news to him.

"Hold up—did you already know that too?" I sounded pissed. I was, a little bit, actually. "Did Finch tell you he was changing representation?"

"Yeah, um, I guess he did. Right after we got here," Derrick stammered. "It didn't seem like my place to, you know, get involved."

I couldn't actually blame Derrick for that. Still, his guilt was my only angle.

"*Get* involved?" I snapped. "You're one of my best friends. You're *always* fucking involved."

"Of course I am. I'm sorry." Derrick shook his head a little. "I've thought for a long time that you and

Finch should go your separate ways. It could be a good thing."

"You still should have told me. Anyway, this isn't like breaking up with some girl you've been dating a few weeks. Finch and me—it's like dissolving a marriage. There are assets and shit that need to be divided, agreements signed. Which is why I need to go talk to him now and clear things up." Honestly, it sounded pretty convincing, even to me. "Just take me downtown and drop me off. Come on, you owe me. And if you don't drive me, I'll walk—dark roads, drunk drivers. Think of the guilt."

Derrick glared at me, but finally he nodded. "Okay," he said. "But I'm staying, and then we're coming straight back here."

I nodded and lied in that way that came so easily to me. "You've got a deal."

Derrick wasn't happy when I said that we were meeting Finch at the Falls. Not that I even knew where I really needed to be yet. But the Falls was at least downtown, so that seemed like a good place to start.

"Finch has just been here all day, hanging out in this bar?" Derrick asked as we were getting out of the car.

"Maybe I'm not the only one with a substance abuse problem."

"But why not go home and hang out in a bar in Brooklyn?" Derrick pressed—he sounded suspicious now, of Finch though, not me. "There must have been half a dozen trains back to the city since this morning."

"Do I look like a goddamn travel agent? Fuck, Derrick, who cares why Finch stayed?"

It was 7:53 p.m. Only seven minutes to get inside and ditch Derrick. I couldn't risk him following me. Trying to stop me. Trying to save me from myself. That wasn't happening, not this time.

"You have fifteen minutes," Derrick said as he pulled open the door to the bar. His stern big-brother voice made my chest pull tight. I should have left Derrick a note too. "Thank you," I would have written, "for being so loyal." Because Derrick was always loyal, loyal to a fault.

I saluted. "Aye, aye, Captain."

Inside, the Falls was even busier than it had been the night before, Aerosmith blasting, wall-to-wall damp bodies, a fucking mob scene near the bar. Something on the TV maybe. Despite all the people, when I looked up I met eyes almost instantly with the contractor sitting at the back. He even lifted his chin in my direction. I wondered if he thought that Jonathan and Peter were with me and had his money. They could already be on their way. *Fuck.* Another reason to speed things along.

Finally, a buzz in my back pocket. The location, had to be. For a second I wondered whether there was any chance this could end differently. But I couldn't see how. I had no money. These people didn't believe in second chances. And I'd already had way more than that. There would never be enough money to dig me out of this mess anyway. Rehab wouldn't be a real fix, either—I already knew that. It would just be an exhausting pit stop on a never-ending downward slide.

"Can you get me a beer?" I asked Derrick. "I've got to take a piss."

"A beer?" he asked. "Are you kidding me? We're supposed to check you into rehab tomorrow."

"Fine, get me a Coke." I smacked him on the shoulder. "And keep an eye out for Finch. He's here somewhere. Sooner we find him, the sooner we can leave. That's what you want, right?"

Derrick looked around. He still seemed nervous. "Yeah, what *I* want, right. You're a dick, you know that, Keith?" he said mildly as he turned toward the bar, looking back at me over his shoulder with that kind of regrettable love that he always had for me somehow, even now. He was a better person than me. All my friends were.

As soon as Derrick was out of sight, I headed into the crowd, toward the bathrooms and the back exit to the bar—toward the dark and the quiet and the night. Alone.

1225 Main Street. Corner of Main and Spencer. That was all the text had said. I was standing on Main already, using my phone to figure out the right direction. Nine blocks from the bar, away from the lights and the sound. Not an accident, of course. By block six the streetlamps were gone, the only light left from the half-moon through the trees.

Twelve twenty-five was a falling-down abandoned house with boarded-up windows and overgrown hedges in front, obscuring most of the porch. They were waiting up there, had to be.

And I wouldn't run. I wouldn't change my mind. I'd be brave once and for all, for my friends who'd tried for so long to save me. I'd finally face this person I had become. This place I, and I alone, had delivered myself to.

Jonathan

Saturday, 8:26 p.m.

"This is insanity," Stephanie snapped as she got out of the car. She'd been complaining, loudly, ever since Peter got the text from the contractors: The Falls, 8:30 p.m. "Are we seriously about to go into this bar to give these people twenty thousand dollars? In *cash*? When does paying people off ever actually turn out well?"

"Stephanie!" I hissed as we crossed the street. "Enough already. Let's get this over with."

She was just worried, though. I knew that. We were all worried. In the midst of everything, Keith and Derrick had also vanished—no explanation, no note, nothing. Surely Keith had talked Derrick into something, and surely it would not be good. They'd presumably gone somewhere Keith could buy, and Derrick had fallen for whatever excuse had gotten him to drive. Though, even for Derrick, this seemed awfully naive. Stephanie wasn't so sure it was that simple.

"Keith got a call from someone when I was with him," she'd said. "Someone who was very angry, he said. He seemed scared, too. And you know Keith, he's usually so—"

"Impervious," I'd finished her thought. And this was true. Keith had a dangerously high terror threshold.

And now neither Derrick nor Keith were answering their phones—and, yes, the signal was spotty up there. But it wasn't a good sign. Maeve had agreed to stay behind to watch for them, but Stephanie insisted on coming along with Peter and me so she could look around herself at the Falls. She had already mentioned going to the Farm if we didn't find Derrick and Keith downtown. But there was no way I was ever going back there. Absolutely no way.

Stephanie disappeared into the packed crowd in search of Derrick and Keith as Peter and I made our way around, looking for our good friend Luke the contractor. I thought it had been crowded the night before, but now there was some kind of fight on the TV, and we had to wade through a sweaty sea of bodies.

"They're not here anymore," Stephanie said, squeezing back out from the crowd almost immediately. "The bartender said he thinks he saw them a little while ago." She looked exasperated. "But I'm not even really sure he looked at their pictures. He might have been trying to get rid of me."

"You said it yourself: at a certain point we have to stop saving Keith from himself. Maybe this is that point."

But I wasn't sure I believed that, and Stephanie's eyes were still darting around, lips pressed tight. She wasn't even listening.

"What are you talking about?" she asked.

"You said that on the way up here, Stephanie, remember? That Keith should have to confront his own consequences."

"Yeah, well, fuck what I said." Stephanie turned to look at me. "I'm telling you, Jonathan, I have a bad, bad feeling. There was just this sound to Keith's voice. And he thanked me for being a good friend. It was like he was saying goodbye."

"Goodbye?" That did not sound good.

"Stephanie, did you happen to see Luke anywhere when you were up at the bar?" Peter asked. "The person we are actually here to find."

"Who is Luke?" she asked.

"The contractor," I said.

"Oh, yeah," she said, waving toward the back. "He's at a table in the corner over there."

Peter immediately moved in that direction, weaving his way so forcefully through the crowd that it was hard for me to keep up. It was sweet, him leading the charge. Though I did worry he was overestimating his ability to match Luke. Peter was young and in amazing shape—but the kind sculpted by a personal trainer at Equinox.

When I glanced behind us, Stephanie was following, but some distance behind, pushing against bodies disagreeably. She paused, looking down at her phone as she typed out a message. Peter gestured subtly for me to hurry—I was the one carrying the money.

"Why don't you give him the, you know . . ." Peter nodded in Luke's direction when I joined him at their table. "So we can get out of here."

"Okay, fine," I said, reaching into my jacket like all of this was an annoyance I was barely tolerating. Careless aggression was a reckless idea, but so was completely rolling over and playing dead.

But already Luke was shaking his head as he looked away. "No, no, you fucking idiot. Have a seat first."

Luke and his friend—a big guy with white-blond hair and oversize pink cheeks—slid over so that there was an open chair next to each of them. The big guy motioned to the one near him.

"Here you go," he said. "Plenty of room."

"That's okay," Peter said. "We can stand."

Luke swiveled his gaze to Peter.

"Sit the fuck down," he said through gritted teeth. "I'm not having the handoff in plain view. In case you boys were hoping to get it on the bar's security film."

"We're not trying to do that," I said, my voice embarrassingly shaky.

Luke kicked the chair nearest him out in my direction. "Then have a seat."

I quickly handed Luke the envelopes under the table. He snatched them away and thumbed through the bills.

"This is twenty thousand. Where's the other eleven?"

"You do know the way banks work, right?" Peter's tone was condescending. "There are withdrawal limits. We'll be wiring you the rest on Monday."

"Thanks for the tutorial." Luke narrowed his eyes at Peter, then turned back to me. "So let me get this clear: you think I'm dumb enough to have you pay me off with a paper trail?"

"Definitely not," I hurried to add before Peter did more damage. "I can get you another eleven thousand cash on Monday if you'd rather that."

Luke was still staring at me. My palms had started to sweat. "Cash," he said finally. "Monday. As soon as the banks open."

"Absolutely," I said. "No problem."

"Also, you should know," Luke went on, eyes still locked on mine, "local police and my family go way back. Way, way back. I'd think twice before I report anything about this. It'll end up turning back hard on you and that drug addict friend of yours."

Stephanie was at the table now, eyes still on her phone. When she looked up, she saw Luke's friend with the big cheeks.

"Hey, look who it is," he said with a lascivious smile.

"Oh, fabulous," she said, turning to me. "And Jonathan, you're sitting. Why are you sitting? Let's do what we came to do and get out of here."

"What's your hurry?" the friend said, pointing to his lap. "I saved a spot for you."

"Ugh." Stephanie groaned and rolled her eyes. "Jonathan, please, can we go?"

Peter looked from Stephanie back to me. "I'm so sorry," he mouthed, pained.

Without thinking, I reached over the table and gave Peter's hand a quick squeeze. He looked up at me then and smiled in the exact way he had the first night we met—shy and sweet. One smile like that, and I'd been done for.

"Are you fucking kidding me?" Luke barked at Peter.

I snatched my hand back like I'd been burned, then felt ashamed for reacting. But Peter was defiant, lips pressed together, a challenge in his gaze as he stared back at Luke. "Maybe if you weren't jammed so far in that closet of yours, you wouldn't care that we're fucking."

"That's funny." Luke's friend laughed. "He just called you a faggot."

I winced, then watched in disbelief as Peter smiled at Luke—a taunting fuck-you smile.

"You think you're funny?" Luke asked Peter.

Oh my God, Peter, I thought. He is going to kill you.

"A little bit," Peter said, still smiling.

"Jonathan," I heard Stephanie say. She sounded nervous. "We should go."

"You know what else is funny?" Luke asked.

I heard the sound before I felt the motion. Felt the impact of my head smashed against the table before the pain. Felt the pain before I registered someone's hand on the back of my neck. Luke's hand. All I could see was black. The table. Maybe.

"Jonathan!" Stephanie screamed. "Let go of him!"

There was a burning at the top of my skull, razors slicing down my spine. Luke was pushing down harder and harder. I felt dizzy. Like I was about to throw up. Or black out. It was hard to breathe.

"Fucking stop it!" Stephanie screamed, even louder this time. "Let go of him, you fucking asshole!"

There was struggling then—Peter must have been trying to help. The hand on my neck was shaking my head, back and forth.

"Stop it!" Stephanie—I could see her feet. Right up against mine.

"Ow! Fucking bitch!" Luke shouted suddenly. "My fucking neck!"

Then, all at once, I was free. Stephanie yanked me up, pulling me through the crowd. "Come on!" she shouted at me, shoving people out of the way.

"Where's Peter?" I asked, as we got close to the door. But when I tried to turn my head to look, the pain was excruciating.

"He's fine. He's fine. Let's just get to the car," Stephanie said as she dragged me outside. "Hurry. Give me the keys. I'll drive."

Stephanie took the driver's seat, locking the doors and putting the key in the ignition.

"Wait. We have to . . ." The throbbing in my head was worse with each word. "We can't leave Peter in there."

"Yes, we fucking can," Stephanie said.

"Luke is going to kill him!"

"I'm the one who fucked up his neck with my nails. If anyone is getting killed, it's me."

"But Peter—"

"He's fine, Jonathan!" Stephanie shouted. She lurched into reverse, then zoomed forward. "Text Maeve. She's at the house by herself. Tell her to lock the doors in case those guys show up looking for us."

Stephanie was really scared, I could see that—even through the screaming pain in my neck. I tapped out a quick text to Maeve. Be careful. Contractors could be on way. Lock everything.

Maeve responded instantly. Are you okay?

Yes, be home soon. "I told her we're on the way."

"Text back and tell her we might be a little while."

"Why?"

"Did you tell Peter where Keith and Derrick left Crystal?"

"Honestly, Stephanie, whatever happened back there, Peter might be a coward, but he's not going to tell—"

"He's in on it, Jonathan."

"In on what?"

"Peter is in on it with the contractors." Stephanie's voice sounded strained.

"In on what?" I asked again.

"And I think they might be *together* together—Luke and Peter. They just looked at each other in this way." She shuddered. "Your neck was about to get broken, and they were—"

"No," I said quietly. And I meant that like *No, you're wrong.* But I already had the worst sinking feeling.

"When Luke grabbed you, Jonathan, Peter didn't look surprised or upset." She gave my forearm a quick squeeze. "I swear to God he looked . . . flattered. Luke was jealous, and Peter was happy about it."

I was quiet for a long time, staring out the window at the passing trees. In the void, there was only my chest getting slowly crushed. Stephanie was right, wasn't she? I could feel it.

"I really know how to pick 'em, huh?" I managed finally. My voice sounded so quiet and small. "I am such a moron."

"What, because you cared about someone? I don't think so." Stephanie's voice was uncharacteristically soft. "However, blaming yourself because Peter is terrible? That *would* make you a moron."

"By all means, don't sugarcoat it."

"You don't need me to sugarcoat anything. That's patronizing." Stephanie said, then stayed quiet for a beat. "Hey, want to hear something that will make you feel better?"

"Sure," I said doubtfully.

"I had a one-night stand with Finch."

"No." When I turned to look at her, she nodded. "Eww."

"A month ago," she said, then shrugged. "Whatever. My point is: we all make bad choices. All you can do is try to choose differently next time."

"Yeah, apparently I'm not so great at that." We were quiet again. "Thank you for stepping in when you did. I think he actually could have broken my neck."

"Anytime," she said.

"Did you hear from Derrick or Keith?"

She nodded. "From Derrick. Apparently Keith talked him into coming to the Falls to find Finch and then gave him the slip. He doesn't think Finch was ever here. He's been driving around looking for Keith."

"So, if we're not going home, what are we doing?" I asked.

"I think we have to move her," Stephanie said.

"Move who?" I honestly had no idea what she was talking about.

"Crystal."

"You can't be serious."

"Did you hear what Luke said about knowing the cops?" Stephanie caught my eye. "We're so deep in now . . ."

"Right, too far to turn back," I said, staring out the window at the passing darkness. "Our specialty."

Detective Julia Scutt

Sunday, 8:12 p.m.

When I return to Jonathan's the house is dark. The two uniforms outside proclaimed "all quiet" when I stopped at their patrol car, parked at the top of the driveway. But it's pretty obvious they've been sitting there with their eyes locked on their phones.

Inside, the house is still. I flip on a few lights, quickly clearing the downstairs—it doesn't hurt to be careful; our driver is still missing—before heading up the steps for Alice's journal. With Finch as my source, I'm skeptical about this guy they supposedly killed in college—that it happened at all, much less that it's got something to do with what happened in that car.

But then, one bad thing does have a way of leading to another.

It's a waiting game anyway until the lab calls with the corkscrew fingerprint results. At least there was one usable print on the handle, which given the shape and the mud is damn lucky. If it does match Luke Gaffney, then I'll have to dig out that rusted tent stake from Jane's file and get that tested, too. I've been trying to prepare for how it will feel to know that I've let my sister's murderer walk around out there all these years. But each time I think about it, all I can picture is myself shooting Luke Gaffney in the head.

They haven't found Crystal's body yet, either. There was evidence that something had gone on in the barn. There were footprints, drag marks—but no Crystal. We'll find her eventually. I'm not giving up until we do. Meanwhile, the officers are holding Luke Gaffney at his house while they finish their search. They haven't come up with much except some pot and a bottle of Percocet with somebody else's name on it. Enough for us to hold Luke, but not for very long.

Upstairs in the room where Derrick and Finch were staying, I find the duffel bag on the floor where I left it. Inside is the manila envelope with the journal. As I slide the pages out, a picture comes with them this time—the group at what looks like Derrick's wedding.

He and Maeve have their hands clasped, and they're laughing. When I look inside the envelope, I find more pictures. Must be the ones Derrick got so angry at Finch over. It is weird that he was carrying them around, but it makes me feel a little sorry for Derrick, honestly. I slide the pictures back inside before turning for the stairs, the envelope gripped in my hand.

Back downstairs, I'm halfway across the living room headed toward the front door when I notice how quiet and peaceful it is being locked away in this beautiful, empty house, no suspects or witnesses—or whatever they end up being—screaming to be released. Could be all for the best if I steer clear of the station until I have that fingerprint report. Everything until then is really just me stalling.

Instead, I drop down onto one of the red leather couches, which is exactly as cold and uncomfortable as it looks, and start reading Alice's journal. Almost right away, there it is: a party on the roof, a fall, one dead guy, and a whole bunch of lies. Alice was tormented by the guy's death, even more so by the fact that the friends decided to keep it a secret. And there does seem to be a fairly straight line between that and her suicide. Alice was never going to make it, keeping that secret, and, according to the journal, she told her friends as much. So they were warned, you could say. They could have cut their losses and told somebody. If they had, it might have even saved Alice from herself, who's to say? No wonder they're all so fucked up.

From the first few entries, there doesn't seem to be anything more complicated than that, though. What the friends did in not calling for help was callous, for sure, criminal maybe, but not outright murder in the way Finch led me to believe. I certainly can't see how it's relevant to the current situation except to prove that they're not the nicest people.

My phone buzzes with a text. It's the lab. Prints on corkscrew NOT A COMPARISON MATCH to Luke Gaffney.

Are you sure? I text back, even though I already know the answer. The lab is very good with manual comparisons.

100%. Inconsistent Loop Pattern.

What the fuck? Thanks. Run SABIS, too, and neighboring jurisdictions. Reach back out if anything pops.

I startle when I hear the front door open, my eyes still on my phone. I stand, hand back toward my gun just in case. The two idiots outside would probably let somebody come straight up the front steps.

Dan steps in, putting his hands up when he sees I'm reaching for my weapon. "Sorry, should have texted."

I drop back down onto the couch. "The prints on the corkscrew aren't Gaffney's."

"Really?" Dan asks, rubbing a hand over his chin. "Then who's LG?"

I shake my head. "I've got no fucking clue. I really thought it was him."

"Me too," Dan says. "I mean, after Hoff's missing statement especially."

I look up at him then, standing there with a concerned frown. "Thank you, by the way, for going back through the files and confirming the alibis and all that. I should have thanked you earlier."

Dan shrugs, then glances at me out of the corner of his eye. "What are friends for?"

"For the record, you're not wrong about Jane, either," I offer. And it really is an offering. I could say more. Except that I can't—at least not yet.

Dan's eyes flick back to mine again, but only for a second. He looks down and nods, quiet for a moment. "So, what's next then on this situation here?" He gestures broadly to the living room.

"Well, I'm holding four people downtown who are apparently all murder suspects again. But if we try to get their prints, they'll lawyer up for sure. At this point, it would be helpful to speed up that ID on the body. At least then, I'd know who it is I suspect they killed."

"Actually, we *do* know that." Dan takes a seat on the couch next to me. "That's why I came by."

"What do you mean?"

"It was Derrick Chism in the car."

"You got the fingerprints?"

He shakes his head. "We just found Keith Lazard downtown. He had his ID on him."

"Holy shit." I sit up straight. "Are you holding him?"

"In a manner of speaking," Dan says. "He was found with a gunshot wound to the back of the head on the front porch of one of the abandoned houses on Main. I'm guessing he was buying. Somebody walking by spotted him lying there."

"Dammit," I say. "There goes our best chance of finding out what the hell happened in that car."

"Not necessarily," Dan says. "By some freak miracle of bullet trajectory, Keith Lazard is still alive. I mean, barely. We're not going to be interviewing him tomorrow . . ."

"Unfortunately, I'm pretty sure the four pissed-off suspects I'm holding downtown aren't going to be willing to wait until he recovers."

"You can at least let Hendrix go, I think," Dan says. "Key card records confirm he was in his hotel room all night. There's security footage, too. The room's been rented for the week, and it's a mess—art supplies, plaster, equipment. Some paintings and what looks like they could be sculptures—pretty weird, you ask me, but what do I know. It all fits with the story he gave—he was making something in there."

"If this whole thing comes down to some drug deal gone wrong, I'm going to be pissed."

"Seldon will be, too," Dan says. "On the upside, maybe a couple dead weekenders will finally make him do his job and clean out the Farm."

"Yeah, right after he fires me."

Dan pops a piece of gum in his mouth. "Nah. I did a little more digging. Guess who was the last person to sign out your sister's file, before you first started on the force. I'll give you a hint: short white guy, big smile, wife that's too good for him."

"Seldon?"

"Yup. He probably buried the Hoff statement because it implicated Gaffney. Seems like there might also be a good reason Seldon doesn't advertise his friendship with Gaffney. Apparently, there are girls up at Gaffney's fishing cabin every weekend—young girls. Officer who checked his alibi was told that by multiple sources. Anyway, when this is all over, might be worth looking into a little more." Dan motions to the pages in my hand. "What's that?"

"Journal of a friend of theirs from college who killed herself," I say. "She felt guilty about some kid who went off the roof at Vassar. Sounds like he was drunk and fell. An accident, but this group—well, I guess they left the scene, didn't call anybody. Seems unlikely that he could have survived, neck broken probably. But you never know."

"Wait, the roof of Vassar?" Dan asks, squinting at me. "When was this?"

"I don't know, ten years ago?"

Something behind Dan catches my eye then. At the back of the living room, the cabinet doors are half open. I can see bottles lined up, glasses arranged on a silver tray, an ice bucket, tongs.

Dan snaps his fingers. "Wait, this is *that* kid? The one I was telling you about, from Hudson."

"What kid?" I ask, getting up to take a closer look at the bar. There's something etched in gold on the ice bucket that I can't make out from across the room.

"That lady in the pink tracksuit. I'm pretty sure that was *her* kid. She was all over the news at the time, wailing about her poor beloved son. Until it came out that he'd actually hated her guts. She just liked being on TV. She lived right behind Bethany, actually. Evan Paretsky, that was his name. He was working some construction job in Poughkeepsie at the time."

"Why didn't I hear about that?" But then I would have been in California at the time.

"It was big news around here, but only for a few days," he says. "Once the college said he'd been breaking into rooms before he fell, people lost interest."

"Well, from the journal, it doesn't sound like he was breaking in anywhere. The group met him in some off-campus bar and invited him back to party on the roof. Guy was drunk, got too close to the edge, and slipped. Bad accident made a whole lot worse when they didn't call anyone. Stupid kids."

"Not drunk, no way," Dan says. "Not Paretsky. He had some kind of metabolic thing or gluten intolerance or allergy or something. I remember. He was a couple years ahead at Hudson High. A single drink, and he'd get real sick. Vomiting and all that. Ended up being everybody's designated driver. Shitty hand of cards, huh? First that and then the roof. That was the first thing I thought when I heard he'd died."

Dan is still talking, but I'm not listening anymore now that I've reached the bar. I lift the ice tongs, the engraving there clear for the first time. Two looping letters, in the exact same font as the corkscrew.

"LG," I say out loud, looking around.

Finally, I see it, the bronze plaque on the wall above the bar: LOCUST GROVE, EST 1883.

Alice

I finally have Evan Paretsky's address! And Hudson is only an hour away from Poughkeepsie.

I'm still not exactly sure what I'm going to do when I get there. Maybe I will just leave a note anonymously at Evan's house, like I told Maeve I planned to. His mom does seem very, very angry—I saw her on the news. Not just about Evan's death, but also about him being falsely accused. It's hard to imagine she'll react well to me admitting I was involved.

And, yes, I know I could just mail a note. But I need to at least see her read it. To know for sure that she got it.

Maeve said to mail the note certified—she wasn't even joking. But she also said that I had to take my medication before she'd even consider helping me.

And I did take it. It was good anyway because I think my mom was planning to come up for a "visit," too—her code for a meds check. I know it wasn't helping anything, me not taking them. But I have now, and I already feel myself settling. Eventually I'll settle too low, that's always the problem—the place where my brain moves like sludge. But for now I'm in that sweet middle ground.

I'll ask Derrick for his car on the way out. I know he'll say yes. He always does. And Maeve will come, I could see it in her eyes—she's already on my side. She knows I need to do this. Besides, she owes me. I let her keep that last shirt she stole from me without even saying a word.

Derrick

Saturday, 8:41 p.m.

I felt relieved when I saw Maeve waiting at the end of Jonathan's dark driveway in her leggings and sweatshirt, arms filled with the jackets she'd brought for us. God, I really was so in love with her. And, no, our conversation earlier hadn't gone as far as I wanted it to, but something had shifted between us. I could feel it.

Maeve opened the back and tossed the pile of jackets in before getting in on the passenger side.

"Are you okay?" she asked as she climbed in.

I nodded, gripping the steering wheel so I wasn't tempted to reach for her. "I feel like a jerk, but I'm fine."

"Keith is the jerk, not you. You were trying to be a good friend. Where have you looked so far?"

I'd looked everywhere, that was the bottom line. I'd been at it for nearly an hour already. And I'd texted Keith at least fifteen times before getting back in the car and driving around town. Of course, if he didn't want me finding him, he wouldn't be found. I'd known the risks—that Keith might be lying about meeting Finch, using me so that he could buy drugs downtown. That maybe he'd even slip away and head to the train station to avoid rehab. But I hadn't been thinking very clearly. I was too worried that Keith was going to see Finch, and that Finch would tell him what I'd done that morning, maybe also about the pictures of Maeve in my bag. What if it all got back to her?

After I left the Falls, I'd made three bigger and bigger circles around downtown, weaving my way up and down the streets, but there was no sign of Keith. There was no sign of anyone besides the customers going in and out of the Falls, including apparently Jonathan and Stephanie, according to her text, but I hadn't seen them any of the times I passed.

Stephanie did tell me that Keith had seemed frightened of something or someone when they last spoke. But she didn't know of who or what, so the information succeeded only in making me feel more stressed. It seemed pretty obvious now that whatever was going on didn't have anything to do with Finch.

And so three times I'd driven past the rest of the stores, all long closed, and the big old Victorian homes on the edge of downtown, disintegrating and boarded up until I finally accepted it: I'd lost Keith. I pulled to the side at the dark dead end of Main Street, alongside those once-beautiful houses, to text Maeve. To make sure Keith hadn't stopped back at Jonathan's house—and because I just needed to talk to her.

Keith's gone.

A response, right away: What?

I know, I'm an idiot. He took off.

There was a long pause. I imagined Maeve sitting in the living room, debating what to say to me. Annoyed, of course. They were all going to be annoyed with me. She was probably wondering how much she should let me off the hook. Maybe even because she felt sorry for me, or obligated. Because of my feelings for her. But I didn't want Maeve's pity. I wanted Maeve.

Come get me. I'll help. We'll find him together. This isn't your fault, Derrick.

Maeve understood. Because she was a good person, a hopeful person. Always seeing the best in other people.

And that's exactly why I was in love with her. And, yes, I did secretly hope that her offering to come with me was a sign that she loved me back.

"I've looked everywhere around downtown. Keith's definitely not there," I said to her now as I started to drive.

"What about at the Farm?"

Of course that could be. If Keith had wanted to buy, he might go there. Maybe it was even somebody there that he was afraid of, like Stephanie had said. I wouldn't put it past Keith to already owe the wrong people in Kaaterskill.

I nodded. "We should check."

We parked on the same deserted strip of dirt road behind the dark barn. I thought of Crystal's legs, so heavy as we'd carried her, the awful soft give of her skin. All of it had been so much worse than I imagined. And yet far easier to forget than it should ever have been.

"Stay here," Maeve said, reaching for her door.

"Are you crazy?" I asked. "That's not safe." I knew better than to say *for a woman.* But I was thinking it. Maeve *was* tiny.

"What's crazy is you risking being seen here again. I'll go quickly, and I'll be careful. If someone sees me, I'll run. These days I'm faster than I look."

I lifted my hands. "Okay. But be careful. Please."

"Just turn the car around and be ready to leave. I plan to be quick."

Maeve emerged a couple minutes later, stride forceful, in one piece, but with a grim look on her face.

"No luck, huh?" I asked as she got back in the car.

She shook her head. "I heard voices down in that other building. But a lot—ten or fifteen people maybe? Like a party. I'm sorry, I know I insisted on being the one to go and then kind of chickened out. But even if Keith is at that party, I don't think it would be a good idea for either one of us to go in. We'd be so outnumbered. Maybe in the morning?"

She was right. We couldn't bust into some party filled with addicts—where Keith may or may not be—and just hope for the best. We had no idea what they were capable of. Look at what *we* were capable of.

"Yeah, the morning is a good idea," I said, pulling out my phone and starting to type an update to Stephanie before starting the car.

"Who are you texting?" she asked.

"Jonathan and Stephanie. We should tell them where we are."

"Oh, I just did a second ago. They texted that they were still dealing with the contractors. Said they might be a while."

Was I a little glad about the extra time alone with Maeve? Yes. Definitely.

"Thank you again for coming with me," I said, still not starting the car. "I mean it."

I put a quick hand over Maeve's for emphasis, but then I didn't let go. Couldn't bring myself to. Maeve was quiet as she stared down at our overlapping hands. And she didn't pull hers away. Finally, she turned toward the window. "Derrick, what did you mean before, when you said you saw what happened on the roof?"

I had upset her, hadn't I? That was the opposite of what I'd intended. "I saw that guy grab you. That's what I meant. He was fixated on you all night. We all noticed. I didn't hear what either of you said, but I saw him put his hands on you, and you—you just reacted. Like anybody would. It was an accident. I just wanted to make sure that you didn't—I don't know—blame yourself for what happened that night."

Maeve nodded, but kept her eyes on the window. "Is that why you sent that email?"

"What email?" I asked.

"The one about the roof," she said. " 'I know what you did.' "

"Me? That was Alice's mom, wasn't it?" I asked. "I was going to ask if anyone else got one, but then I thought we were all just agreeing not to talk about it because of Keith."

"Oh, right," Maeve said quietly, still looking at the window. She didn't sound like she believed me.

"Maeve, I would never send you an email about that night. *Never.* That's my whole point. I would never tell anybody. I'll take it to my grave."

When she finally turned to look at me, she smiled. "Thank you. I appreciate that." I thought she believed me now, but I wasn't sure. "I think we should drive a little farther down that way just to check for Keith before we go back." She pointed into the night. "Maybe he got turned around and is, I don't know, walking around lost or something."

"That's probably a good idea," I said. And Keith had threatened that exact thing—walking on the road. I could easily imagine him getting hit by a car.

I pulled out of the dirt track behind the Farm. We drove on, scanning the dark woods, for another ten minutes. But it was impossible to see anything except trees.

"Wait, stop," Maeve said suddenly, her arm going to my chest. "I think I just saw something. Somebody in the woods. I swear to God it was Keith, and there was somebody behind him, in a hat. A red hat, like the contractors."

I swung the car to the side of the road. "Where?"

I rolled down the window, looking where Maeve had pointed for movement, listening for sounds. But the night was still. I didn't see anyone, anywhere.

"Where?" I asked again.

"I don't know—I thought I saw someone. But it's so dark. Maybe I just want to find Keith so badly I'm imagining things." Maeve reached over and put her hand on my knee. She shook her head. "I'm sorry, Derrick."

"That's okay. It's no problem. It's impossible to see."

"No, I mean: I'm sorry that I haven't been completely honest with you," she said, staring down.

"About what?" My heart had picked up speed.

"I, um, have feelings for you, too. I think I didn't realize it until this weekend. And it's just . . . complicated."

Keep. Calm.

"Bates?" I asked, trying not to sound overeager.

"I don't even know. I thought I knew what I wanted." When she looked at me finally, her eyes were gentle, searching. "But I don't feel sure about anything anymore."

Maeve reached out then and put her other hand on my cheek. A second later we were kissing, her fingers twisted in my hair as she moved toward me in the driver's seat, her soft mouth over mine. When she tried to move closer, the steering wheel was in the way. And I wanted nothing more than the feel of her on me. We moved over in an awkward passing of body over body. But soon she was on top of me in the passenger's seat, her thighs straddling mine, my hands on the curve of her waist as she kissed my neck.

And all I could think about was all the time we'd wasted, pretending that we were just fr—

There was a sudden stabbing pain in my neck. A pop. Then a jolt of an even worse pain, shooting down my arm. Had I been shot? A rushing in my ears. Maeve was slumped over, and she'd stopped kissing me. Someone had shot her, too? Finch and the gun. Keith. Who was he afraid—

I tried to blink, to focus, to move. But I was underwater, held there. Drowning fast. I reached for the door, needed air, to shout, to get above the tide. But there wasn't enough oxyg—

Three Weeks Earlier

I'm on my way to meet Bates at Minetta Tavern when I get the email. I stop halfway across Washington Square Park to read it.

I know what you did.

Alice's mom, that's what I assume. At least at first. She's been sending us anonymous emails for years, accusing us each time, in slightly different words, of being self-centered, selfish, cruel monsters. We were responsible for Alice's death because of the things we *didn't* do: *You were supposed to watch out for her. You were supposed to protect her. You were her best friends.*

I always braced myself for Alice's mom to shoot some extra blame specifically my way—*and you, Maeve, the roommate.* Back at Vassar, she once tried to saddle me with the responsibility of making sure that Alice stayed on her medication. How could you put that on somebody so young? And I wasn't a mental health professional. I had no training.

But luckily, all these years later, Alice's mom has still never singled me out. There's never been any mention of the roof either. Alice said at the time she hadn't told her mother about what happened, and that seemed true. Her mother certainly would have brought it up. Her messages were never short on words.

Which is what makes this new email different—only one sentence? And "I know what you did"? That certainly sounds like it's about the roof. Even the email address—friendslikethese212—is unlike any that Alice's mom used before. Some of her emails have been from cryptic addresses, but usually they included Alice's name. I'm actually not sure this new email is from Alice's mom at all.

I'm only a block away from the restaurant when I google Alice's mother. Her obituary comes up right away—natural causes related to pancreatic cancer. She only died a few weeks ago, and now this email?

There's that podcast, *The River*, too. Somebody at the foundation mentioned the Alice episode, though she had no way of knowing our connection. None of my friends seem to have heard about it. True crime podcasts are a dime a dozen these days. But maybe this email has something to do with that?

Or there is the other possibility. The most obvious one, which I'm trying not to think about as I finally open the door to Minetta Tavern. I step inside, drinking in its elegant Parisian charm. Was this email sent by one of my friends? Did one of them see what really happened on the roof that night, and now here they are—after a decade of silence—threatening me?

I have no choice but to wait and see if someone else mentions getting the same email. It'll be the only way to know for sure whether it was directed specifically at me.

Finally I spot Bates seated at the bar, an open stool saved there next to him, just for me. Even in his standard-issue trust-fund jeans and sport coat, Bates looks adorable. Because he *is* adorable, and charming and sweet. I sometimes worry that he's out of my league, even though I look much better now than I ever have—best shape of my life, my hair and body finally the way I've always wanted them to be. Even my features are so much more defined these days, especially my cheekbones. Sometimes even *I'd* swear that I must have had work done.

But no, nothing nearly that easy. Instead, I've worked hard to become the person I am, to forget the past and move on. Not to let negativity or guilt drag me down. That takes real strength. It's worthy of admiration. It's worthy of Bates—even if I worry sometimes that he's not 100 percent convinced, not yet.

Of course it's impossible to know the truth of someone else's heart. The best I can do is keep on being the best Maeve I can be. And trust that Bates will keep on seeing a future with me. I'll do whatever I have to, to protect that.

Detective Julia Scutt

Sunday, 10:59 p.m.

"You can let Hendrix go," I say to Cartright when we're finally back at the station. He's behind the front desk, stuffing his face.

"Thank fucking God." He tosses his sandwich into a wrapper. "That guy is a serious pain in the neck. You can hear his whining all the way down the hall."

As I turn toward the other interview room, I double-check that I have everything I need—the journal, the complete fingerprint report, the photos, which I've studied much more closely. It's taken a couple hours, but I've finally put all the pieces together. Took me a bit longer to process the full picture once everything had been snapped into place.

"You ready for this?" Dan asks, then quickly adds, "I mean, I know you're ready. I just meant—"

"I know what you meant," I say. And I do. He meant well. That's all that matters.

I peer into the interview room through the little window, reaching inside my shirt for Jane's ring. Let it lie outside finally, in plain sight. Maeve is walking the perimeter of the room, her back to me, one balled-up hand pressed against her mouth, the other clasped around her waist. I don't see it at all. That's the weird thing—even now, knowing what I do. I still don't see it.

Finally I reach for the door. "Let's do this."

As I step inside, Maeve turns, eyes welling up instantly, lower lip trembling. I have to bite back a flash of rage.

"You know something by now. You must," she pleads. "I understand you're just doing your job, protecting the investigation. But can't you tell me something?"

"Actually, I can. I have some good news," I say to Maeve. "He's alive."

"Alive?" Maeve asks. "Who's alive?"

Excited, but wary. Even her shock walks the right line.

"Keith," I say. "We found him downtown, but he's been—"

"Wait, if you found Keith, then that must mean . . ."

"Yes, it was Derrick in the car. I'm afraid it does mean that," I say. "Would you like to know about Keith?"

"God, yes, please." She blinks her big blue saucer eyes, still shiny with tears. "What happened to him?"

"He was shot in the head," I say. "But he's alive somehow. Sheer luck. From the differences in location and method, we're assuming that what we have here is actually two unrelated crimes."

"Oh, thank God . . . But does that mean Derrick . . ."

"Yes," I say. "Derrick Chism is definitely dead. He was murdered." Her shoulders sink as she slowly lowers herself into her chair. "But, come on, Maeve, you already knew that."

When she looks up at me, it is only with mild confusion—no defensiveness, no concern. No alarm. Perfectly executed. Enraging, too. I clench my teeth. I have to keep it together. I want to do this myself. I need to. I owe that much to Jane.

"I don't understand what you're talking about," she says.

Of course, this is her only real option: complete denial. At a minimum, she needs me to put my cards on the table first. So she can figure out how to use them against me. That's okay. She can try. I have a lot of cards.

"You've known this whole time Derrick was dead. That Keith was never even in that car."

Her expertly tweezed eyebrows pinch. It's only then I see it for a second. Maybe. Like a quick flash and then gone.

"And how would I know that?"

"Because you killed Derrick."

Her eyes brim with tears again. "That's sick," she says in a wounded but slightly defiant voice that pokes at me again. "I know it's your job to get information by saying these terrible things. But there is a line, and that crosses it." She leans back in her chair and juts out her chin. "I'm not answering any more questions."

Luckily, she hasn't actually said the magic word *lawyer.* I did read Stephanie, Maeve, and Jonathan their rights when they first arrived at the station—informing them that it was procedure prior to any questioning, even of witnesses. That's not exactly true, but true enough. It's always useful to have a signed waiver on hand before you question anybody. And both innocent people and overconfident guilty people will often sign away their rights without hesitating. But in New York State, when a suspect mentions a lawyer, all questioning must cease, signed waiver or not. Still, Maeve hasn't said lawyer, not yet.

I lay the journal pages down, spin the stack so that it faces Maeve. This is what will help me not kill her with my bare hands—getting on with it.

"Derrick's research?" she asks, and I wonder whether she actually has no idea. If she knew it was Alice's journal, she'd probably have found a way to destroy it.

I shake my head. "It's a journal," I say. "Alice's journal."

"Alice?" she asks sharply. "What are you talking about?"

I nod. "Yeah, apparently Finch got his hands on it. You are right, he is a real jerk. And he kind of hates all of you. Anyway, he's using the journal to do some art project. At your expense I'm afraid."

"What art project?"

"You'll have to ask him for the details," I say. "I'm more interested in what happened that night on the roof."

"What roof?" This confusion is not as well executed. At last, her mask is slipping.

"I've read the journal, Maeve," I say. "Alice was very upset. She wrote all about what happened."

When Maeve shifts uncomfortably in her chair, it

slightly eases my rising fury. "That guy was drunk, and he fell from the roof," she admits finally. "And we didn't call anyone, that's true. But we did think he was—his neck looked broken." She shudders dramatically. "We should have called someone anyway, obviously. It was a stupid, stupid thing."

"Evan Paretsky," I say.

"What?"

"That guy who died—he had a name. It was Evan Paretsky."

"Oh, yeah." Maeve looks down. "Of course he had a name. I'm not trying to dehumanize him."

"You know what I think?"

"What's that?"

"I think he recognized you."

"Recognized me?" She looks up, almost serenely, mask perfectly affixed once more. "What are you talking about?"

"The Paretsky family house was right behind yours," I say. "I think Evan saw you that night at Vassar, and he recognized you. I think he knew who you were and threatened to tell the others. So you pushed him off that roof."

"I *pushed* him? He 'lived behind me'? I have no idea what you're talking about." She laughs a little and glances over at Dan. He looks stunned—eyebrows lifted, hand over his mouth. I think he's finally recognized her. "That guy fell. It was an accident. You can ask anybody who was there."

I nod, frowning skeptically. "In the end, you went with Alice that night, didn't you? To keep her from getting all the way to Hudson. Because you were worried about her talking to Evan Paretsky's mom and somehow it all getting traced back to you, which I've got to say was kind of unlikely. You ask me, you should have just let Alice go. No one would have ever found out about you—about the rest."

"The rest of what?" Maeve asks, with a kind of amused exasperation, except there's a little flicker of rage in her eyes, too.

"Who you really are," I say. "That you've been alive all this time. Right, Bethany?"

Her face is still. She blinks once. "Who's Bethany?"

I slide toward her one of the pictures I eventually found at the bottom of the envelope with the journal. A candid shot of the whole group—Maeve, Stephanie, Jonathan, Derrick, Keith, and a tiny girl with strawberry blond hair in two braids who must be Alice. They all look so young and happy and alive. Much better than they do now. Everyone except Maeve. Today, Maeve is much better looking than Bethany ever was, some would probably say beautiful. She's also better looking than in the picture, which I'm guessing was taken freshman year. In the photo, Maeve's face is rounder and softer, her body shapeless, dull brown hair unflatteringly short. And the sweater she's wearing—the distinctive vivid green cropped cowl-neck knitted by Jane—is doing her no favors. And hey, I can relate. Mine never suited me either.

Maeve is staring down at the photo, silent.

"That's my sister Jane's sweater," I say, leaning closer. "She was wearing it the day you killed her."

"Who's Jane?" Maeve asks, fingers pressing down on the table so hard the tips have gone white. That's when I notice for the first time: she's ripped off her acrylics and chewed her nails, some of them right down to the weeping cuticles. "I see a picture of all of us from back in school, but I don't understand what you're saying."

I point to her image. "I'm saying *that* is Jane Scutt's sweater. I'm saying that you must have pulled it off my sister Jane before you stabbed her more than twenty times with a rusted tent stake. You were her best friend, Bethany."

Maeve assesses me curiously. Crosses her arms. *Don't slap her.* "I don't know a Bethany."

I open the folder containing the fingerprint reports from Connecticut and New Jersey. The different jurisdictions slowed down the identification process. "Do you know a Jezebel Sloane or Jessie Jenkins or Jackie Jones?" I slide the print run in front of her, and the mug shots. They all look much more like Bethany than the person sitting in front of me. But similar enough—there's no doubt they are all one and the same. "You look great these days, I have got to hand it to you, Bethany. Gorgeous and young, even though you're what—three, four years older than your Vassar friends? You've done a great job maintaining your looks. But man, you were sloppy as a criminal. You got arrested a lot at first—petty larceny, grand theft, bribery, prostitution. All in the six years after killing Jane and before you enrolled as one Maeve Travis at Vassar College. And let's not forget the murder charges that are on the way for Derrick and Jane. You got so lucky with all the rain we had right after you killed Jane, the flooding. I imagine it made them quick to assume that accounted for any missing evidence." I slide another page in front of her. "But I think your luck just ran out. We have prints matching all three of these women on the corkscrew that killed Derrick. And I just sent the tent stake that was used to kill Jane down to the lab. What do you want to bet those are going to match, too?"

Bethany looks up at me then, without blinking. "I want a lawyer."

"Good idea." I close the folder and stand. "I think you're going to need one."

Six Months Later
Bethany

They were all accidents. Really. Well, I guess maybe with Derrick—but that was a decision I was forced into, by *him*. Well, him and Finch, it turns out—I've learned since that it was Finch who sent that stupid email. But how was I to know that everyone else had gotten the same email, when they were keeping it to themselves? A terrible coincidence, like Jonathan buying a house here, of all places. As soon as Jonathan mentioned looking for houses in the area, I tried to redirect him. Peter won out, of course, and he'd had his own reasons for fixating on Kaaterskill. Turns out, he and Luke met in college, too—Buffalo State, a SUNY school.

I'd known the risk of going back to Kaaterskill, even with my family long gone. But how could I have explained not coming along for Keith's big intervention? He needed us. All of us. Did I also maybe want to prove something to myself? That this chapter of my life really was closed, that nothing was going to stand in the way of my future with Bates? Could be. I definitely second-guessed that decision when Jane's little sister Julia introduced herself as one of Kaaterskill's finest. Luckily, it didn't seem like she recognized me—but then she'd been so young back then and I looked so very different now.

If only I'd been more cautious, less willing to push the envelope, maybe everything could have ended differently. And that makes me sad, because I did love Derrick as a friend—in my own way. But love and happy endings are often mutually exclusive. Despite what people like to believe.

It was all much more complicated than it seems, too. I guess that's why I've agreed to talk to you, Rachel and Rochelle—over my lawyer's objections. Because I want to be sure people know the truth. My lawyer says it doesn't matter that we have a plea deal and that I already have my sentence and all that. He says that they can *still* find a way to use your show against me, at a parole hearing for instance. But I'm not worried. People will understand. I'm sympathetic, and believable. Always have been, always will be. You're right, too, my perspective matters. And I agree that it would be good for me to finally tell my side of the whole story.

I mean, I know this: people change. And what starts out as a story you made up about yourself can eventually become the truth of who you are—if you want it bad enough. I am Maeve now. That's the bottom line. And I have been her for a very long time.

But I didn't forget everything that came before. I remember what it felt like to be Bethany. How miserable I was. And how sad.

I remember Jane, too. I loved her, by the way. So much. She was my best, best friend. She was fun and silly, and she really got me. I know what people thought back then: what a mismatch, Bethany and Jane. Why was perfect and popular and golden-hued Jane slumming it with someone like me?

That's why that day down by the river crushed me so—when Jane started saying in her gentle, nice, well-meaning way that maybe I should think about improving myself. That she'd even be happy to help. I was beautiful, she said, especially on the inside. But there were things we could do to make my inner beauty really shine. She held my hands as she said it, beamed that dazzling smile of hers my way. And I felt her love. Limited, though, as it was by how beautiful she was—her hazel eyes glittering in the sun, her blond hair a bright gold. I'd always known it was only a matter of time before Jane came to her senses and saw me the way the rest of the world did.

And there she was, finally admitting it. Jane might have loved me, but deep down she thought I was just as ugly as everybody else did.

I didn't realize what had happened until it was over, that rock gripped in my hand, Jane in an awkward pile on the ground. Well, not completely over. Jane was just unconscious then. The rest of what I did—I did after. I had no choice. And they needed to think some real sicko was responsible. They needed to at least find my bloody shirt to believe that I was dead, too. Of course, if they'd done their jobs and run tests, they'd have found Jane's blood on that shirt, not mine. All that rain really did feel like the universe sending me a sign—I deserved a fresh start.

It was a risk enrolling at Vassar, so relatively close to Kaaterskill. I'd known that at the time. But when that married customer I was sleeping with bragged about how working in Vassar's admissions office gave him so much power over so many young lives, it was too good an opportunity to pass up. By that point I was way past tired of the waitressing job I'd found in Yonkers and it was shockingly easy to blackmail him into helping me. In a way, I was honoring Jane's memory by going to

Vassar. It had always been her dream to go there. And, let's face it, risk is always part of the thrill.

I didn't plan things with Alice either. Yes, it had been my idea to stop at the Vanderbilt Mansion on the way from Poughkeepsie to Hudson. But I swear, when we got out of the car to sit by the river in the deserted park, I was still convinced I'd be able to talk Alice out of going to Hudson and that idiot Evan's house. Because obviously she couldn't do that. Alice was impulsive. She might go there with every intention of only leaving a note, but then something in the woman's expression might grab her and next thing you know, she'd be throwing caution to the wind and knocking on the woman's door. Alice was *that* consumed with making amends for something that *definitely* wasn't her fault.

Under no circumstances could Alice end up inside Evan's house. Apparently they had a *picture* of me in their kitchen—a framed newspaper clipping of the dead neighbor girl. That's what Evan had said to me that night on the roof: "I've been looking at your fucking picture at the dinner table for the past ten years. Your face was fatter then. But don't tell me that's not you."

I hadn't recognized him at all until he said that. But his mom had apparently been obsessed with the murders, seeing as how one of the girls had lived right behind them, and she was also a true crime aficionado. She kept the framed clipping on the wall as a reminder to cherish life, she said. (Creepy, if you ask me. Evan thought so, too.) The worst part was that I knew the picture Evan was talking about, with my hair back in a headband and my face extra puffy. Still, it was one of the few where if you looked hard enough, you could almost see *this* me already, waiting in the wings.

Alice completely freaked when I brought up the subject of going back to campus instead of continuing on to Hudson. She started screaming at me. She even tried to leave me behind at the Vanderbilt Mansion, running toward the car with the keys. Though that was after I'd slapped her—just hard enough to get her to come to her senses. But apparently Alice was going to Hudson no matter what I said. No matter what I did. Except, of course, for the thing I did eventually do: make it so that Alice couldn't go anywhere ever again.

She was light, but she was strong—I'd forgotten that—and it got ugly. I had to chase Alice down. I think she even made some calls at one point, hoping to get rescued. After it was over, what choice did I have but to leave the car someplace where suicide would be presumed? The Kingston-Rhinecliff Bridge was an obvious choice—people jumped from there all the time. Honestly, though, I was surprised as anyone that they never found Alice's body. Her parents were incensed, blamed gross incompetence. But with the powerful current and all the commercial barge traffic on the massive Hudson River, the police never seemed that surprised. Bodies weren't always that easy to find, apparently. Of course, maybe they would have found her if they'd started searching twenty-miles downriver instead of wasting all that time up by the bridge, a place Alice never was to begin with.

But the most awful of all was Derrick. That was the worst, because he really did love me, for me. And yet in the end even he didn't give me a choice. The way his empty eyes stared at me after, so accusingly—just like Jane's. I couldn't bear it. It hardly counts as a thing you've done when a person leaves you with no alternative.

And, really, what kind of friend does that: leaves you with no good way out?

One Year Later
Detective Julia Scutt

I don't have to be doing this, going through everything again. But it will be my last chance. Jane's case files are on their way to long-term off-site storage, where the files of all the closed cases go.

And so I've looked through the bagged evidence one last time—the bloody clothing and the dried remains of Jane's favorite lip gloss and that rusted tent stake. I've felt the weight of each object in my hands. I read through all of the old witness statements again, too, and looked over the ME's report in detail for the first and last time. It wasn't easy, but I owe at least that much to Jane. To bear witness to her loss. To allow myself to fully feel it finally, after all this time. It turns out, there is a certain solace in sadness. Solace, and maybe freedom.

It's unfortunate that Bethany didn't have to sit in front of a jury and spectators and be called to account for Jane's murder at a trial. So the whole world would know the monster she really is. But Bethany wouldn't have felt bad anyway. She might have even enjoyed the attention. And with my parents gone, it would have only been me there to genuinely care. I knew about the plea deal in advance, of course. The prosecutor is a good guy. I've known him for a long time. And so I trusted him when he counseled against risking a trial, given how good an actress Bethany is. A jury can get easily swayed by a defendant's outward appeal. And Maeve is outwardly appealing, that's for sure. It's her insides—Bethany's—that have always been rotten to the core.

In the end, Bethany pleaded guilty in exchange for a reduced sentence for the four homicides—Jane, Evan, Alice, and Derrick. Thirty years with the possibility of parole. I can live with that for now. Because she's not going anywhere. I'll be at each and every parole hearing to make sure.

Stephanie, Jonathan, and Keith pleaded out, too, after telling us where we could find Crystal, in a remote forested area twenty minutes from the Farm, sheltered carefully at least under some trees. Keith pleaded out from his hospital bed. Even now I've heard he still has some lingering physical damage, but no permanent brain injury. And I'm guessing, on the upside, the lengthy hospital stay also helped him get clean. Felony improper disposal of a body was the charge in the end related to Crystal's overdose and the hiding of her body, pleaded down to a misdemeanor, no jail time. Word is, though, that Stephanie has left her firm, and that Jonathan's defense team wasn't funded by his parents—so there have been other consequences. There were no charges against anyone other than Maeve for Evan Paretsky's death. The others weren't actually legally obligated to call for help, believe it or not. Morally? That's another story. They'll have to figure out a way to live with that for the rest of their lives.

The door opens, startling me. "Oh, sorry, Lieutenant, I didn't realize you were still in here," Cartright says. "The record storage guy's here for the files. You want me to hold him off?"

Cartright is growing on me. He's trying, at least. Not that he's got much of a choice. I'm his boss now. *The* boss, until Seldon's replacement arrives. It took a while to find an underage girl willing to testify against Seldon and Gaffney about the *extra* extracurriculars on their fishing weekends. But I did eventually. I am tenacious. I know how to sink my teeth into something until they knock against bone.

Dan appears in the doorway next to Cartright. "You're still here," he says, his eyes moving to the files. "Take your time. I can meet you at home."

He gets it, of course he does. Dan's been exactly what and where I needed him to be this entire time. Patient and kind, but honest, too. A really good friend. And, it turns out, so much more.

"No, it's okay. I'll come," I say, rising slowly to my feet. "I'm ready to go."

Acknowledgments

Endless thanks to my supremely talented editor, Jennifer Barth, for bravely stepping into this book—well, before it was a book and for doing so with indefatigable grace and profound generosity. I am grateful for your wisdom, creativity, and compassion and for your unwavering ability to see past what is, to the glory of what could be.

Much gratitude to Jonathan Burnham and Doug Jones for your relentless passion and deep commitment. To everyone else at Harper in the marketing, publicity, sales, and library departments—thank you so much for your hard work and dedication. Special thanks to Leah Wasielewski, Tina Andreadis and Amelia Beckerman. Leslie Cohen and Katie O'Callaghan—I adore you both. Thank you for being so gifted at what you do and for being such delightful people. Thanks also to the very talented Sarah Ried, production editor Lydia Weaver, copyeditor Miranda Ottewell and the rest of the Harper managing editorial team for always working so hard on my behalf. My deepest gratitude to incredibly talented designer Jaya Micelli for my beautiful cover and to Robin Bilardello for so patiently shepherding the process. Thanks also to Kyle O'Brien for the lovely interior design.

To the world's best literary agent, Dorian Karchmar—it's a gift to have you on my team and in my life. I'm grateful to be the beneficiary of your immense creative skills, your keen judgment—about *all the things*—and your boundless empathy. Sincere thanks to the lovely and dedicated Anna DeRoy for all your hard work and your belief in me. My appreciation also to Matilda Forbes Watson, James Munro, Alex Kane, Jessica Spitz, Christina Lee, Megan Pelson, and everyone else at WME. Thank you for all your efforts on my behalf.

Thank you to my beloved lawyer and law school bestie Victoria Cook—such a gift to always have you in my corner. Thanks also to the ever-fabulous Mark Merriman. To Katherine Faw, my own personal savior, I have absolutely no idea what I'd do without you—so

I'm afraid you can never leave. Thanks also to Claudia Herr, Darren Carter, Deena Warner, Brendan Kennedy, and Harris Davis.

To my best friends and beautiful beta readers—Megan Crane, Cara Cragan, Elena Evangelo, Heather Frattone, Tania Garcia, Nicole Kear, and Motoko Rich—thank you for always dropping everything to read and then finding a way to be both truthful and kind. I'm so lucky to have you all in my life. An extra thank-you to Tara Pometti and Jon Reinish, who not only served as early readers, but tracked down experts for me. Huge thanks to Parky Lee for taking my out-of-the-blue call and helping with such generosity and warmth. Thank you also to Joe Daniels, Teresa Maloney, David Fischer, D. Ann Williams, and Zhui Ning Chang. And remember everyone: only the good parts of this book are about my friendships with all of you.

To my amazing experts without whom I would be hopelessly lost—thank you for so patiently answering my endless questions about how art is sold, how guns go off, how many plastic gloves you actually use at a crime scene and whether you really can pull an IV out your own arm. Bless you: Stanley Dohm, Dr. Ora Pearlstein, Jim Reinish, and Professor Linda C. Rourke. A special thank-you to retired detective Peter Frederick for combing through the manuscript in detail, for always being there to consider even my most outlandish follow-up queries, and for being kind enough to make me laugh while telling me I got things totally wrong.

As always, thank you to the miraculous Nike Arowolo for everything you do and much gratitude to Martin and Clare Prentice for your unfailing support.

Thank you Tony, Harper, and Emerson for allowing me the space to write this book in an insane lockdown world—when space was precisely what none of us had to give. I can only imagine how hard it was. And I will be forever grateful.

About the Author

KIMBERLY McCREIGHT is the *New York Times* bestselling author of *Reconstructing Amelia,* which was nominated for the Edgar, Anthony, and Alex Awards; *Where They Found Her*; and *A Good Marriage*. She attended Vassar College and graduated cum laude from the University of Pennsylvania Law School. She lives in Brooklyn, New York.